New York Times Bestselling Author

MAGGIE SHAYNE

THE RHIANNON CHRONICLES

Edited by Jena O'Connor

www.practicalproofing.com

Ebook formatting and Graphic Design by Jessica Lewis

www.authorslifesaver.com

Cover Photo: Paige Wisenbach

paigewissenbach.com

Cover Model: deadlynghtshde13@aol.com

www.facebook.com/deadly.nightshade.model

All characters in this book have no existence outside the imagination of the author and have no relation whatsoever to anyone bearing the same name or names. They are not even distantly inspired by any individual known or unknown to the author, and all incidents are pure invention.

ISBN: 1517056713
ISBN-13: 978-1517056711

PRAISE FOR MAGGIE SHAYNE

"My inspiration has always been Maggie Shayne and her Wings in the Night Series. Sexy, thrilling, a must-read!" ~* * *1 *New York Times* Bestselling Author CHRISTINE FEEHAN

"Maggie Shayne's books have a permanent spot on my keeper shelf. She writes wonderful stories combining romance with page-turning thrills, and I highly recommend her to any fan of romantic suspense." ~KAREN ROBARDS

"Readers will feel as if they can touch the connection sizzling between the duo. This story will have readers on the edge of their seats and begging for more." ~ RT BOOKCLUB MAGAZINE (Review of Twilight Fulfilled)

"One of the strongest, most original voices in romance fiction today." ~ Bestselling Author ANNE STUART

"Creepy, chilling and compelling. Simply spellbinding!" ~ New York Times Bestselling Author SHANNON DRAKE

CHAPTER ONE

I stood on the deck of the ship we'd stolen from the US government, the sea wind rinsing my hair with the scent of every creature she held in her briny womb. If our enemies found us, they would, as my young friend Charlotte put it, "blow us out of the water." And they wouldn't care about destroying the seven hybrid children who were still onboard. That was Charlotte's opinion, at least. I rather thought they would try to take those walking, talking little experiments alive. They were, after all, bred and trained to be weapons. Vampire killers.

I could only hold the glamour I'd cast for so long. I had to rest. And my attention was divided, to say the least, by the little ones who had been known as The Offspring.

One in particular.

Sooner or later, the government's secret anti-vampire troops would find us. We had to get the children off the ship.

But right then, at that moment, we were safe. The night was beautiful. And I was in the arms of the man I loved beyond reason. My Roland.

"If it can't be Egypt, my love, then it must be the rocky coast of Maine. I'll have it no other way," I told him.

Roland crooked a dark brow at me as if I'd claimed it was raining in the Sahara. Momentarily, that distracted me from our dire situation. He was so incredibly beautiful, standing there with the silent night sky, glittering stars, and ancient rolling ocean as his backdrop. He had the strong jawline and proud nose of nobility, the cheekbones and full, sensual lips of a leading man, with a deeper than usual dip in the center of the top one. I had a hard time keeping my own mouth away from that sexy upper lip of his. Furthermore, he had the body of a god and the piercing, hypnotic eyes of a vampire–for that's exactly what he was. As was I.

Roland sensed the arousal in my blood. I knew he did because he smiled very slightly, and his eyes sparked. Then, knowing he had me at a disadvantage, he tried his ever-present logic on me.

"Rhiannon," he said, "we are in the northern Pacific Ocean. Pacific. Not Atlantic."

"The Pacific and I do not get along," I said. "She's full of predators who make our kind seem mild by comparison, one of whom took your leg, lest you forget."

"Not bloody likely to forget that," he said with a resigned look down at the ingenious mechanical prosthetic the vampire Killian had made for him, all from items found aboard *The Anemone.*

I touched his arm, sorry to have brought up what was, for him, a painful subject. We still didn't know if his leg would grow back. Our kind regenerate and heal during the day sleep. But I'd never known of a vampire with an injury so severe who'd survived long enough to make it to his bed. If Roland's limb was going to grow back, we'd seen no sign of it.

I dragged my fingertips over his cheek, down his corded neck and across his chest to distract him from his pain. "I far prefer the rocky cliffs of the northeastern coast. There's an entirely different energy to the Atlantic. She feels younger, friskier, lighter somehow. She has a restlessness about her, a vibrant, feisty eagerness."

"Does she now?" he asked. I nodded in reply and he gazed at me with love in his eyes, amused, I thought, by my uncharacteristic whimsy. "And what personality do you attribute to the Pacific? Besides her children's hunger for vampire limbs?"

That he could joke about his loss made me love him even more. I'd been finding reasons to love him more for century upon century. I used to think my love for this man would reach its maximum at some point. But I'd come to believe it was capable of growing infinitely. Every day, somehow, it was more.

He was awaiting my reply—not impatient, only eager—standing directly behind me, and I was enjoying our moment on the midnight sea. After all, they hadn't found us yet.

I leaned on the ship's rail and looked out across the massive swells, rising and falling like the lungs of a giant, slowly, with an ancient and timeless rhythm. "The Pacific is older, deeper, calmer, perhaps even wiser. But deadlier, too. She holds immense power, and secrets–unfathomable secrets."

"She's like you, then," Roland said softly, his arm curling around my waist to pull me closer. "How can you not love her? How could anyone?"

I turned in his embrace to welcome his kiss and thought again of the miracle that was our love as I tasted his lips and he tasted mine.

As he lifted his head, his eyes as alight as the stars above us, he said, "Short of heading southward all the way to the Panama Canal, I don't see how we can—"

I pushed at his chest, cutting him off as he stumbled a little. "You can't sweet talk me out of this, Roland. I'm tired of being at sea. We are not safe on this stolen ship, and I'm not even certain that *The Glamourie* can hide us from our persecutors with their radar and sonar and whatever else they're using to search for us. I want a safe place, a haven where we can...settle down."

He blinked precisely twice, and then his entire being softened. "I never thought in all the centuries we've been together, I would hear you say you'd like to settle down."

I lowered my head, embarrassed I suppose, at my own weakness. I didn't have many. In fact, until recently, Roland had been the only one. "Not forever, of course. Just for a short while. A dozen years, perhaps fifteen. Just until Nikki is grown." I looked past him then, at the seven children playing on the deck. "She's never had a home, Roland. Never had a family, nor any of the things children need in order to thrive. None of them have."

He turned, looking at them as well. We'd found thirteen children in kennel-like cages below decks when we'd taken control of the so-called research vessel *Anemone*. According to the files we'd found, The Offspring had been produced in a lab in four batches. The oldest batch included just two—a girl and a boy, both seventeen years old—but they were no longer onboard. The second batch were all eleven years of age, and there were four of those, two boys and two girls. Next, there were the seven-year-olds, two boys and a little girl who had stolen my heart after nearly killing me. I'd named her Nikki.

There had been four more, just two years old, mere babes, but they too, were gone.

It had not escaped my notice that each group of children included equal numbers of males and females, likely siblings. Which meant my Nikki probably had a sister who had not survived. And that thought infuriated me.

When we'd taken this ship, we'd also found nearly a hundred vampires, half-starved and locked up in cells. They'd been captives, used to train the killer children. Most of them had left the ship by now. Every time we dared venture near enough to shore, another group would take to the water to make their way to land. Our friend Devlin and his dwindling gang had headed out to a private island to take refuge and begin to build what he referred to as "the resistance." We were not at war with mankind, exactly. But there were elements among them who were determined to wipe us out of existence, and Devlin intended to fight back. When he left, the two eldest Offspring, Wolf and Sheena, had jumped into the sea after him. I'd had time to shout a mental warning, but we'd been spotted and had to flee. Devlin said he would go back for the two. And it killed me that I didn't know whether he'd managed to save them or not.

Another group of vampires had taken the two-year-olds with them when they'd left the ship, to find a safe haven in which to raise them. We couldn't give them back to the mortals. The children were powerful. How powerful, we still didn't know. But they'd been bred to be used as weapons against us. Mortals could not be trusted with such a powerful force, nor could they be counted on to raise the children as souls deserving of love and kindness, rather than as a pack of killer dogs.

For two weeks, we'd had control of the ship. I thought the seven remaining children were beginning to understand that we were their friends, here to care for them, to save them. Bribing them with chocolate from the galley helped, as did having a few mortals among us who insisted vampires were neither evil nor in need of killing, as the children had been taught.

Seven-year-old Nikki was perched in the miniature crow's nest Christian had built, while he stood nearby, attentive, his big arms outstretched below in case she fell. Dear Christian. Despite his lumbering size, he had the heart and soul of a child himself. He'd been experimented on by those animals who called themselves scientists, as well.

"Look how Pandora watches over them," I said to Roland. My cat pretended not to like the little ones mauling her, but she was never far from them, always guarding, watchful, protective, as if they were her own cubs.

"The sight of a small child flung across the back of a black panther might be alarming to some," Roland said, and I heard the smile in his voice.

"To me, it's a sight that deserves to be painted by a master."

I sent Nikki a wave and she smiled hugely and waved back, her sleek black hair falling into her eyes as she did. I wanted to shower that little girl in precious gems and swathe her in fabric spun of gold.

"Your eyes, when you look at her," Roland whispered, "shine in a way I've never seen, Rhiannon."

I shifted my gaze back to my mate. "I've never felt this way before, Roland. I want to give her a home. A childhood of magic and wonder, of luxury and delight."

"You love her."

I nodded, blinking down an uncharacteristic swell of emotion. "I guess I do. I never thought I would have the chance to raise a child. This is a gift that might never come again."

He pushed a hand through my hair in that way he so often did, lifting the long dark length of it and tucking it behind my ear. "I'll make arrangements to get us to Maine."

My smile was fast and bright. "Thank you, my love." I kissed his cheek, but when I pulled away, his strong arms closed around me, tugging me hard against him and holding me there, pressed tight, chest to chest, thigh to thigh.

"That sad little peck was hardly a thank you at all, my goddess."

Oh, he knew how to get to me, my Roland did. I smiled slowly and, leaning up, whispered into his ear, "Once we're in the privacy of our cabin, I'll thank you properly." Then I nipped his earlobe and felt a rush of pleasure course through him.

Perhaps I was asking the impossible of him, but I knew my Roland. Even if I asked for us to go and live on the moon, he would make it happen. Besides, he was as smitten with Nikki and her brothers Ramses and Gareth, as I.

I leaned into his chest there on the deck, feeling blissful

and even optimistic.

And then there was an ear splitting sound, the blast of a deep-throated horn, repeating itself over and over. I spun to face Roland. "What–?"

"It's the alarm. Something must be wrong."

The hatch flew open; Charlotte and Killian burst through, wide eyed. "We intercepted a transmission," Charlotte shouted. "They've found us, Rhiannon. They're heading this way. We have to get the children off this ship!"

"We're miles from shore and we haven't a single lifeboat," I cried. "For the love of the gods, Roland, what are we going to do?"

"Rhiannon." Roland put his hands on my shoulders, squeezed firmly. "You don't panic in the face of attack. You never have. You're more than equal to this challenge."

"But the children—"

"Imagine the children aren't here. Imagine it's just you and me and a few mortals who can't swim. What would you do? Hmm?"

I blinked slowly, knowing he was right. It was completely unlike me to panic. And moreover, in order to use the skills that made me more than just an ancient vampiress, skills I'd learned in my childhood. I needed to calm my mind, settle my spirit.

I shut the children out of my thoughts, a cold but necessary act. I detached my awareness from my body and connected to the gods.

As the others gathered around me on the deck of *The Anemone*, I stood near the rail, facing the midnight sea. My eyes were closed, my arms up and open wide in a crescent-like arc meant to emulate the moon. It was known as the Goddess Pose among practitioners of magic. I spoke in the ancient tongue of my ancestors and called down the strongest power I had ever channeled. Directly from Isis, I called it down, and She poured it out for me as She had never failed to do. I felt Her energy rushing through me.

"Look at her," I heard little Nikki whispering. "She's all light."

Roland said, "Yes, child. Rhiannon is more than a vampire. Before she was ever changed, she was a powerful priestess of Isis. Maybe the most powerful ever to train in the temples of Ancient Egypt."

I lowered my arms, opened my eyes, gazed down over the rail into the water. I could see with the Eyes of the Goddess. I could see far beneath the waves. And I scanned further and further from *The Anemone.* And then I spotted her; a shipwreck lying at the bottom of the Pacific. I focused on her, extended my arms out over the waters, palms down until the seas began to churn. And then slowly, I turned my palms up, and raised them inch by trembling inch.

"They're fifteen minutes from us," Charlie whispered urgently, but I tuned her out. Tuned all of them out, or nearly all, as the water became a bubbling froth.

"Roland, we have to do something," the fledgling insisted.

"We are, Charlotte. We are." I was vaguely aware of Roland's voice. Him, I could never tune out entirely, nor would I. Then he said, "Tell Killian to head *The Anemone* closer to where all that churning is."

"What *is* that?" she whispered.

"I believe it's our ride."

I opened my eyes and saw the old ship rising from the deep, first her mast, bent and cracked. And then her body. Seawater cascaded from her deck as she broke surface and bobbed there beneath the midnight sky, shuddering, groaning, but staying afloat by the power of my magic.

The Anemone headed toward the ghost ship, and everyone around me was muttering, whispering. Charlotte's mortal mother Trish and grandmother Roxanne, the oldest living member of The Chosen, so far as anyone knew. Christian was there, and Larissa, a timid young vampiress of exceptional beauty. Lucas, a former DPI officer, stood off by himself. He was always by himself, and I suspected he would leave our little band as soon as he could. Killian had gone to the bridge to maneuver *The Anemone* nearer. None of them had ever seen anything like what they were seeing now; a ghost ship rising from her grave.

Nikki looked up at me, her raven hair styled exactly like my own, long and black and straight, with bangs. Her eyes were wide. I think I had finally impressed her. I would drape the child in jewels and silks when we managed to get ourselves back to civilization.

She was my child. She was my daughter. No matter who had made her or how, she was mine. I would kill for her.

"Get us closer. Right up alongside," Roland called out.

Charlotte cut loose a whistle, and within seconds the huge white owl that had become her companion swooped silently from the darkness to alight on her forearm.

"If she cuts you, you'll bleed out, Charlotte," her mother warned.

Roxanne made a "psssh" sound. "Olive would never cut flesh. Would you, girl?" And she stroked the bird's head.

Killian managed to maneuver the modern ship as close to the ancient one as anyone could have. There was still a thirty foot gap between *The Anemone* and the broken-down wreck. She shouldn't be floating. Only my energy was keeping her above the waves. And somehow, those of us with the strength to do so were going to have to toss or carry everyone else across that chasm of ocean. And fast.

I turned to look for my cat. Pandora was nearby. She never wandered far from the children. She was pacing, her long tail twitching now and then. Clearly, she sensed the danger. "Roland, Killian, Charlie, jump across," I said. "Larissa and I will throw everyone else to you."

"I can help," Christian said. He wasn't a vampire. He was another government science experiment. One of The Chosen, he'd been given a drug called BDX to give him superhuman strength. But he was never told it would dramatically shorten his life expectancy. Charlotte had been the same, but she was a vampire now, and out of danger. Christian was going to have to become one of us soon, or his heart would explode from his chest. Stress, battle, even fear, could initiate the end for him. He knew this, but he kept saying he wasn't ready. However, he'd also been treated with a chemical that made imbibing his blood toxic to vampires.

We had expected to have more time to solve this challenge. But none of the ship's records had provided an answer.

"We can make that jump, too," Nikki said, tugging my sleeve and looking up at me. "We're as strong as vampires."

"No, you're not, darling. You're–"

I stopped when Roland touched my cheek, a whisper of his elegant fingertip, lovingly brushing over my skin. "We don't know how strong they are at all, do we?" he asked.

I looked at him with wide eyes. "No, but–"

"Perhaps we should let them try," Roland said.

Horrified at the thought, I wrapped Nikki in my arms and shouted, "Pandora, come!" Then I ran and jumped. The night wind whipped my hair, razed my ears, and made my eyes water as we rocketed. I aimed for a solid looking section of the decrepit ship's deck and landed, light and easy. Pandora landed right beside me a fraction of a second later. I set Nikki down, looked back, and saw Killian and Charlotte run and jump across, hand in hand. Killian landed in a springy crouch, but Charlotte came down hard on the deck beside me, boards cracking beneath her.

Fledglings.

She sent me a sheepish shrug. "Hey, I'm not even two weeks Undead yet, Rhiannon. Cut me some slack, will you?" She bounced upright and went to the rail, waved, and one of the children, the seven-year-old boy I'd named Ramses, gave a running leap. He came flying at Charlotte. Not to her, but *at* her, like a missile. He landed so close that she ducked, then he threw his dark head back and shouted, "We are as strong as you, vampire. And we'll get stronger!"

Then the rest of the children came leaping across the

chasm. It seemed as if the ghost ship was under fire and they were the cannonballs. They soared out of the night and onto the ship, all four of the eleven-year-olds, and the one remaining seven-year-old, Gareth, who crossed his arms and sent a disparaging look Nikki's way.

Nikki tugged her little hand from mine and when she looked up at me, her dark eyes were angry. "I could have jumped, too. I'm as strong as you."

Perhaps she was, I thought. Perhaps she was. "Next time I won't hold you back," I told her. But I wasn't altogether sure it was a promise I could keep. When Roland had suggested I let her jump, the image of her missing her mark and plunging into the sea had been vivid and cold in my mind's eye. I'd panicked.

The thought of losing her....

I crouched to put myself at eye level with her, while Charlotte shouted, "Throw the mortals across and let's get out of here!"

I put my hands on Nikki's shoulders and met her eyes. "I'm sorry I didn't let you jump, Nikki."

She crossed her arms over her chest, thrust her lower lip out. "What means, 'sorry'?"

"Sorry means–I wish I hadn't done that."

"Rhiannon we have to move," Roland said.

"Yes, yes, I know, love." I straightened, saw Larissa wrap her arms around Lucas, the former traitor to his own kind, and jump across. Roland hugged Roxanne to him and did likewise, and finally Christian gave a mighty leap, carrying Trish in his beefy arms. They all landed safely, Christian hitting so hard our boat rocked to one side. And I frowned as I saw *The Anemone* heading away from us, out to sea.

I shot a questioning look at Killian.

"I set her course before I jumped," he said. "She should lead them away from us, give us a head start. But we have to hurry. They've deployed jets."

"Rhiannon, *The Glamourie*," Roland urged.

"Yes, of course." Raising my arms, I cast the concealment spell I'd been taught as a child, *The Glamourie*, over the ghost ship on which we now sailed, and glimpsed the subtle shimmer of the space around us that told me the illusion was in place. While I, and everyone onboard could still see the ship on which we rode, anyone not aboard would see only ocean.

Quickly then, I went to the very front of the ghost ship and leaned out over the prow, lifting my hands toward the bit of coastline I could see in the distance and willing the old wreck to move in that direction.

And she did. Slowly at first, and then faster as the wind blew my hair back away from my face. I felt the kiss of brine on my skin, and the smell of land, of trees and earth, grew stronger. Then suddenly, my concentration was broken by a whirring, whistling sound overhead.

Every one of us looked up in fear as missiles appeared out of the empty sky, their tails flaming against the dark. They angled sharply downward, aiming themselves at the ship we'd been aboard only minutes earlier. We could still see her heading away from us in the distance.

The missiles hit their mark and *The Anemone* exploded in a series of deafening booms and blinding blue-white flashes. The impacts rocked our own vessel, and the reverberations thudded in my chest.

"Roland—" I reached out for him, my gaze fixed to the distant red-orange flames and black roiling smoke that had been *The Anemone.*

He clasped my hand immediately. "I know."

"They never intended to arrest us. They intended—and still intend—to wipe us out."

"I know, love."

"And the children—they knew the children were aboard!" I stared into his eyes, horrified, and he stared back into mine.

Nikki squeezed between us. "Rhiannon, you have to do that thing again! My feet are getting wet."

I looked down at her, realizing, as was everyone else

aboard, that our ghost ship was rapidly sinking. I had let go of the spell I'd cast.

"It's okay," Nikki said. "I can do it." She leaned into the cradle of the prow, looked out over the water, closed her little eyes and lifted her hands just as I had done to raise the vessel in the first place.

"It's sweet, the way she mimics you, love," Roland said, "But truly, you need to—"

"It's rising," I whispered. I felt it. I couldn't look away from my little girl to watch the seawater withdrawing from around our feet, but I knew the others were. I heard them whispering, sensed their awe.

Quickly, I recast *The Glamourie* to conceal our wreck from prying eyes. And then I moved to stand right beside Nikki. Softly, so as not to break her concentration, I said, "Very good. Now guide her toward shore. See it? It's closer than ever."

Her little eyes opened, mere slits, and she nodded once, then squeezed them shut again. She made fists of her hands, jabbed her forefingers straight forward. And the ghost ship resumed its journey toward shore.

"How are you doing it, Nikki?" I asked, keeping my voice low and level, so I wouldn't break her concentration.

"I saw you do it."

"But there's more to it than just how you stand or where you point. How did you know about the...the other parts? The parts that come from inside?"

"I *listened* to you do it. Not with my ears. You know." Then she grinned. "Watch this." She swung her arms right, and the ship tilted and turned, veering sharply that way. Everyone stumbled, grabbing anything to keep from falling. Then she looped her arms back again, and the hulk obeyed.

Clinging to a broken mast and looking ill, Roxanne shouted, "Unless you want us all barfing over the side, ladies, knock it off already!"

I smiled, I couldn't help it. Nikki looked up at me. "What means barfing?"

I opened my mouth, poked a finger inside, made a gagging sound, and she smiled. One of the first expressions of emotion I'd seen cross her face. The ship shuddered, though, so I quickly pulled her back into control, adding a burst of speed and pointing us toward what appeared to be a deserted stretch of forested shoreline. I had let my little protégé practice her newfound skills long enough. Our lives were at stake.

When I felt the hull dragging over sand, I knew we would have to swim for it, but then Roland touched my shoulder, and when I looked, he nodded toward the stern. There was a dinghy, still attached after so much time. It was no more seaworthy than the ship, but certainly no less. We could make the final part of our journey that way.

Killian and Christian saw where we were looking and hurried back there to start freeing the smaller vessel from its age-frayed bonds, and Charlotte came to us, held out a hand. "Come on, Nikki. You can sit with me."

Nikki went, not seeking my permission first. She was a free spirit, despite the fact that her entire life had been spent in captivity. And she was far more, I realized. Far more. Who knew how much?

As she ran off with Charlotte, I said to Roland. "Did you hear? She said she knew how to do the spell because she observed me doing it. Sensed me doing it."

He nodded. "So in addition to incredible strength, agility, and speed, they have powerful psychic skills."

"I wonder if she can read my thoughts? I wonder if she could, even if I were blocking them?"

"We'll try it and find out." He caressed my cheek and I closed my eyes at his touch, which never failed to elicit shivers of pleasure in me. And never would. "When we've found our haven, we'll have time to help her explore her abilities and master them."

"She could've made that jump from *The Anemone*," I said softly. "You were right, Roland, I should not have stopped her."

He took my arm as we quickly walked the length of the ship to where the others were gathered around the smaller boat. "You've been her mother for all of ten days, my love. There's bound to be a...what do they call it? A learning curve?"

"Mother." I stared at Nikki, who was climbing into the rickety lifeboat with Pandora right behind her. The cat looked dubious about the idea. "I'm not sure I'm comfortable with that word."

"Big sister?" Roland teased. "Youthful aunt?"

I smiled. "Guardian, perhaps."

"Guardian my ass," Charlotte called with a grin. "She's your Mini-Me. Now let's go, huh? Before those idiots figure out the ship they just blew up was empty."

Roland met my eyes, his message for me alone. *They will figure it out. And it will not take very long. The moment they do, they'll be after us again. We cannot let our guard down, Rhiannon. Not for a second.*

I nodded, knowing he was right.

We made our way to shore in the dinghy, sixteen of us crammed into a lifeboat designed to hold twelve, and as we did, I released my hold over the ghost ship. I pushed her out into deeper waters with my will, and then watched as she sank slowly beneath the waves, returning again to her saltwater grave.

When she was gone, leaving but a telltale hissing and frothing above her, the only things that remained on the horizon were the smoke and flames of *The Anemone*, and the silhouettes of several vessels now speeding toward her. Coast Guard or military, I couldn't be sure. DPI had the entire force of the US government at its disposal these days.

As if further proof of that, we were startled by the deafening sound of helicopters, like massive, prehistoric insects, pounding over our heads to join in the grim search for our remains.

And for the remains of the seven innocent children.

Our enemies were ruthless, and they were powerful. For

the first time I wondered if we truly had a chance to survive now that the world knew of our existence and had deemed us monsters in need of annihilation.

CHAPTER TWO

We took shelter three hours before dawn in an abandoned candle factory not far from the sea. Our best guess was that we were in the state of Washington, but we did not yet know where. Our refuge was small for a factory—two levels of brown brick in a perfect square, surrounded by a time-dulled chain-link fence that leaned drunkenly one way and another. Weeds and a broken up patch of pavement stood between the fence and the building. We only knew it was a candle factory because of the tall smokestack that still bore the fading image of a white taper candle with an orange and red flame. Inside, the place was barren aside from broken glass, shredded insulation, and rodent droppings. It was not ideal, but we needed shelter before dawn, and so we had little choice but to take the first viable option, though we had another three hours of darkness remaining. Being caught out in the open as the sun rose would prove fatal, even to vampires as old as Roland and I, to say nothing of the younger ones among us; Killian, Charlie, Larissa.

"The boat was nicer than this," Nikki said, looking around the dim, dirty place and wrinkling her nose at the scents of mildew and mice.

"At least we're not in cages," said Gareth, one of the two boys I considered her brothers. He had a soft heart, I thought. Ramses and Nikki were both hard edged and bore streaks of the cruelty they had experienced. Gareth was tender, more easily wounded, I thought, though I had only my instincts and his expressive brown eyes to judge by.

Roxanne had excused herself shortly after we'd arrived, saying she was going out for supplies, and she'd taken Lucas and Larissa with her. That had been two hours ago, and I was starting to worry. I trusted Roxanne above any mortal I had ever known. She was more than just the oldest living Chosen. She was a friend. But as for Lucas, I didn't trust that one as far as I could throw him. He, too, was one of The Chosen. But he'd willingly worked for those DPI forces that were neither military nor law enforcement, but something else. Something dark.

The vampires aboard ship had taken to calling them Crows, because they dressed all in black. I rather thought the moniker was an insult to corvids.

We had left everything behind. We had no clothing, no telephones, no sustenance, neither for us nor for the children. We were desperate. And a desperate vampire is a dangerous thing. The hungry looks in the eyes of Killian and Charlotte were not lost on me.

"We should find some humans to feed on," I said to Roland. I, too, was hungry to the point of distraction. We'd expended a lot of energy making our escape. We needed to replenish.

"Let's wait and see what our intrepid explorers come up with first, all right?" Roland suggested. "I've seen no fewer than three raggedy looking males scuffling past our hideout in the past two hours," I told him. "Easy prey."

"I've seen them too. Drunk, addicted, homeless, mentally

ill, or some combination of those things, more than likely."

"Does it matter?" I asked. "They could still spare a little blood without suffering harm. And the buzz of intoxication it might carry would frankly be a welcome break."

He looked surprised by my comment, but before he could respond, the sound of a motor distracted us both. We ran to the nearest broken window, keeping to one side, so as not to reveal ourselves. It wasn't one motor, but two. Two nearly identical vans stopped just beyond the chain-link fence that surrounded this place. Lucas emerged from one of them, and after looking around, he opened the gate. It wasn't easy. The thing was lopsided and looked as if it hadn't been moved in years, but he managed it, despite being a mere mortal.

"Motor cars," Roland said, using the same tone one might use to say, "Spoiled fish." He'd done well at sea, which had surprised me. The man had a powerful aversion to modern modes of transportation. Always had.

Within moments, Roxanne was coming inside, Larissa and Lucas right behind her, their arms laden with sacks from a fast food chain. Roxanne returned my questioning look with a wink, and said, "Gather 'round if you're hungry. We brought back dinner."

The children mobbed her. Our four eleven-year-olds and three seven-year-olds didn't have a clue about manners or sharing. Roxanne laughed while handing out paper-wrapped fast-food sandwiches, boxes of fries, and bottles of water. She couldn't blame them for their lack of etiquette. They'd been raised like animals. It wasn't their fault.

Then Lucas shrugged off a backpack and held it out in my direction. Frowning, I moved nearer, taking it. "What's this?" But already the scent was reaching me. Blood. The luscious, precious stuff of life. My mouth watered.

"We borrowed a phone," Lucas said. "Used it to track down the nearest blood bank. Security's never great at those places."

"No doubt that will change soon, like everything else."

I unzipped the backpack and took out a bag containing a full pint. Without hesitation I pierced the plastic with my fangs and drank. It wasn't warm, and it wasn't pulsing into my mouth with the force of a still-beating heart. But it bore the essence I needed to survive, to replenish, to regain my strength. Charlotte, Killian and Roland gathered round to do the same. I could tell that Larissa had already fed by the nearly mortal pinkness to her flesh.

The children wolfed their food, though I paid little mind to any of them. As I drank, the bloodlust rose up in me, causing my eyes to glow red, and my body to heat with a need for other sorts of fulfillment. In our kind, sexual desire and bloodlust are intertwined, each stoking the other until they become difficult to tell apart.

I lowered the bag, licking my lips, my eyes seeking out my mate.

Roland threw his empty bag to the floor and came to me, snapping his arms around me and kissing me so passionately that the few remaining windows in the place began to rattle with the energy we emitted.

A throat cleared loudly. Roxanne's.

We parted just enough to note that everyone in the place was staring at us. Charlotte and Killian included, although they looked flushed themselves, and their eyes were glowing, too. And poor Larissa had no one to focus her desire upon...though the looks she was sending Lucas's way spoke volumes. They were not lost on him, either. And they made him nervous. I could feel it in him.

Roland licked his lips, his eyes on mine as he got himself under control. The man sometimes exercised a bit too much of it for my taste. "Roxanne," he said, "Where did you get all of this? Surely someone will notice two missing vehicles, a break-in at a blood bank, and—"

"Come on, Roland, you know me better than that by now," she said with a toss of her flame-red hair. "The vans belong to a local grocer who's closed on the weekends. He won't even miss them 'til Monday. And I discombobulated the in-dash GPS systems."

"There must have been security cameras," Roland went on.

"Yes. And I didn't bother breaking those. Kept my face concealed," she said, tugging up her hood to demonstrate. Then she tugged it down again, smiling. "I figured, let 'em see their car thief on camera. That should prove it was an ordinary human, not a vampire."

Lucas was nodding as she spoke, agreeing with her every word. "I was very careful at the blood bank," he said when she finished. "Easy in, easy out, didn't damage anything, and they might not even notice the missing bags."

"And the food?" Roland asked.

Roxy shrugged. "All right, all right, I had to pick a pocket for that. The fellow was drunk, staggering along the sidewalk. I didn't clean him out. Just took a couple of twenties, and slipped his wallet right back where I found it."

"We even returned the cell phone when we were finished with it," Larissa added.

Roland didn't look as if he approved. I did, however. "Did you happen to find out where we are, Roxanne?" I asked.

She nodded. "Near the Canadian border," she said. "I have a safe house fifty miles northeast. It's in the middle of nowhere, and like most of my places, it has everything we need. Weapons, untraceable cell phones, a computer with a constantly changing ISP, and satellite internet. There are moose for neighbors. We'll be safe there indefinitely. I can work from there to get us some convincing false identities while we figure out what to do next."

"What we do next is nothing," I said softly. "We just get there, and we give ourselves some blessed rest. The gods know we need it."

Everyone nodded in agreement.

"And as for false identities, Roland and I have those in abundance," I went on with a look his way.

"Indeed. We need only make our way to one of the safe

deposit boxes we have scattered about the country under various names."

Our bank accounts were set up in much the same way. We had money to burn, account numbers and passwords committed to memory.

"I don't have any of that," Killian said.

I shot him a look. "And you've survived as a vampire for how long now?"

He shrugged. "Thirty years or so."

"Well, that explains it. Lesson One, fledgling. Build many identities. Set up many bank accounts under many names. And put aside piles of emergency cash and precious metals, driver's licenses, passports, debit and credit cards in many places. That's how our kind gets by in the mortal world."

Killian sighed and Charlotte leaned her head on his shoulder and said, "I hope it won't always have to be that way. I hope someday we can live our lives in the open, use our real names, our real bank accounts."

"I wouldn't hold my breath," Roxanne said. Then she looked at Roland and me. "We should hit the road now, get as far as we can before sunrise. We might even make it all the way. We still have a couple hours 'til dawn. Those vans are both full of gas, and there are no windows in the back. I have another vehicle garaged at the safe house. So we can return the borrowed ones tomorrow before the grocer even knows they were gone."

Roland nodded and I could see him releasing his worry and doubt. "You're the smartest mortal I know, Roxy."

"Maybe the smartest there is," she said with a wink. "Now let's get a move on."

* * *

When I fell asleep, I was lying down in the back part of a dark colored van beside my beloved Roland and young Larissa. The third row seats had been folded down to make room for us. Lucas was driving. Christian sat in the front passenger seat, and the three seven-year-olds, Nikki, Ramses, and Gareth, were in the second row of seats, staring out the windows in wide-eyed silence. It occurred to me that they had never seen much of planet Earth before. They'd been created and raised in a floating laboratory at sea. They had never set foot on dry land. I had noticed them swaying now and then, sensed their bouts of dizziness since we'd come ashore. But that seemed to be lessening with time.

The other van, the one leading the way, carried the four eleven-year-olds, who were probably as mesmerized by the passing scenery as their younger counterparts. Charlotte and Killian were in the far back of that vehicle. Roxanne was driving, and Trish rode shotgun.

Three generations in that van. Charlie was a vampire, her mother Trish, an ordinary mortal. And Roxanne, Charlie's grandmother, Trish's mother-in-law, was the oldest living Chosen. She could become a vampire, but she claimed she didn't want to. I often wondered why. It was not something she had confided to me. By all rights, she should've been dead years ago. The Chosen rarely lived to see forty, unless they accepted the Dark Gift. Roxanne was well beyond forty, though she refused to say exactly how old she was, and it was impossible to tell. The woman was ageless.

Those were my thoughts as the day sleep claimed me as swiftly and surely as death itself.

When I woke again, I was still in the back of the van, though in a different position. Someone had lowered the second section of seats and rearranged our bodies to give us more room. That same someone—Roxanne, I suspected—had covered the van's front windows with dark green trash bags and duct tape to protect us from the sun.

I usually take my time about rising in the evening. But that night, I was too nervous to languish in my lover's arms. I sat up quickly, gathered up my discarded shoes, and clambered over my now-waking beloved, to open the sliding side door and jump out onto the ground.

My bare feet sank into cool damp grass. I gave my senses

permission to relish that feeling as I looked around at rolling hills and dense forest. Old trees, giant conifers, made the air almost sticky with their piney aroma. I turned around, my senses delighted as the stars winked to life in a cloudless dark blue velvet sky. There was a large log cabin that had perhaps been a lodge of some kind once. It was a stunning building, its portico supported by logs so huge I doubted I could wrap my arms around a single one of them. Its arched front windows gleamed with a warm yellow light from within. It felt welcoming, that light. And I saw too, the oversized shutters that bracketed each window and could be closed to block sunlight by day.

Roland exited the van and came to stand behind me, his hands curling over my shoulders as he joined me in admiring the place. I followed his gaze to the eastern horizon, where the uppermost curve of the biggest, roundest, most beautiful moon imaginable was just inching her way up for the evening.

The other van's door slid open and Killian and Charlotte emerged from it, met my eyes and nodded a greeting. Larissa came out next and said, "So this is it, then? The safe house?"

"By the gods, I hope so," Roland whispered.

The front door of the log cabin opened. Roxanne stood on the other side, her hand on her hip. "Well? You gonna come inside or stand there star-gazing all night?" And then Nikki squeezed past her and came racing down the broad front steps toward us. I opened my arms. She sped right past me and directly to Roland, but she stopped short of running into his ready embrace, looking uncertain.

Roland scooped her up in his arms all the same, but I saw him watching her face, ready to put her down should she seem uncomfortable.

"I wanted to spend the day outside with you, but Roxy wouldn't let me." She said it as if she was fully expecting Roxanne to be punished for committing such a despicable offense.

"That's just as well, little one," Roland said. "Roxy's a smart lady and you should always listen to her. She was protecting us from the sunlight. We can't allow it to touch us."

"Or what?" she asked, resting on his hip and searching his face.

"Or they go up in flames, that's what," Ramses called. He had come outside as well, made his way to us, and stood close beside me. There was no rush, no hug, but something told me to take his hand in mine, and when I did, he didn't pull away. Instead he looked up at me and asked, "Right?"

By the Gods, this one was making inroads into my heart, as well. "You could've put it more delicately than that, Ramses. But yes, we are quite susceptible to sunlight."

Gareth, named by Roland after a man he had both served and loved back in his human days, had come out as well, but he stood uncertainly, halfway between us and the cabin's door.

"So you've been cooped up indoors all day, have you?" Roland asked, setting Nikki on her feet, taking her hand, and walking up to Gareth to take hold of his.

"It's all right. It's a nice house," Gareth said. "And the bedrooms are bigger than the ones we had on the boat."

"And way bigger than our cages were," Ramses added.

"You will never be in cages again," I told them. "Never ever."

"And tonight, we are going to teach you to play tag," Roland said.

I widened my eyes at him. He smiled and shrugged. "They need exercise and distraction. And we need to see what they're capable of. Roxy, get the older children out here. They'll enjoy this too."

"Roland, your leg–" I began.

He waved a dismissive hand. "The prosthetic Killian made for me is more than capable of a game of tag, Rhiannon. You worry too much."

Odd, I was usually the one accusing him of that.

I gave in, though. And so it was that I, Rhiannon, daughter of pharaoh and queen of the vampire race, played tag with my beloved Roland and seven genetically engineered children, one full moon night in a forested bit of glorious western Canada.

* * *

Roland watched his beautiful Rhiannon running around with the children over grassy lawns, beneath star-dotted skies. She seemed to be glowing from within. Motherhood suited her. The love in her eyes for the young ones did something to him, made him feel larger and stronger, more protective than ever.

They had shut Pandora inside, in case things became too exciting. The cat had very little experience with children, the past two weeks aside, and it would be horrible if she took a swipe at one of them. A game of tag could easily arouse her instincts, cause her to revert to hunting mode.

Pandora didn't mind. Last he'd glimpsed her, she'd been stretched in front of the fireplace, soaking up its heat as if it was her sustenance.

Ramses sped toward him, having noticed him standing still, and Roland waited until the boy was almost within reach to step out of the way, moving so fast, it must seem he'd vanished from Point A and reappeared at Point B. Ramses gave his head a shake, then looked around and spotted him.

This was no ordinary game of tag. The children were nearly as fast as Rhiannon, and equally matched with him, due to his missing leg. They ran and jumped, leaped and tumbled, climbed trees as nimbly as chipmunks and leapt from limb to limb like spider monkeys.

Rhiannon outran little Nikki, caught Roland's eyes and wiggled her brows at him. Then she pressed her back against a tree trunk, closed her eyes, and vanished just as the little girl reached her.

Nikki stood still, frowning and tipping her head to one side. "You're still there," she said. "You only made yourself look like the tree's skin."

"It's called bark," she said, stepping away from the tree, her colors returning.

"I want to try!" Nikki said. She quickly turned round, and backed up until her body was pressed to the tree trunk.

Teaching your child how to become invisible might not be the best idea, Rhiannon, Roland warned.

Nikki frowned at him–had she heard his thoughts just then? Then she shot a look at Rhiannon again. "You don't have to show me anyway. I've seen you do it two times."

She shifted her little weight against the tree, closed her eyes, and Roland thought she started to shimmer, but then Ramses ran at her, grabbed her around the waist, and jumped up onto the lowest limb, shouting, "Why learn to disappear when you can run faster than anyone who might be after you?" he demanded.

He sounded truly agitated.

From the cabin, Roxy called, "If anyone's hungry, I've got enough to feed an army in here!"

Nikki sprang down from the tree and zoomed toward the cabin, a seven-year-old blur of motion and energy. Her brothers looked at each other, shrugged, and went after her. No goodbye or parting words. No eager laughter or joking. They were such stoic little things.

"We'll teach them," Rhiannon said. "Seven years in a cage will take some time to undo. But we have time. We'll heal them."

"And they us, I think."

Rhiannon tilted her head to one side, and Roland found himself wanting to trace the lines of her royal cheekbones and deceptively delicate jaw. "Do we need healing, Roland?" He could see the worry appear in her eyes. Rhiannon's emotions ran high. She couldn't conceal them if she tried. Her eyes were like compasses, pointing him to the direction of her mood. He loved her so much it was like an ever-present ache in his soul. Yet, somehow, a good ache. A vital ache. An ache he would not wish to live without.

"Roland?"

Now her brows furrowed over her piercing onyx eyes. She

could see to his soul. "I don't know what made me say that," he said. "Something's got me feeling a sense of...I can't put words to it. Trepidation?"

"You're worried?"

"More like what I've heard described as the sensation of someone walking over my grave."

She hunched her shoulders. Gave a shiver. "Roland, you're frightening me."

"I'm sorry. Maybe my brain is having a bit of trouble accepting that we're safe here." He looked around, inhaled to smell the air. It was redolent with pine, fresh as the water from a melting glacier. "It's force of habit, my love," he said, taking her hands and willing her to look around. "This is a good place, Rhiannon, I can feel it."

She smiled then, leaning into him, tipping her face up beneath his. "We got away. The children are perpetually ravenous and will spend the next hour devouring everything Roxanne has prepared and asking for dessert. Now we can focus on each other for a little while."

Her hips rocked against his, pelvis brushing pelvis. His physical reaction was instant and demanding. She need only get that look in her eye for his body to react that way.

And what man, living or undead, wouldn't have a similar reaction? He suspected a great number of women would, as well. He clasped her backside in one hand, cradled her nape in the other, and tipping her head back, lowered his mouth to hers.

She sighed his name into his mouth, clung to his shoulders, and lifted one knee upward to hitch over his hip. He moved his hand over her hip, and down the back of her dress, lifting it. Then he replaced his hand on her buttock, nude this time. Rhiannon did not believe in undergarments.

She drew her hands up to his shoulders, then around his collar, pulling at him and tangling her tongue with his.

He brought his other hand down to free himself, as she unbuttoned his shirt and shoved it down his shoulders. Her nails raked his skin just short of cruelly, on the way back up his arms and across his shoulders. They dragged over his neck as he kicked free of his remaining clothes and then scratched a light trail down his chest. She shoved him away, then peeled her dress over her head and tossed it to the ground. And then she was on him, licking the tiny beads of blood her nails had drawn from his chest, and setting his very soul ablaze.

She licked her way lower, then dropped teasing kisses all over him from head to root and back again, until he thought his brain would melt. When he was at the edge of his endurance, she took him into her mouth, but that only intensified his need.

Clasping her hips, he urged her upward. Then he slid his hands to the backs of her thighs and lifted her around him. She locked her legs behind him and pulled him into her. Naked, they clung, body to body, heart to heart, soul to soul. She was everything, by the gods, she was.

They moved together, their beings synchronized, their rhythm as ancient and deep as the waves upon the sea. They kissed, and they clung, and they whispered love words that couldn't begin to describe what was truly between them.

And together they found release, they found bliss, they found heaven itself in each other.

* * *

Colonel Patterson of DPI had been starting to think he would be returning to the East Coast headquarters empty-handed. And then he got the call. Now he sat watching an interview through one-way glass at the local police department, and his hopes began to rise once more.

Independent Grocer Alvin Schultz sat across the table from a police officer, explaining again what he had already explained three times before Patterson had arrived. His frustration was understandable, but the colonel needed to hear this story for himself, straight from the grocer's mouth.

"Yes, two vans," Mr. Schultz said. "Almost identical. I've given you the make, model, year, plate number, VIN, and the photos on record with my insurer." He tapped his forefinger repeatedly on the table. "I would really like it if *I* could go home now, and *you* could start looking for my vans."

The cop said, "Look, I'm not trying to be a pain in your ass, Mr. Schultz, but I've got orders to report any stolen vehicles, break-ins or other suspicious activity to the Feds. Which I did. And they say you're stuck here until they show up. And you better believe I'm gonna have every i dotted and t crossed when they do. All right?"

The grocer's defiant expression melted away like a snowball in July. "Like what kinda Feds?" he asked. "FBI or something?"

Officer Tenny shrugged and Mr. Schultz seemed to get a little hitch in his breathing and whispered, "DPI?"

Clearly the guy had been watching the news. Officer Tenny's determinedly blank expression probably confirmed the grocer's suspicion. "Hell, it's those vampires from the hijacked ship, isn't it?"

"I don't have any information about that, sir."

"Bullshit. It's going around that some of the vamps jumped overboard off the Oregon coast. News can't confirm it yet. Or won't. I heard a couple of them were shot in the water… young ones, I heard."

"Where did you hear that, exactly?" Officer Tenny was not smiling, but his eyes were.

He'd be a better cop when he developed a more convincing poker face, Patterson thought.

Averting his face, the grocer shrugged. "I read it on Facebook. Posted and reposted. Who knows where it started out?" He shrugged and changed the subject. "The news says that ship was blown up not too far down the coast from here. You really think some of them survived?"

"I have no reason to think anything about any of this since it's all rumor and speculation."

"Except that the boat blew up. That's not rumor."

Officer Tenny nodded once. "That's being investigated by the Coast Guard. But I repeat, I don't have any reason to think the theft of your vans is related to that."

The cop would make a terrible politician.

"Well who else would steal two vans in the dead of night like that?" Schultz asked.

Officer Tenny shrugged. "Car thief?"

"Hell. *Hell*, I don't want any trouble with their kind. They can keep the damn vans." Schultz got to his feet. Colonel Patterson knew it was time to step in. "I've heard about them," the grocer said. "I watch the news, read the papers. Vampires are for real, have been all along. And the government *knew*." He shook his head hard. "Never mind," he said. "I withdraw my complaint."

"A little too late for that, sir," said Colonel Patterson, who had opened the door and entered the room almost silently and now stood right behind the grocer.

Mr. Schultz turned so fast he almost lost his balance.

The colonel flipped a badge. "I'm Colonel Patterson with the DPI."

"Ah, hell, I knew it." Alvin Schultz sat back down. "Dammit, I don't want any trouble with vampires."

Another cop opened the door and leaned inside. "We just pulled up the surveillance footage. It clearly shows the car thief, probably female, wearing jeans and a hoodie. She drove one van out, came back for the other, even closed the door behind her. Never shows her face to the camera, though."

Officer Tenny nodded and said, "Colonel, I'm sorry I got you out here for nothing. The thief clearly wasn't a vampire." He sounded almost heartbroken. Probably thought he was going to get a promotion for calling this in.

"Why not?" the grocer asked, his eyes jumping from one man to another.

"They don't show up on camera," Officer Tenny said.

Schultz sighed heavily, and Patterson thought every muscle in the guy's body relaxed a notch. "Good. Good. Just an ordinary thief. That's good." He leaned back in his chair and his legs sort of melted out to full length.

"That really doesn't prove anything," the Colonel said. "They sometimes use human accomplices. And we know for a fact there were several humans with the group we're hunting."

"The ones from *The Anemone*?" Mr. Schultz asked, relief turning back into fear right before Patterson's eyes.

"That's classified," Patterson said. "Sir, I really just have one question for you, and then I'll let you go on home. Are your vans equipped with GPS?"

"Of course they are. What car isn't these days?"

"I wouldn't know, Mr. Schultz." Patterson's heart beat a little faster. This could be the break he'd been waiting for. "Are the GPS systems in your vans factory-installed or aftermarket?" he asked.

"Both, and that's two questions. I really want to go now."

"You can leave when you've told me what I need to know, Mr. Schultz. Now explain what you mean by both."

The grocer didn't try to hide his impatience. He glanced Officer Tenny's way, but Patterson said, "The sooner you answer, the sooner you're out of here, Mr. Schultz."

He sighed, but conceded. "The vans have factory installed, in-dash nav systems. My drivers use those to get around. But I used to have a lot of trouble with the systems getting shut off during the day."

"By the drivers?"

"Not that they would admit. But yeah, I figured they were taking unauthorized breaks, going home for lunch, stopping off at a bar or whatever. So I had backup systems installed. They stay on all the time. Drivers don't even know they're there."

"You're a smart businessman, Mr. Schultz," Colonel Patterson said. "How are the backup systems working out for you?"

"Good enough that I had to fire two drivers."

The Colonel felt the urge to high-five someone, but there was no one around who knew the importance of this. So he just kept his stoic face in place, and celebrated on the inside.

"So we just need the info on those extra systems so we can track them, and then you're free to go."

Mr. Schultz got to his feet. "I already gave all of that to Officer Tenny." He turned toward the door, then turned back again. "I *really* don't want any trouble with their kind," he said. "Can you try to keep my name out of this?"

"I'm sure as hell not gonna give them your name," Colonel Patterson said. "But they know perfectly well where they stole those vans." He handed the grocer a card. "Don't leave town, Mr. Schultz. Call me directly if you think of anything else. And, uh, I don't recommend spreading it around that this is anything more than a garden variety, run-of-the-mill car theft. You don't need to mention that DPI is involved or any imagined connection to anything you might have seen on the Internet lately."

Mr. Schultz swallowed hard, his Adam's apple bulging, and tried to ask, "Why not?" but the words came out like a croak.

"Well, it's like you said, you don't want trouble with their kind."

Schultz looked scared. Truly scared. He grabbed his jacket off the back of the chair, and headed for the door.

"Remember," Patterson said, and when Schultz looked back, he put a finger to his lips. "Shhh."

CHAPTER THREE

Nikki was stretched out on the floor near the fireplace, playing a game of Trouble with Gareth and Ramses and eating potato chips, a treat she'd never had before. By the way she was eating them, I guessed they were a new favorite.

It was a peaceful night for us, the most peaceful in recent memory. Roland and I had even managed to slip away into the nearby forest for an hour of woodland lovemaking that left me weak-kneed and sappy, a state that was far from normal for me. By Isis, how I loved him. And then we'd gathered in the cabin's large living room for games and conversation.

Roland and I needed this haven. This rest. The past two years and especially the past few weeks, had likely been the most tense period in our lives together. We'd been pursued, even in our sleep, hunted like animals. This cabin in the woods provided a rare and desperately needed respite from all of that. It felt like bliss to us. I looked around at the others in the room. My beloved Roland sat beside me, watching over the three younger children; Ramses, Gareth, and Nikki, my precious Nikki. Pandora lay beside them, ever vigilant for she adored them as much as I, though she tried to pretend otherwise. She also adored the fireplace, and was basking in its heat.

Roxanne and Christian were arguing playfully over which type of pizza was the best and laughing. Every now and then I saw the children look their way during a burst of laughter, their eyes curious. I was sure they were talking amongst themselves, communicating without words. I could tell by the looks they exchanged. Laughter was a puzzle to them. I decided to let them work it out on their own. It was good that they were noticing expressions of emotion and wondering about them. It was very good.

Charlie and Killian snuggled together in a love seat near the fire. Trish and Larissa were admiring the wood and stone of the hearth.

These people around me were my family. There was no other way to describe this band of survivors we had formed. It was family. Well, with the exception of Lucas. I still did not trust him.

The older children, the eleven-year-olds, were restless. They wanted to know everything. Particularly Iris, with her blood red hair hanging dead straight past her shoulders and eyes as bright green as emeralds. "How does the television work? How do you read all the countless books around this place? What lies beyond the next hill? What are the cities and towns like?" All of that and more. And with every question she asked, her siblings gathered round to listen to the answer. They were like the thirsty desert absorbing the first spring rainfall. The other girl, Damiana, had hair just as red with a more bronze tint. It was thicker, and wavy, but her eyes were just as green, her skin just as pale. The boys had auburn hair and eyes of cerulean blue. Thorn's face was a little more angular, and Sage's eyes were bigger, the curves of his face a bit softer.

Trish had taken charge of them, with help from Charlotte and Killian. Charlotte had helped them choose their names from one of Roxy's books about the medicinal and magical properties of plants. They'd taken names they thought emulated the qualities they saw in themselves.

It had been a truly brilliant exercise in self-discovery for the children, I thought. Charlotte was going to be a wonderful guardian for them.

Sage, the herbal kind, represented wisdom and protection. And while it was Iris asking all the questions—her plant also denoted wisdom tempered by purification—Sage was the one who seemed to be most intent on hearing the answers. Iris was usually interrupting the answer to ask another question, unless the topic utterly fascinated her. She was more of a sifter, where Sage wanted it all.

"Did they sleep at all while we rested today?" Larissa asked, apparently noticing my eyes on the older children.

Trish smiled and shook her head. "I keep thinking they'll drop from exhaustion, sooner or later."

"They need structure, is what they need," Roxanne said with a firm nod. "And an education. They need to socialize with regular kids. Maybe a nice private school, one pricey enough that they don't ask too many questions. They could pass as mortals, if no one paid too much attention."

"Perhaps," Roland said, "if we taught them to hide what they truly, are—"

"And if we could be sure they wouldn't murder the first classroom bully or arrogant cheerleader who deserved it," I interrupted.

"They won't do that," Roxy said. "They haven't tried to kill any of us yet, have they? Or even any of you! And that's saying something, isn't it? Since they've been raised to think that's their reason for being."

"What about St. Michael's in Portland, where I went to middle school?" Charlotte asked. She shot a look at Killian. "Could it work, do you think?"

"A little mental manipulation of the mortals in charge, and anything can work," he said. Then he frowned. "Are you saying you want to…break up the band?"

It was a topic that had been on my mind, on everyone's mind, I thought, though no one wanted to broach it. So I cleared my throat and said, "It's time we each decide what we intend to do next and where we intend to do it. There is no requirement that we remain together. Roland and I, for example, intend to journey to the East Coast. Maine. We have friends there and it's familiar territory to us. We can make a home for Nikki, Gareth and Ramses there. A good one, I think." I glanced down at Nikki and her brothers as I spoke, but they seemed too immersed in their game to pay what I said any mind.

Trish nodded. "I've been thinking along the same lines as Charlie," she said. "I want to take the Elevens back to Portland and give them the most normal childhood possible for as long as I can. Roxy's had a false identity set up for me for months now. I'll change my hair color and style, maybe finally give in and get some reading glasses. I should be able to stay under the radar without too much trouble."

Of them all, she was the least sought after by the authorities. She was neither Undead nor one of The Chosen like Lucas. Neither was she a BDXer like Christian, nor one of The Offspring. She was an ordinary mortal with an extraordinary love for her daughter.

Roxanne's eyes took on a look of worry. "You don't have any idea what they can do, Trish. None of us have. Neither do they, though I have a feeling they know more about it than they've shared with us."

At that, Nikki stopped in the midst of moving her peg over the game board, but quickly resumed. I do not believe anyone else noticed the slip. But it was clear to me that, despite outward appearances, the children were listening intently to our every word.

"You might not be able to handle them on your own," Roxanne went on.

"That's why I'm hoping my daughter and new son-in-law

will come with me." Trish sent a longing smile Charlotte's way. "We've been on the run too long. It's time to try to get our lives back. Or rather, start new lives. That's really what we're talking about here." Then she watched the Elevens calmly close the books they were each reading, get up onto their feet and walk to the back of the oversized living room, which spanned the depth of the cabin's ground floor. They went out through the French doors and onto the cabin's rear deck.

Charlotte and Killian exchanged a long glance, speaking mentally, I suspected, though they kept it to themselves. At length, Killian gave a nod. Then Charlotte smiled at Trish and said, "Yes, we'll come with you, Mom. We were planning to take the Elevens ourselves and try to raise them anyway, and we'd be grateful to do it with you."

Trish arched her brows. "I guess that makes me a grandma, doesn't it?"

"Not if it makes me a great," Roxanne said, but she said it with a smile in her voice. The three of them then looked at Roxanne after she stopped speaking, and I realized they were waiting for her to say she was coming with them.

Charlie's grandmother didn't give in. Instead she turned and said, "What about you, Lucas? Larissa?"

Lucas spoke first, possibly because of the lost and confused look in Larissa's Arctic blue eyes. He said, "I've been thinking that the best way I can help your kind, and my own, is from the inside. I'm going to report back to my unit or what's left of it. I'll say I escaped *The Anemone* before it was blown to bits and made my way to shore. I might even drape myself in seaweed and lie on some deserted beach until someone finds me, just to make it convincing."

I studied him, looking for signs of a lie, and I heard Roland in my head saying, *I think he's right, don't you? We need someone on the inside, secretly working with us. He's a Lieutenant, a DPI officer. He can help a great deal from that position.*

I'm not so sure he'll help at all. I think he hasn't made up his mind where his loyalties lie, Roland. I do not trust him.

"And you Larissa?" Roxanne asked.

"I don't...I don't know."

Christian was looking fretfully from one person to the next. "I don't know, either," he said.

"You'll come with us, then," I told him. "Both of you, if that's what you want, Larissa." And then I looked at the ageless mortal redhead. "Roxanne? What about you?"

"She's coming with us, of course," Charlie said. But there was uncertainty in her voice.

Roxanne sent a resigned look her granddaughter's way and shook her head. "Not just yet, Charlotte. I need to go with Rhiannon and Roland. They can't raise the Sevens without help from someone who can be awake by day. And we all know Christian can't remain mortal much longer."

"I'm still doin' okay," Christian said. The idea of becoming one of the Undead terrified the big man. Apparently, more than the notion of his heart exploding from his chest did. But it was a ticking time bomb, whether he was willing to admit it or not. The stress of battle could bring him to a rapid and gruesome end.

Trying to change him over could bring one of us to the same.

"I can find someone to help us once we get to Maine, Roxanne," I told her, ignoring Christian's ongoing state of denial. "You should go with your family."

"I'll go with my family once you've found someone else. 'Til then, you need me. "

I wanted to argue, but could not deny her logic. She was right. And as I was forming my next words, Nikki slowly got up from her game, turned to face the front door, and said, "Someone's coming."

A chill went up my spine at the calm certainty in her voice. I rose and went to her, clasping her tiny shoulders gently in my hands while my mind scanned for the energy signatures of mortal intruders. I found none. "How do you know?" I asked, not even thinking to doubt her.

"I just do." She took a backward step, shaking her head left and right rapidly. "They're coming, and they're bad. They want to put us back in those cages. Don't let them, Rhiannon!"

"How could they have found us?" Roland asked, his expression as shattered as our peaceful interlude.

"The vans. Has to be the vans." Killian ran to the door and outside. Every vampire in the room was scanning for humans with evil intent, but I didn't feel them yet. Which meant they were not yet close enough for a vampire to detect. But close enough for The Offspring to sense them. Nikki felt them.

So, apparently, did the others. Her two brothers were on their feet, looking just as alarmed, and the Elevens came back inside. It was clear in their wide eyes that they were also sensing the approach of something dark. Something menacing. Damiana's face reflected none of the love and passion that her plant name evoked. Instead she seemed afraid.

Roland went outside behind Killian. I stood in the doorway watching as Charlotte's young mate opened the hood of the nearest van and poked around the engine. The breeze brought the scents of pine and that unique aroma of nighttime in the forest. The stars dotted a black velvet sky. It was too beautiful here to be dangerous. And yet...

"I disabled the GPS units," Roxanne called, coming to stand beside me in the doorway. "I made damn sure of it."

But then Killian turned, holding a small electronic box in his hand. "There was a backup unit hidden in the engine." He jogged over to the other van, opened its hood and pulled out an identical device.

I stepped outside, down the front steps to the grassy lawn, my heart sinking. There was no doubt that we had been located. Our enemies had found us. Our pursuers were on their way, and who knew how much time we had before they would arrive?

Our respite had been blissful, but all too brief. I clenched my fists so hard my nails dug into my palms. "When will we have relief from this constant struggle? When, dammit?"

Roxanne vanished into the depths of the house, then only seconds later, came back outside with several large zipper bags crammed full of items. "There's no time to monkey around here," she said, each word like the crack of a whip. "It's happened. They've found us. It's time for action. Trish, Charlie, Killian, take the Elevens and one of the vans and get the hell out of here." She handed Trish several of the bags and a set of keys. "There are birth certificates and Social Security numbers for all of you in here. Driver's licenses, even a few credit cards, all under false names. A couple of pay-as-you-go phones, as well."

Trish took the bags with trembling hands. She looked scared to death. "You just have these sorts of things lying around?"

"I've been around the block a few times. I know what's necessary."

Trish nodded, then herded the Elevens into the van without even a token argument. Charlie snapped her arms around Roxy's neck, hugging her hard. "Thank you, Gram. For everything."

"I love you, girl." Roxy hugged her back, blinking hard against the moisture in her eyes that she would not allow to spill over. "Take Olive with you, all right?"

"Yeah. I'll take good care of her, I promise." She gave a whistle, and the white owl came gliding silently from a nearby tree to land on Charlotte's forearm.

Roxanne latched onto Killian and hugged him, as well. "Be smart. Ditch that van and get another vehicle just as fast as you can."

"I will," Killian said, then as he turned Lucas clapped him on the shoulder.

"Give me those GPSs units, and I'll lead the Crows away from you."

"Smart thinking," Roxanne said. "Take the car from the garage, Lucas. The keys are in it and there's a clean phone in the glove box with my number programmed in."

Lucas gave a firm nod and headed for the garage attached to one side of the log cabin. I heard him opening the overhead door, and shifted my focus to Nikki, who'd come to stand close to my side. She was terrified. I could feel her fear emanating from her little body in waves.

Gareth and Ramses stood close to her, and all three were staring at the Elevens, who were staring back at them from inside the van. The van started to move and Larissa, shouted "Wait!" and ran toward it. It stopped, and its side door slid opened. She climbed inside with a last look back at us, and a lingering one at Lucas, who was already pulling Roxanne's sleek black Lincoln out of the garage.

Nikki smiled very slightly, lifted a hand and waved goodbye as the van's side door closed and then it sped away. The Lincoln took off as well, leaving a trail of dust illuminated by red taillights, before the night closed in behind them.

Roxanne turned to Nikki and asked, "How close are they, child?"

"I don't know. I only felt them for a second."

"Close," I said, sensing the humans at last as my stomach knotted. And then suddenly, far too rapidly, the sense of them became immediate and I realized they were not arriving by land, but by air. "They're here!"

My answer was punctuated by the sounds of helicopter blades beating the dark skies above us as they came swooping in low over the cabin and hovered over the front lawn. And before I could even guess at her intent, Nikki dashed off at a dead run for the forest, Pandora speeding behind her.

"I'll get her," Roland shouted. "Get the others the hell out of here." And then he was gone, too.

Grabbing the boys, Roxy and I dashed through the cabin's door while dust and dirt whipped the air, driven by those blades as the choppers landed. Christian slammed the door behind us and threw the locks. The fire was still snapping happily in its grate The board game still lay on the floor. The bowl of potato chips, too.

I turned to Roxanne. "Is there an escape route?"

"Have we met?" She took off at a jog, leading us upstairs at a brisk pace, down the hall and into the rear-most bedroom. She opened the bedroom window and pointed at the cord beyond. I stuck my head out and saw the line that was attached from the highest peak of the cabin, angling sharply downward over an entire mountainside, ending, I couldn't even guess where.

As Roxanne started gathering hardware from a closet, a man's voice came to us on a bullhorn–as if vampires couldn't have heard him even if he'd whispered. Idiot. "We have you surrounded." They did not. No one had gone to the rear of the house yet. But even now they must be beating the woods in search of my precious Nikki. And my beloved Roland would not leave her, not if it cost his life.

"Come out now and no harm will come to you."

Roland's voice came to my mind. *Use* The Glamourie, he said, and he said it fiercely. *Cloak yourselves and go if you can.*

We can. Roxanne has an escape route, a cable by which we can apparently glide down the mountainside behind the cabin. But what are you saying, Roland? My chest was near to bursting with emotion. *What about Nikki?*

She's climbed a tree around back. Grab her on your way. There's not much time.

Never! I will not leave you!

I looked out the rear-facing window then shoved everyone aside as I saw armed troops sneaking around behind the house. We were truly surrounded now.

You have to go with them, Rhiannon. The Glamourie—*you have to be with them, hold the spell over them powerfully enough. Get them out of here.*

I can cast it over them from here.

And if you fall the spell falls with you, and they're found. Captured.

Gareth tugged at my skirt. I looked down into the terrified pools of his eyes. The first sign of emotion from the child was ice cold fear. "I don't want to go back in the cage," he said as tears spilled onto his cheeks. "Don't let them take us back."

My own eyes welled, and my heart felt as if it were being sliced by razors. *I love you, Roland,* I told him. *I love you!*

And I you. Forever, Rhiannon. Then I felt him come nearer and dared to peer out the window. He dashed out of the woods directly behind the cabin, moving far faster than humans could move, but not fast enough to be invisible to them. Even with his missing leg, I knew he could move faster. Using a tree limb as a crutch, he ran across the lawn. He was trying to clear a path for us.

The Crows shouldered their weapons and opened fire as he raced unevenly around the house toward the woods on the other side. And his plan worked. They stampeded after him with blood in their eyes, and we had a chance to escape.

I had no choice but to take it.

* * *

Roland blocked his mind as forcefully as he could from Rhiannon's just before he was hit by a bullet, right in his one remaining leg. He tumbled and rolled for several yards, momentum carrying him. He came to a stop near the edge of the front lawn. Twenty men formed a living barricade around him. Behind them two helicopters rested, their propellers still whipping autumn leaves and dust into the air. Birds and wildlife had long since scattered. Roland remained prone for just a moment. He needed to give Rhiannon time to get away. He used those seconds to reinforce the barricades blocking his mind from hers. It was not an easy thing to accomplish. She was his soul. To block her from his mind felt obscene. But he needed her to focus on getting herself and the children to safety. Not on the vengeance that would burn through her like hellfire if she sensed that he had been shot.

A man in the center of the Crows raised his bullhorn. "Put your hands up and get to your feet. Slowly!"

Slowly would not be a problem. "The bullhorn is unnecessary," he said, taking his time to get up onto one wounded leg and one prosthetic, worrying about the slow but steady pulse of blood coming from the fresh bullet hole. "I could hear you if you whispered."

"Come forward, vampire."

He nodded, and took another step, and then another. He tried to feel for Rhiannon without letting her in, but sensed only anguish, heartache, and grief.

As he moved nearer, the armed men kept their rifles trained on him. A few of the weapons were different from the others, and he recognized them as the sort that fired those tranquilizer darts with which he was all too familiar. Only a few, though. Most of them seemed to be the same high-powered weapons that they used in combat. He was familiar with those, as well.

"I am not going to resist." He moved another few steps forward, then stopped with ten feet still remaining between him and the Crows. Then he knelt and put his hands on the back of his head. "You have me. I'm tired of running."

Two men rushed forward, one keeping his rifle pointed at Roland's head, while the other shouldered his and pulled out a pair of handcuffs. Their metal—titanium, Roland thought—was cold against his wrist, and the man squeezed it too tightly. Then he pulled Roland's arms downward, behind his back, and snapped a cuff around the other wrist.

Only when he was cuffed did the leader come forward. He wore black fatigues like the rest, but his were decorated with colorful patches, one of which bore his name. Patterson. "Where are the others?"

Roland memorized his face, which was large and long and very angular. Square jaw, prominent brow ridge, ice blue eyes and brown hair cut to within a half inch of his scalp. He memorized Patterson's energy, as well. It was dark, but sparking with tiny ignitions, firing off randomly, many at the same time. It was a violent energy, and perhaps not an entirely sane one.

"I asked you a question, vampire. Where are the others?"

"There are no others. I'm alone here. Honestly, I never expected you would find me all the way out here in the middle of—

Patterson's rifle butt connected with Roland's chin, sending him backwards onto the ground. Instinct told him to rub the pain away, but of course, he couldn't move his hands.

"Fine," Patterson said. "You don't want to tell us who's inside, and we're clearly not going to walk in there to be ambushed by a horde of blood drinkers."

As Roland got himself upright again, Patterson said, "Burn it."

Roland's stomach knotted up. *Please be gone*, he thought. *Please be as far from here as you can possibly be.*

"On your feet, vampire."

Roland got up onto one knee, then awkwardly all the way upright again. He wouldn't fight. He would do nothing to further anger these men. Not until he was sure Rhiannon and the children were safe. He heard small explosions and breaking glass as men fired incendiary rounds through one window after another. Twisting his head around, Roland saw flames erupting inside.

And then Patterson jerked his shoulder. "Face front, vampire. Get moving. We've got plans for you."

Looking ahead of him at the smaller of the two helicopters, Roland barely restrained himself from moaning out loud. It had no doors, just openings. Apparently that was going to be his conveyance.

But then a truck rumbled up behind it, large and green. Obviously military. It stopped, and its passenger door opened. A woman stepped out of the rig. She was not wearing a uniform nor the familiar black fatigues of DPI muscle, but rather a white coat such as a doctor would wear, hanging unbuttoned over black trousers that sat higher at the waist than was currently fashionable. They seemed to strain at the seems to contain her substantial backside. She was a middle-aged mortal, perhaps forty-five or fifty human years in age, with chin-length blond hair which she wore parted deeply to one side.

She walked right up to him, looked him up and down, and said, "You're Roland de Courtemanche, aren't you? What happened to your leg?"

"I lost one to a shark. The other was just recently shot."

She frowned, her gaze shifting from the prosthetic leg to the bleeding one, and then taking on a hint of alarm. Quickly she removed the thin, patent leather belt from her high-waisted trousers, and kneeling, wrapped it around his thigh and pulled it so tight a grunt of pain escaped him. She watched the wound, and when she seemed assured the bleeding had stopped, she nodded and turned to Patterson. "This is better than I'd hoped for."

"I don't see how. The others apparently got away."

"Doesn't matter," she said. "We have all we need right here." Then she took a syringe from her coat pocket. "I'm going to have to tranquilize you for the flight."

"Thank you," Roland said. "I was not looking forward to riding in that contraption."

She blinked, perhaps surprised by his calm, even polite tones. "That's not your ride. We have a small plane waiting." Then she sank the needle into his arm, right through his shirtsleeve, and dizziness flooded through him at once.

"Get him into the truck," she instructed, and some soldiers took him by his arms, one on each side, and mostly dragged him toward the waiting truck.

Roland didn't fight them, and as he was carried toward the vehicle he was able see the flaming cabin. Heat seared his face, acrid smoke burned his nostrils. The flames crackled and roared as they devoured Roxanne's woodland haven.

Rhiannon was safe. She had to be safe. Patterson said the others got away, and he'd sensed no outcry of pain, no heavy shadow of death, no crippling feeling of loss.

His eyelids dropped heavily as the men heaved him up and into the back of the truck.

"Ride up front, Dr. Bouchard," Patterson said. "I don't trust him."

"I appreciate your concern, Colonel, but I prefer to ride with the subject."

"I don't rightly care what you prefer. You are essential personnel, the only person besides me who even *knows* about this project. I can't complete it without you. So get in the front like I told you. I'll meet you at the field."

Roland felt the two of them walking away. The last words he heard were the woman's as she muttered, "It's a real shame about the cabin. Must've been a beauty."

Then a door closed, and Roland felt the truck lurch into motion.

CHAPTER FOUR

The instant the Crows cleared the back lawn, I cast *The Glamourie.* I cast it beautifully, despite my broken and bleeding heart. Roxanne handed out little devices that snapped over the zip line, with wheels to roll over the cord and handles to grip, and two by two, we went down. First Christian, with little Gareth wrapped around him like a spider monkey. Then Roxanne with Ramses. I left last of all, crying out to Nikki as I did, *I'm coming for you, darling.*

Hurry, was her only reply.

But it was enough to give me a bearing on her location. The tallest pine tree in sight. As soon as we sped into the woods I let the spell falter, so Nikki would be able to see me. As I sped closer I called to her mentally, *Can you jump to me, Nikki?*

She jumped, but too soon, and the poor little thing was clinging to the cable in front of me as I sped toward her.

On my word, let go. I will catch you. If I hit her at this speed, I would likely tear her little fingers from her hands, or at least skin them where they gripped the cable. *Now!*

She closed her eyes and released her hands just as I hit her, and I clung to the handle one handed, wrapping her tight to my body with the other.

Her arms locked around my neck, and I quickly cast the spell again to make us all invisible. Aloud I dared a single shout and hoped it wasn't loud enough for the Crows to hear. "Pandora, come!"

I caught a glimpse of her then, a darker shadow in the night. She raced along below us, and I expanded the glamour to include her.

We soared through the night, invisible, soundless, undetected by those mortal beasts. I cast my spell over the cord and hardware, so the Crows wouldn't even see *them* for as long as the magic held. I focused with all my strength on holding the spell, despite my grief and fear for my beloved.

As we flew, I sought Roland's mind with mine, tried to feel what was happening to him, but he had closed me out. And that hurt nearly as much as the rest. But his motives were clear, and they were true. He wanted my attention on protecting the children. He loved them as much as I.

The line Roxy had rigged wound itself ingeniously among the trees without smashing us into their trunks or their limbs even once. It seemed we went on forever, and every second took me further away from my love.

And then suddenly, the line leveled off so that we slowed and eventually, stopped with ten feet between us and the ground. I let go, as did the others. The soft, grassy ground welcomed us and smelled of dying pine, its sappy resin, autumn wildflowers, and water. I felt as if I had left my very soul behind.

Roxanne sprang up onto her feet, ran to a post, and hit a button. There was a mechanical whir. I realized she'd activated a winch that was rapidly rolling up the zip line after apparently detaching it from the house. Brilliant.

Nikki tugged on my arm. "Not another boat," she said. "I don't like boats."

I looked where she was pointing. There was a lake before us, though my attention had still been on what lay behind. Bobbing serenely on the water was a bright yellow airplane with pontoons instead of wheels. "That's not a boat, little one. It's an airplane. It flies through the sky."

I looked at Roxanne. She looked back at me and nodded. "We'll taxi 'til we hit the far end of the lake and take off from there, so they'll be less likely to see us."

"You mean to say you can fly this thing?" I asked her

"I can. I can fly it all the way to Maine, Rhiannon, with a couple of stops for fuel."

I looked at her, at the plane, and then back toward the cabin where I had left my heart. Pandora came loping out of the woods. Her speed never failed to amaze me. She stood there, mouth agape, panting softly. Then she came closer and sat down right beside Nikki. Nikki hugged her neck, and Pandora chuffed and rubbed her head against the child. Nikki said. "We can't go all the way to anyplace, Roxy. Not without Roland. Right, Rhiannon?"

A cellphone rang. Frowning, Roxy started patting herself down, and eventually pulled out one of the zipper bags she'd shoved into the canvas sack she carried. I presumed she'd prepared one for each of the children, just as she had for the others. She fumbled inside, extracted the phone, looked at the screen. "It's coming from the phone I gave Lucas," she said, and she answered and tapped the speaker icon.

"I saw what happened," Lucas said. "I had just turned off onto a side road, when I heard choppers heading for the cabin. I headed back in case you needed help."

"And what did you see, Lucas?" I asked, every cell in my body yearning for his reply.

"They took Roland prisoner. I think he was wounded. And then tranquilized." *Either that, or dead*, was what I heard whisper through Lucas's mind. "Did everyone else get away?" he asked

"For the moment." My words came out choked and raspy. "Roland sacrificed himself to allow our escape. Do you know where they're taking him, Lucas?"

"No, but I hid in the woods near the road, and managed to toss one of those GPS units into the back of the truck they put him into as it pulled away. We can track them."

I met Roxanne's eyes. She read my expression and muted the phone, then nodded at me to say what was on my mind.

"I haven't trusted Lucas from the beginning," I told her. "If he's working for them, it could be a trap."

"I've been with you on that, Rhiannon," Roxanne said. "And I agree, it's possible, though I'm leaning toward believing in Lucas. I think he's truly changed his stripes."

I wasn't so sure. "Either way, I have to go back. Will you take the children to safety in the plane?"

"I will," she promised.

"No!" Nikki stomped her little foot. "I won't leave without Roland. What if they put *him* in a cage on some stupid boat out in that stupid water?"

I gripped her tiny shoulders and stared into her eyes, and even with all that had happened, it wasn't lost on me that she was showing emotion. Anger. "You will listen to me and do exactly as I tell you for once, little one. I love you beyond reason, but that man is my world. I cannot help him and protect you at the same time. If you care for him at all, you will go with Roxanne and Christian and do as they tell you."

She gaped at me, shocked, I'm sure, that I was being this firm with her, when I hadn't yet. Then Christian said, "I can come with you, Rhiannon."

"And risk your heart exploding in battle? No, Christian. And I have no more time to argue. Take the children and get aboard the plane. Do it now."

Nodding, Christian rushed to obey, and for once, Nikki didn't argue or resist, nor did the boys. To my shock and surprise, Gareth came to me, wrapped his arms around my waist, and hugged me awkwardly. Ramses stood a few feet away, staring hard at me, and I heard him clearly inside my mind. *Get him back.*

I will, I promised, and I saw from the flash in his eyes that he heard me.

I nodded at the phone Roxanne held. She pressed the mute button again and handed it to me, then she turned and climbed onto the yellow pontoon plane.

"I'm coming back, Lucas," I said as Christian helped the children up into the craft, though they could easily have done it on their own. Pandora looked at me, then at the children, clearly upset.

"You have to stay with me, girl. We'll get them later. They'll be all right," I told the cat.

Roxy fired up the engines. The propellers whirred, stirring the water around them into a froth and the huge yellow beast began skimming across the lake, slowly at first, then faster. I turned away, not allowing myself even the luxury of watching them move out of sight, and started back through the forest, my cat by my side, but looking behind us over and over. The poor thing was traumatized. We'd separated her from her newfound cubs.

I brought the cell phone to my ear. "Lucas," I said, "Tell me where to meet you."

* * *

Lucas picked me up, along with my cat, and I let him continue driving, since he was more practiced at it than I. We used autos only when absolutely necessary. Roland detested them.

Roland.

I ached for him as strongly as he must ache for his lost limb. He was a part of me. There was nothing in me that had not been shaped and altered by our love for each other. All of his softest parts had been toughened by my grit, and all of my sharpest edges had been buffed down by his tenderness. My temper had been cooled by Roland's wisdom. My impulsiveness, calmed by his patience.

And yet I could easily rip his abductors limb from limb with my bare hands. And would, if I caught up to them. No, not if. When. *When* I caught up to them.

"He'll be okay, Rhiannon. He has to be."

I looked across at Lucas, one of The Chosen, a man I did not trust but could not harm. He was driving the car while Pandora lay stretched across the large backseat. Lucas might be driving me straight into the hands of those DPI men-in-black for all I knew. They'd always wanted me. Had me once, tortured me with their experiments until I was nearly mad. Perhaps *was* mad. A lot of them died when I made my escape.

More would die this time.

I was beginning to believe that our friend Devlin's notion of fighting back against humankind with all of our power and minimal mercy might be preferable to Roland's idea of diplomacy and peaceful coexistence. One could not make peace with a people who wanted to wipe out one's entire race.

"They've stopped," Lucas said. His face, I noticed, was scruffy with a couple of days' growth. His eyes were ringed with worry. I'd been feeling him but not truly looking at him for the past few days. I'd been sensing for lies and betrayal. But now that I was using my physical senses, I could see that he was under stress. He looked just the way I felt. Truly haggard.

He glanced my way, saw me looking at him, and nodded toward the cell phone he had propped up on the dashboard. It was serving as a GPS, tracking the truck that had taken Roland.

I followed his gaze with alarm.

"The truck hasn't moved in the past ten minutes," Lucas said. "And I seriously doubt they'd take a bathroom break with a thousand-year-old vampire in the back."

"Eight hundred sixty-seven," I said softly.

He looked at me for a long moment. "And you've known him all that time?"

"Most of it. When he was very young, he saved a little boy from a wolf attack. When he returned the injured, frightened child to his home, his father, a knight called Sir Gareth, rewarded Roland by taking him as squire. Two years later Gareth was cut down in battle. And my Roland, at the tender age of fourteen, donned his master's armor and fought in his place. He was knighted by the king for his valor."

"Gareth," Lucas said. "That's why he chose that name for Nikki's brother."

I nodded.

"And how did he become...what he is now?"

I looked at Lucas, pulling myself out of the depths of my memory. So many years. Centuries. Lifetimes. Neither of us were the same people we'd once been. And yet we'd grown together rather than apart. Our bond had become ever stronger.

Lucas seemed genuinely interested, not fishing for information. I plumbed his mind a little but found no ill intent there. Though some DPI spies were trained in blocking us from their minds, I encountered no barricades.

"I found him in the dirt after a nasty battle, one of the few he ever lost. He was dying. I loved him even then, though he was a little slower to come around to the fact that I was his destiny." I smiled softly, remembering how difficult it had been to convince Roland that he loved me. But eventually, love won out. "I could not let him go. Let him die."

"You were the one who...changed him," Lucas said, his voice a whisper that felt, perhaps, reverent.

"I was." I looked at the road. "You've stopped driving."

He seemed to snap to attention, realizing he had brought the car to a halt in the middle of a narrow country lane. Then he got it moving again. "DPI teaches its trainees that vampires don't have feelings. Emotions. That they're soulless and incapable of love. I've always known that was wrong, but now I think it's more than inaccurate. I think they have it backwards. Maybe your kind loves more deeply than humans can comprehend, much less experience."

I sighed. "Only enough that if he leaves this life, I will follow him."

"But what about the kids? What about Nikki?"

"I will follow him," I said. "Now please make this thing

go faster."

He obeyed, and within a short time, we rounded a very sharp curve, and I saw a large green military-style truck sitting as if abandoned in the middle of a hayfield. There were two clear paths where its tires had flattened the tall golden grass as it had trundled out to where it now rested. And where that path met the road, two armed men wearing the typical black fatigues of DPI forces stood guarding it.

I opened the door and leapt from the car before Lucas had a chance to bring it to a stop, and I strode toward the men, my steps long and powerful. They shouldered their rifles, aimed them at me and shouted, "Stop where you are! This is—"

I exploded into motion, and when I stopped again the two of them were on their backsides in the dirt, wondering what had happened. I stood over them, holding their rifles, one in each outstretched arm. The night wind whipped my hair and fury heated my blood. Lucas was on his way to my side, Pandora already there, growling low, crouching and ready to rip out their throats at a flick of my finger. "What have you done with my husband? Where is he?"

"I don't—"

I dropped the weapons to the ground and was on the man before he could finish his lying denial. I closed my hand around his neck and lifted him up off his backside and into the air. The rifles clattered as Lucas picked them up. Beside me, Pandora swished her tail back and forth like a whip, shifting her weight from one haunch to the other as she prepared to spring.

Staring into the man's eyes, my own heating with my rage, I commanded his mind with mine. *Tell me what you know. Open your mind and show me what is there.*

But there was only a dark emptiness. He'd been trained very well by DPI, to resist the mind control of the vampire.

"Believe me, Crow, I will fit your weapon entirely inside your body if you do not tell me what I wish to know."

"I…I—"

Before he could speak, the other one, trembling, said, "Don't say anything, Jim."

I slid my gaze toward the second man, who was picking himself up off the ground, and I probed his mind, then recoiled at the sheer hatred I found there. Hatred for me, for my kind, though he knew nothing about us. It was ignorance and bigotry. And more. He wanted to kill me. He wanted me to give him an opportunity to do so. And I would not be his first such victim. And yet, no information. Nothing about Roland, or what DPI had done with him. He too, was a well-trained, black hearted bastard.

"You won't tell me anything, will you?" I asked that second man. "No matter how much I might torture you, you'll never break."

He stood erect, lifted his chin, sent a worried glance at Pandora, but even her menacing presence didn't seem to deter him. "No, I won't. I know what you are."

"Then you're of no use to me." I gave Pandora a nod. It was all she needed. She sprang from where she stood, clamped her jaws around his throat and took him down to the ground. His eyes widened, hands clasping at her fur as she tore at his flesh, shaking him. He screamed and kept on screaming, but not for very long.

"Rhiannon!" Lucas lunged toward the man as if he would try to save him.

"Do not interrupt my cat when she's eating, Lucas, or you will end up as her dessert."

I turned my attention to the one I still held, while Pandora enjoyed her meal. The other man's suffering had been all too brief.

"Where have they taken my husband?" I asked the one who still lived.

"East!" he shouted, but his voice was strained by the tightness of my hand around his throat. I lowered him to his feet, eased my grip.

"Go on."

"They—they had a small plane. Took off f-f-five minutes ago."

"Bound for where?"

"White Plains. DPI headquarters."

"We burned that place to the ground more than a decade ago."

"They rebuilt. They call it The Sentinel now. I swear, I swear, that's where they're taking him. Please, please...." He looked past me at what remained of his comrade, an eviscerated, bloody mess that no longer resembled a human being. Pandora was stretched out, gnawing on an arm.

"Let me probe your mind, so I know whether you're lying to me."

And when I tried again, I found no resistance. He was telling the truth. And I saw more. So much more.

"I believe you. And you'll be rewarded for your cooperation." I pulled him closer, just enough to reach his throat with my mouth. And then I bit in and drank him.

Lucas was shouting, arguing that I should show mercy, perhaps, but to me it was only a faint din. I was feeling the man's ecstasy as I imbibed him, and more. I was seeing the vampires he had killed, the ones who'd been tortured while he stood guard, the ones he'd helped to throw into cages, the ones he'd hunted down and executed, the ones he'd burned in a vigilant rage before he'd joined the DPI Crows. I drained the man until he was no more than a husk, filling myself with the power and strength that only came from fresh, living, human blood. Then I tossed his lightweight shell into the field and pressed a fingertip to the corners of my lips.

Calmer now, my cat came and sat down beside me when I called, though I knew she would have preferred to continue feeding.

"No time, my pet," I said as the red haze slowly cleared from my vision, but my eyes still glowed.

Lucas was staring at me with horror in his eyes.

Ignoring him, I tugged out the cell phone Roxanne had

given me and sent her a text message, hoping her small plane was near enough a tower for her to receive it.

Return for me. DPI taking Roland to NY.

I waited, tapping my foot impatiently. At last, came the reply.

On my way. Same place.

Pocketing the phone, I headed toward the car.

Lucas stepped into my path and met my eyes, which had by now ceased their glowing. I felt them cool and regulate themselves. "That was—that was—"

"What?" I demanded, preparing myself for his condemnation. "What you did to those men....that was...."

"Inhuman?" I asked.

"Inhumane," he replied.

"Those men were killers. They've done far worse to my kind than I did to them."

"How do you know that? Just because they wear those black uniforms? I wore one, once."

I gazed steadily into his eyes. "You're one of the The Chosen, Lucas. I *can't* kill you. If I could, you'd likely already be dead."

He stumbled backward as if the words were blows.

"Pandora, come." I turned to continue to the car, or back to the lake on foot if need be. But then I stopped, my back to Lucas. I felt an unusual stab of guilt. Rolling my eyes I spoke again. "That is untrue, what I just said. Even though you were once with them, you have helped us when you needn't have. Those two...." I tilted my head toward the field. "They were not like you, Lucas. They were evil. And I am angry."

"I got that."

Turning, I looked him in the eye. He had a conscience. I respected that, because my Roland had one too. As much of a hindrance as it was, it was also part of what made me love him. And he would not have approved of me letting this young man think I had murdered two men in cold blood.

"They were not innocent men misled into serving. They

were killers with hearts as black as tar. They've murdered innocents, and took pleasure in it."

"Are you sure?"

"I am. I saw their crimes. That is the truth."

He took a deep breath, nodded once. "Then they deserved what they got."

Lucas walked to the car without another word, got behind the wheel, and started the engine. I opened the rear door for Pandora, pointed at the backseat, and she leapt obediently inside, stretched out across the seat, and began licking her paws in utter contentment.

"Where to?" Lucas asked, as I got into the passenger seat beside him.

"There's a lake at the base of the mountain on which the cabin rested. We need to make our way to the far end of it. Roxanne will meet us there in a small yellow airplane. The children and Christian are with her."

He nodded. "And then what?"

"And then we're going to the East Coast to find Roland, free him, and mutilate his captors."

* * *

There were only flashes of awareness for Roland as the tranquilizer must have begun to wear off. In them, he was not in an airplane, but in a room with brilliant white light and white coated humans all around him. There were sounds like drills or saws, and muted voices, but those were soon obliterated by excruciating pain that permeated his entire being, but seemed to radiate outward from his head.

After three or more such nightmarish flashes, he experienced the sensation of motion again. He was lying on his back on a flat surface that moved. He heard squeaking wheels, smelled manmade chemicals, cleansers and such, and the energies of humans permeated his surroundings. His head was screaming, one eye felt as if it was trying to pop out of its socket from some kind of pressure that made him want to scream.

And then he was moving again—directly downward, and someone said, "He's coming around. Should we give him another shot?"

"Sun's coming up as we speak, rookie. He's gonna wake up in a nice, cozy cell without a clue. They heal up by day, you know."

"I know that."

The downward motion stopped. Elevator, Roland thought as the doors opened. His ride bumped over something and his skull seemed to split into several pieces and pour his throbbing brain out onto the floor.

Then the day sleep came calling, pulling at him, and he rushed willingly into its gentle embrace.

CHAPTER FIVE

Roxanne piloted the plane through the daylight hours. When night came again, I roused in the cramped cargo hold. The plane was motionless, resting on the ground, empty. Its hatch stood open and I could see the ocean rolling beneath the night just beyond it. Waves hurled themselves against the familiar rocky shore, then hissed away again. My heart lifted in something like joy, something like relief. The Atlantic. God, how I'd missed her.

Climbing out of the hold, I sank my bare feet into the cool sand that wound its way, riverlike, amid the dark rocks of Maine's coast. Even as I relished the sensation and breathed the fresh salty air, I realized that my shoes had been removed and a blanket wrapped over my shoulders, covering me like one of Roland's beloved cloaks. I held it around my neck without thinking. Roxanne, of course, always seeing to my comfort. No matter how many times I told her we feel nothing during the day sleep, she always acts as if we do. Whenever we spend time with her, she buries us in down comforters and fluffy pillows, even though we would sleep just as soundly were we resting upon a cold, flat rock, so long as it was out of the sun's reach.

I adore her for that.

Turning my gaze away from the ocean, I faced the cliffs and spotted the path that led up them to the house far above. It was a restored mansion, and familiar to me, having once been the home of the Gypsy vampire Dante, and later, of the woman who would become his bride, Morgan de Silva. Morgan was an award-winning screenwriter. But that was long ago, back in the days before anyone realized her vampire films were based on reality. She'd found Dante's diaries, forgotten in the house's attic and penned screenplays based on what she'd read in them. One of them had earned her the industry's highest award. It had been given "posthumously," because everyone had to believe she'd died. She had, in fact, only become Undead. Now the pair traveled, as we all had to do, lest we be found out and murdered in our sleep. She'd willed the house to her only sister.

Maxine, otherwise known as "Mad Maxie" was Morgan's twin, and yet not one of The Chosen. Her husband Lou Malone was a retired policeman and together they'd created a detective agency that specialized in things that go bump. Supernatural Investigations Service, SIS for short. They were friends to our kind and I trusted them more than any other mortal, save Roxanne.

I was eager to see them again, but more eager to rescue my beloved Roland from those who had dared take him from me.

There would be blood tonight.

I didn't bother making my way up the steep, zigzag path that led from the beach to the top of the cliffs. Instead I jumped, springing upward like a rocket and landing easily at the top. There, Pandora sat awaiting me. I should've known she would be there. She knew my routines as well as I knew them myself. When the sun went down, she would always come to my resting place and wait for me to awaken.

I stroked her sleek head. "Was it very awful, being crammed into that cargo hold with me, my pet?"

She chuffed and pressed her head up against my palm. I bent to kiss her face, and she licked my cheek in return.

My cat kept pace as I strode toward the pristine white mansion, across lush green grasses, past flourishing gardens with stone benches and fountains.

The three children came bounding out the back doors and across the patio, Christian lumbering along as if he were one of them. Maxine and Lou came right behind them. Roxanne remained in the still-open glass doors, ever watchful.

Nikki raced forward, slamming into me like a wrecking ball and hugging me around my waist, but quickly pulling away and looking almost confused by her own actions. Emotion. She was feeling emotion.

"I hate when you sleep, Rhiannon."

"What a strange thing to say. Why do you hate it?"

"Because...because what if you never wake up?"

I hugged my little girl close, stroking her hair, and wondering if Nikki had witnessed my deathlike slumber and been frightened by it. I must see to it that such a thing did not happen again.

"I will wake up for as long as I am meant to wake up, my darling. We all live just as long as we are meant to live. And when the time comes to stop living, we awaken to another life. A different life, where everything is good and peaceful and kind." I planted a kiss on the top of her head, then took her hand and began walking toward the others, and when I reached the boys, I hugged them, too. And they hugged back, though they pretended not to want to. I patted Christian's shoulder, and thought he might prefer a hug as well. Though large and powerful, the man was childlike in many ways.

Maxine was shaking her head slowly. "Never thought I'd see the day. The great Rhiannon in the role of Old Mother Hubbard."

I shot the perky redhead my most fearsome scowl, knowing

it didn't scare her in the least. In fact, she grinned and came to me.

"It's so good to see you again, Rhiannon," she went on. "So good." She held out her hands.

I took them and accepted her enthusiastic cheek kiss stoically. "It's good to see you, too. I only wish it were under better circumstances. How are your sister and Dante?"

"They're good. Staying off the radar. Traveling the globe, never remaining in one place very long. They say it's a bit easier in Sweden and Canada, where attitudes are more liberal. But they visit often."

"It is good to know they're all right," I said, and meant it. These days, those we hadn't heard from in a while were, more often than not, no longer in existence.

"We know what's going on," Lou said, standing beside Max. His brown trousers and cream colored button down shirt seemed a bit too big, just as they always did. The only thing about him that had changed since being with a bride eighteen years his junior, was that he looked younger than before. He stood straighter, smiled more widely, had new a sparkle in his eyes. He seemed more alive than before. Life with the hellion was good for him, I thought. "Roxy filled us in," he said, pretending not to notice my perusal. "I hope you're not going to argue against us coming along to help you with the rescue."

Maxine nodded with enough emphasis to strain her neck. "We've been keeping tabs on that freaking place ever since they started rebuilding it a couple of years ago," she said. "No matter how many times we destroy them, DPI just won't stay dead." She elbowed Lou. "Didn't I tell you? Didn't I?"

He sent her a long suffering, but utterly loving nod.

"I was hoping to leave the children with you, Maxine," I said. "They are...special."

"Special, how?" she asked, eyeing the kids. Apparently Roxanne had told her nothing of their origins, nor their abilities.

"It's...complicated. Suffice it to say that DPI is after them, as well."

Roxanne spoke up from behind Max. "Christian and I can stay with the kids. No one's going to bother them here. They won't even make the connection between the Malones and the Undead. Max and Lou have been extremely discreet, as have Morgan and Dante. This is truly a safe place, Rhiannon."

"That's what we thought about your woodland cabin, Roxanne," I said softly.

Maxine was looking at the kids, then at Lou, as if wondering what they were, and why DPI would be after them. She didn't ask, but I knew she would, sooner or later. Her curiosity was just shy of legendary. It was a miracle that it had not yet got her killed.

"Lucas called a few minutes ago. He'll be here in twenty," Roxanne said. He'd booked a commercial flight, since there hadn't been room enough in the small plane for him. "You may as well come inside and get something to eat."

"I do not want to eat. I want to get to White Plains as fast as possible."

Maxine put a small hand on my shoulder. "You must be going crazy worrying about him. But you want to be at full strength when you get there. It'll only take a couple of minutes."

Nikki tugged on my dress. "Where is Roland? How far away?"

I shot a look at Lou, because I did not know the distance.

"A good five hours by car," he said.

I walked with the others across the patio, through the glass doors and into the house. "That's unacceptable," I said.

We wound up in the kitchen, which was huge and entirely done in darkly stained wood and hammered copper. It was stunning, old looking, and beautiful. It had not been this way when Morgan had lived here. Maxine had apparently changed things to suit her own tastes.

"The only way faster is to take the plane," Roxanne said. "And I can't fly it if I'm staying here with the kids."

Maxine put a mugful of sustenance into the microwave and pressed a button. I tried not to grimace. Microwaved blood was nothing compared to fresh from the tap. But beggars could not be choosers. "We can't take the children near that place," I said. "DPI considers them a greater prize than any of us. I intend to keep them as far from their headquarters as possible."

The timer pinged, and Max handed the mug to me. I thanked her and drank deeply. The red-headed conspiracy theorist had been right about one thing; I would need every ounce of strength for the battle I would wage on this night. I needed to get to Roland. My beloved. Every instant we delayed brought with it the risk of greater suffering for him. I was all but trembling in my eagerness to go.

"How fast could the airplane get us to White Plains?" I asked.

Roxanne said, "Two hours, give or take."

"Then we must take the plane. Maxine, you'll have to stay behind with Christian and–"

"No one knows that place like I do," Maxine argued.

"It is not up for debate, my mortal friend. Roxanne is the only one who can fly the plane."

"I can fly the plane." The voice came from the patio, through the still-open glass doors, and it belonged to Lucas. He had a duffel bag slung over his shoulder, and he came in, dropping it on the floor. It clunked loudly.

"You can?" I asked.

"Absolutely. The only question is, is there room for all of us in that little seaplane?"

"I rode in the cargo hold underneath on the way here, but only to avoid the daylight."

"You'll fit," Roxanne said. "I fueled her up while you rested today, Rhiannon, so she's good to go."

"Then please, let's be on our way."

Maxine heaved a sigh, rolled her eyes at my hastiness. "I'm Max," she told Lucas, extending a hand. "Have you eaten?"

"Lucas," he said, shaking briefly. "And yeah, fast food while driving. I'm in a big hurry to get to old Peg-Leg, too."

"Peg-Leg?" Maxine looked at me, her brows raised, her eyes round.

"It's a tale for the trip." I headed for the door and heard Lou asking Roxanne how much weight the cargo hold could handle for weapons, including tranquilizer darts to keep the kill count down.

Keeping the kill count down was not among my priorities.

"We don't want to be under-armed," he said.

"When are we ever?" Maxine asked him.

"Let's leave then," I said. "Roland is even now awakening in captivity. The gods only know what those animals might do to him before we arrive."

* * *

Roland awoke slowly, arising from a sleep deeper than any living mortal would ever know. There was a brief, blissful instant when he expected to open his eyes and see the face of his Rhiannon. She'd be lying beside him, her head pillowed by softness, her eyes open but sleepy. She liked to take her time about waking up. Often, she preferred long, slow lovemaking to bring her around to full wakefulness.

But this night, when he opened his eyes, he saw iron bars in front of him, and he wondered if DPI had become so stupid in its latest incarnation, that it expected them to hold a vampire. He could bend those things like a human could bend coat hangers. He rose, grabbed hold of the bars and a bolt of electricity blasted him right back into his bed. His head cracked the wall behind it, and then he sat there for a moment, dazed and shaking with the after effects.

I tried to shout a warning, Roland, but you're too fast for me.

The energy of the male vampire addressing him was vaguely familiar, but Roland's mind was foggy and not functioning the way a vampiric mind ought to. *I'm sorry,* he replied. *Do I know you?*

It's hell the havoc their damned tranquilizer wreaks on our brains, isn't it? This mental voice was female, and he did remember her. She was one of Rhiannon's.

Cuyler Jade? he said. *The Flapper, yes?*

I'm flattered you remember.

How could I forget? Rhiannon used to go to that speakeasy every night to watch over you. She sensed something was coming. And then she'd return to me after closing time and insist on teaching me whatever silly dance steps she'd learned from you that night.

She was a natural, Cuyler replied. *And she was a knockout in fringe and feathers. And believe me, I'm glad she was there night the G-men came in shooting up the place. I wouldn't have survived if she hadn't turned me.*

Roland missed his bride. It welled up in him as he recalled how she'd looked in her red sequined dress, with its layers of fringe that moved whenever she did, and the matching headband with the long black feather. *Then that's Ramsey with you,* he said, trying to distract himself from his grief. *I'm sorry I didn't recognize your energy, Bachman.* And as he said it, he opened his senses and realized they were not the only other vampires imprisoned in this place. He felt others, all of them alert and paying attention to him, though he'd been keeping his conversation private up to now. He mentally lowered the protective gates of his mind to allow the others access. *How many vampires are here?* he asked.

Eight, including you, Ramsey replied.

Hey, fellow captives, Cuyler said. *The newcomer is Roland de Courtemanche.*

He felt their emotions, surprise and some kind of hope. One by one they introduced themselves. Besides Cuyler and Ramsey, there were Samuel, Lorna, and Jonathan Jacob.

That's only seven, Roland replied after each of them introduced themselves.

The eighth can't answer, Cuyler Jade said. *She's imprisoned in a way we are not, and there's barely any life left in her. But you can feel her, intermittently, and when you can, her energy is kind of...well...insane to be blunt about it. We don't know what these bastards did to her. She's in the furthest cell back.*

The word "cell" prompted him to take a more careful look around him. Walls of concrete on three sides, and electrified iron bars across the front. Inside, there was a cot, green fabric stretched across a wooden frame. No pillow. No blanket. No comfort of any kind. And there wasn't another item in the cell with him.

Lorna asked, *Did they get Rhiannon too?*

No. She's still free. And there's very little question in my mind that as soon as she can figure out where I am, she'll arrive with an army to tear this place apart brick by brick, and its keepers limb from limb. I wish she wouldn't risk it, but I've known her for too long. His head throbbed and he pressed the heel of his hand into the spot between temple and forehead, as if he could press the ache away. After touching the bars, he'd hit the wall just now with the *back* of his head. Odd that this was the place hurting as a result.

If Rhiannon comes, we'll all be free, Samuel said.

And DPI will be no more, said Jonathan Jacob. *Her temper is legendary.*

Roland secretly hoped that she wouldn't come here. Perhaps she didn't even know where *here* was. But that wasn't a logical thing to hope. He knew her too well. She would find him, no matter what it took, and when she did, there was going to be hell to pay. He prayed she wouldn't get herself killed trying to rescue him, but knew there was nothing on this earth that would stop her from trying.

* * *

"We're very strong, you know," Nikki said to Roxy.

The others had all trooped out across the lawns, carrying duffle bags filled with weapons and ammo to the waiting plane. The kids had helped them pack. It made them feel useful, Roxy had thought. But the little girl was going on about how strong she was now, and Roxy didn't much care for the look in her eyes.

"We can help save Roland. Probably better than they can," she said.

Roxy frowned at the beautiful seven-year-old child, tilting her head to one side, then she turned slowly, realizing that one of the boys, Gareth, was standing behind her while Rhiannon's mini-me stood just in front of her. A shiver raced up her spine. Where the hell was the other one, the brooder?

Ramses was in the next room with Christian. Roxy could hear them talking. "Why don't we find something fun to do, kids, to make the time go faster until your parents get back hmm?"

"What means parents?" Nikki asked, drawing Roxy's eyes to her again.

"What does the word 'parents' mean," Roxy corrected. "You're forgetting all that grammar we've been teaching you.

"I didn't forget." Nikki nodded at Gareth and before Roxy could even turn again, something jabbed her in the backside.

"Son of a–!" She twisted her body to look down and saw a dart sticking out of her butt-cheek, and as she reached back to pull it out, the children grabbed her arms and held her still with surprising strength.

"Rhiannon will be mad at us for leaving you like this," Nikki said. "But we have to hurry or they'll go without us."

Roxy's knees turned to jelly as she realized the little rugrats must have stolen one of Lou Malone's tranquilizer darts from the stash of weapons they'd helped pack up. She heard Christian yelp, and then there was a loud thud from the next room that had to be the big guy hitting the floor. They'd stolen two darts, then. Her head swirled. "Take it out, Nikki. The dose is too..." She struggled to form words. "Too much for a human. Those are v-vamp tranqs."

The children lowered her gently to the floor, handling her weight as easily as if she were hollow. Then they ran out the door and sped across the lawn toward the cliffs.

Fighting to cling to consciousness, Roxy managed to pluck the dart from her own ass. But there was already enough of the drug in her bloodstream to put her down for the count, and fast. She dragged herself past the glass doors and saw the kids reach the edge of the cliff and jump over. She heard the plane's motor turn over, heard it growl softly, wondered if Rhiannon could feel her, sense the alarm she was trying to emit. But she was so weak, and Rhiannon, so focused on rescuing Roland….

Oh, God, the little monsters are going to try to stow away in the cargo hold, assuming they survived the jump from the cliffs. It'll be cold and rough. Dangerous as hell. Lord of mercy, keep those kids safe. Anything happens to them, Rhiannon will hate me forever.

Weakness washed over her, but she knew she had to get to Christian so he didn't overdose on DPI's vampire tranquilizer formula. Her eyes kept falling closed, her head nodding, as she crawled into the next room.

Christian lay on the floor, a very large, very blurry lump. Just a few more feet, Roxy thought, placing one hand and then one knee in front of the other. Slowly, she inched closer, and finally she could reach the dart she saw sticking out of Christian's flank. She grabbed it and yanked it out, dropped it from rapidly numbing fingers onto the carpeted floor.

"Thanks, Roxy. Why did Ramses do that to me?" Christian asked. His words were as slurred as if he'd been drinking whiskey all night.

"Li'l brats're stow-stow-stowing away on the plane."

"We sh'try'n stop'em"

"Nuttin' we can do, buddy." *I just hope we wake up from this shit so I can kick their little asses up and down the street.*

It was her final thought before she surrendered to the darkness.

* * *

Lucas landed the plane far from DPI Headquarters, and I focused my senses on Roland. I sought his energy with every cell in my body, straining to feel any sense of him. We had to travel from the landing site to DPI's so-called Sentinel on foot. It took more time with mortals in tow than it would have taken me alone. It was maddening to me, traipsing through brush and woodlots to remain out of sight, at the snail's pace that was the fastest the humans could manage. Pandora padded soundlessly beside me, and I sensed she was as impatient as I. Not once was she distracted by the myriad sounds and scents of the east coast woodlands on a late autumn night.

They were familiar to her, and to me. The northeast was my favorite part of the United States. Its forests were dense with young growth and even the mature trees were saplings when compared to the ones in the northwest. The air was cooler, not as heavy with humidity, and the scents of pine and sugar maple all mingled with those of the brown leaves that created a carpet of softness beneath our feet. Every step we took, released that evocative fragrance of fall.

It was delicious, that scent. In other circumstances, I would have taken pause to bask in it. But not tonight. Tonight my goal was my husband, and may the gods have mercy on those who held him.

DPI had placed its headquarters in an out-of-the-way area, back in the days when its work had to remain clandestine. One couldn't have the general population finding out about vampires, and the government's research on them, after all. Panic would ensue.

The general public had found out, though. And panic had indeed followed. Too many had died among my kind as well as among the mortals.

At last, we arrived atop a hillside far above the DPI building. I stroked my cat and looked down at the place. The entire perimeter was surrounded by a tall fence that was clearly electrified. Every few feet, cameras and possibly motion detectors were perched atop high metal poles. The building itself was made of reddish-brown stone blocks, polished to an artificially high gloss. Neat rows of tinted windows had the same effect as the sunglasses on a federal agent—cold, dark, revealing nothing. The Sentinel stood several stories high, and who knew how many more extended below ground level? That was where my beloved Roland would be. Below, somewhere in the sub-levels of this nightmarish place. It was all I could do not to race down the hill, leap the fence and charge in screaming like the storm god Seth raging across the desert.

But I knew that would only result in my own capture. I must do this correctly. I must use every possible advantage to get my Roland out alive.

"The best way in will be the loading dock in the back," Maxine said. She stood beside me on the wooded hillside in the dead of night, unafraid of the myriad sounds of animals, and of the wind moving the limbs of the leafless trees and causing the berry briars to scratch against one another.

I said nothing.

"You know this place has always been an obsession of mine," she went on. Chit-chat had always been one of her most irritating flaws. "I was just a kid the first time I got onto the property to do a little snooping. Research center my ass."

I almost smiled. I knew the tale, of course. My kind owed the girl for her conspiracy theorist tendencies. Her perkiness and chattiness were small enough things to tolerate, given her courage, sharp mind, and heroism. She'd have made a wonderful vampiress.

"I've surveilled the place several times since it was rebuilt," Maxine chattered on. "I don't know what's going on in there, but I *have* figured out the best way in. It's not going to be easy."

She was good at snooping, and she was a friend to the Undead. I trusted her. "Tell me about this loading dock in the back, then."

She nodded, her coppery red hair moving with the motion. "Trucks go in through the front gates, then all the way around to the rear. If we circle to the back you can get a look—"

"Tell me first."

She bit her lip, met my eyes, maybe sensed what I was thinking. It would take forever to hike to a good vantage point for surveilling the rear of the building with all these mortals along. Alone, I could do it in minutes. I needed to go in on my own. And I would, by fair means or foul.

The night wind lifted my hair and carried with it the scents of pine boughs and rotting bark, rapidly crumbling from downed trees to merge with the earth. I closed my eyes and thought of Roland, called out to him with my entire being. Even listened for a reply. But my love couldn't hear me through the walls of a DPI fortress. They had technology that made telepathy ineffective, had been using it for years.

"...and then use those elevators to go down to the sub-levels," Maxine said.

I blinked and realized I'd missed most of what she'd said. Then I blinked again, because moisture dared to flood my eyes. Whoever said vampires couldn't cry was an idiot. We wept. I was weeping now on the inside. But I needed to keep it together. I needed to hold my imagination in an iron grip, and not let it conjure images of what might be happening to my Roland in that foul place.

"Zoned out, didn't you?" Maxine asked. And when I nodded, she repeated herself. "Trucks go in through the front gate and drive around to the back," she said softly. "The overhead doors go up, the truck rolls through, the doors come back down. There's time, while the doors are open, for a vampire to slip inside."

I nodded. "For a vampire. Not for a human?"

Maxine shook her head, her red hair swinging. Her hair, I thought, matched her spirit. Spunky.

"No human could move fast enough. We'd be seen for sure. I've watched those doors go up and down, though, from a distance, using high powered binoculars. There are elevators on the farthest wall from the overhead doors, and a stairwell door too."

"Then there's no point in all of you coming with me."

"I think we'll be more useful serving as backup, providing diversions if necessary. I think one vampire alone is going to have the best chance to get in there undetected."

I glanced back at the thicket where her husband Lou and my unwanted sidekick, Lucas, were speaking softly to each other. "They'll argue against it."

She shrugged. "Give their brains a little vampiric nudge if you have to. Just don't leave them too mushy to do what needs doing out here."

Sighing, I approached the men. They stopped talking the instant I drew near. As if I couldn't have heard every whisper, had I wanted to.

"We'll need a place to rest for the day," I told them. "It's already late and we have no idea how long it will take me to locate Roland and get him out. Or...." I had to lower my lids, conceal my eyes. "Or what kind of condition he'll be in when I do."

Lou looked at me, frowned, then shifted his gaze to Max, his question in his eyes. She said, "Look, to get inside undetected, we'd have to move too fast for human eyes to see, and we'd also have to not show up on those cameras. There's only one of us here who can do that."

Lou pondered that in silence, but the frown he wore made his opinion of the plan clear.

"I don't like it." Lucas was apparently his opposite, speaking too loudly, too emphatically and too immediately. "Suppose you get yourself captured too, Rhiannon?"

"Getting myself captured is far more likely if I have mortals to look after. Especially you, since you're one of The Chosen."

"Right," Maxine said to her husband. "Cause she has no choice but to help him. Us, she could leave to die." The comment was an effort at levity that fell flat. No one laughed nor even cracked a smile.

"I couldn't leave any of you behind," I said. "Unfortunately, that makes each of you a liability."

Lou nodded, not liking it but unable to argue against my logic. I'd always liked the man's slow-walking, slow-talking, deep-thinking ways. They reminded me of Roland's.

"Maxine, I'll leave it to you and Lou to find us a safe place to spend the coming day in case we don't have time for the flight home before dawn," I said. "I will meet you there with

Roland."

"If you can get him out. What if you can't?" Lucas argued.

"If I can't get him out, I won't be coming out either, Lucas. I'll either die trying or join him in captivity. Leaving him there is not an option."

"Rhiannon, you can't mean that!" Lucas grabbed my arm.

I jerked it free, rounding to face him. "Oh, I mean it, Lucas. When you find your life mate, you'll understand. Until then, do not deign to advise me on the lengths to which I should or should not go for mine."

Maxine said, "She's right. I'd do the same if Lou was in there."

"And I'd kick your ass for it," Lou said softly, but the way he looked at her took the sting from his words.

Their love for each other only made my heartache that much more pronounced. I wanted my Roland. I wanted the man who looked at me the way Lou was looking at his Mad Max just then. I had to avert my eyes. "I'd appreciate it if you all would help Roxanne, Christian, and the children as much as you can, should I fail to re-emerge from this place."

Maxine rolled her eyes. "Jeeze, Rhiannon. Morbid much? If you don't come back out, we'll descend on that place with the biggest, ugliest horde of blood-drinkers we can find. For us, leaving *you* in there is not an option."

I stared at her, admiring her just as I always had, in spite of myself. Spunk irritated me. And yet, on this one, it fit.

She thinned her lips, but nodded. "And yeah, sure, you know we'll see to the kids if anything goes wrong. Right, Lou?"

"Or course we will," he said. "But listen, Rhiannon, even if you have to go in alone, someone should be outside. In case you need a diversion or…something."

Lucas pulled his backpack around, opened the flap, and pulled out a hand grenade. "I've got that covered," he said. "I brought along a dozen of these babies, and some other goodies as well."

I nodded, approving of his preparedness, neither knowing

nor caring where he'd come by the arsenal. "I only wish I could speak to you all mentally. It would make this much easier."

"Who needs telepathy when you've got technology?" Max dipped into a pocket and brought out a cell phone, handing it to me. "Lou's number is on there. Call it if you need us. We'll text you the location of the hideout the minute we're sure it's secure."

"Text me, too," Lucas said. "Give me your phone, Lou."

Lou handed it over, and Lucas programmed his number in. He held out his hand for the phone I held.

I handed it to him, feeling so impatient I could barely stand still. He poked at the screen with what felt like agonizing slowness, and then finally handed the phone back to me. All told, the operation had taken perhaps five seconds. But five more seconds away from my Roland was the same as an eternity to me.

"Are we ready then?" I asked.

They all nodded, grim faced.

"All right, then. Pandora, go with Lucas." I said it firmly, adding a mental command and pointing at Lucas as I did. My cat hung her head, but she obeyed.

Maxine lunged at me, her arms going around my neck and squeezing. "Please be careful, Rhiannon. Don't get dead." Then she released me, and she and Lou headed off to find us shelter. I smoothed my blouse, unused to such shows of affection from mortals.

Lucas was watching me, trying hard not to smile at my discomfort. He gave me a nod, then he and Pandora began looking for a good vantage point from which to observe what happened below.

Alone, I started down the hill toward the enemy stronghold. The way I felt just then, I was certain I could kill every human in the place without much trouble at all.

Overconfidence, Roland would tell me, could be a fatal mistake.

I hoped he'd be able to lecture me for it thoroughly before

this night had ended.

CHAPTER SIX

Alone, I raced to the fence, jumped it, and sped around the building whose large and impressive sign pronounced it "The Sentinel" in shiny red-brown granite. DPI had a new name for its headquarters. I'd have come up with a different one. *Center for Imprisonment and Torture*, perhaps. Or *Genocide Central.* Oh, I knew what went on beyond the stone walls and tinted glass windows. I knew.

My Roland was in there now.

It was as dark as ink around the building, despite that there were spotlights on the ground at intervals that seemed to be for the purpose of lighting the grounds and the building itself. There were lights above on poles, as well. That DPI had left the lights off, possibly in anticipation of my arrival, did not trouble me. I neither knew nor cared what their reasons were. I just wanted my husband back.

I sped around to the rear of the building, too fast for human eyes to detect, much less identify. Trucks came and went, rolling slowly in and out of tall overhead doors manned by armed guards. That was going to be my way in. It was the most vulnerable portal in the entire building.

As I crouched low, my back pressed to the cool red stone wall, a truck came rumbling by, and at the same time, I caught the scent of another vampire—no, two of them!

The overhead door rose slowly, emitting a mechanical hum. I thought it must have captives onboard, and focused my senses more sharply, feeling inside the rear of the vehicle.

But there were no vampires inside the truck. Something else was being taken prisoner by DPI this night, something I'd encountered only a handful of times in all my years of existence. Unconscious. Probably drugged. My God, DPI had discovered their existence, then. It stunned me. Lycanthropes were rare and tended to be the most elusive of creatures. They were so seldom seen that most vampires didn't even know they were real. But I knew. I had little experience with them, zero trust of them, and even less use for them, uncivilized wild things that they were. But they were there, in that truck.

The two vampires I'd sensed, however, were beyond the truck, just on the other side of the big door, doing exactly what I was doing. Waiting for a chance to get inside. I aimed my senses at them and felt a familiar energy. Devlin. A vampire I'd wanted to kill once. More than once. And then he'd saved my Roland's life and put me forever into his debt. He had been blocking heavily. I had not, so he sensed my presence first. I felt him drop his guard just slightly to let me sense him and understood that he was going inside.

I did not know what had brought Devlin all the way across the country to this hellish place. He'd been planning to build a resistance, an Undead force to fight back against man. But I didn't think it possible he'd done so this fast. It had been only weeks since I'd seen him.

And yet I hoped. I hoped with all my might that he had an army of vampires lurking in the woods, ready to rain down hell upon this place.

He didn't, of course. An army of vampires could hardly

have escaped my notice. But whatever Devlin was up to, I trusted that he had his reasons.

The truck rolled inside, and Devlin and his companion, a newborn fledgling female, flashed inside after it. I stood there a moment, unsure whether to join them or give them a head start and then enter the next time the door opened. As the door began to descend, I was torn, and then Devlin spoke to me mentally. *We need a distraction, Rhiannon. If you're still out there–*

They have Roland, I replied. *Bring him out in case I cannot.*

The truck was already reversing, the door closing again. I pulled my favorite dagger from my tall black boot, held it at the ready, and aimed my energy at the truck's fuel tank. I could start fires, light candles. I'd never attempted to ignite gasoline before, but it would only take a small spark, surely.

There was a whoosh, an explosion, and I sailed backward and landed hard, my head cracking against the side of the building with so much force that it split one of the stone blocks. The door closed before I could get up and get beneath it. An alarm began to sound, deafening and intermittent blasts coming from some deep, earsplitting horn. Spotlights flashed on from the roof, and men surged onto the rooftop, wielding rifles.

I scrambled to my feet, dizzy as hell, and pushed myself around the corner to the other side of the building. Several armed men converged near the explosion, helping the truck's driver to the ground, their rifles aiming around them as they herded him inside. I had mere seconds before they would discover me. Zipping up the side of the building toward the front, I paused at the corner with my back to the wall, and peered around.

When I saw them, I swore my blood turned to ice. There, standing in the middle of the front lawn were three small children—Nikki, flanked by Ramses and Gareth. They stood there in the dead of night, calm and still and completely defenseless while bullets rained all around them from the rooftop. Fear such as I'd never felt before wrapped around me like a deadly constrictor.

Little tufts of grass exploded around the children, shocking me out of my stillness. I shot toward them as fast as I could run, opened my mouth to shout at them to get down, but my voice seemed frozen in my throat. I saw little Nikki clasp her brother's hands, close her eyes. And then they vanished. Just rippled and disappeared. Muzzle flashes from the roof were like strobes in the darkness and the deafening shots were fired in such close succession that they sounded like machine gun fire. I veered to the nearest cover I saw, the sign on the front lawn, and I crowded my body against it.

Nikki! Ramses and Gareth! What in the name of Isis are you doing here?

Don't be mad, Nikki returned, speaking to me mentally, and just as proficiently as we vampires did with one another. *I did the* Glamourie, she told me, using the name I called my invisibility spell. She'd seen me do it twice. Apparently that was enough. *They can't even see us,* she went on, sounding very pleased with herself.

We came to help you save Roland. That was the voice of Gareth, the gentle one.

Bullets peppered the ground between me and the place where I'd last seen the three children. I clung to my only scrap of cover, calling upon the old gods to protect them. *Do not move. Being invisible will not stop bullets. Stay perfectly….*

I heard glass shattering, and dared to peer around the sign just in time to see several vampires hurling themselves through a broken window. One was dear and familiar, and landed unevenly on the ground. He lifted his head. I saw his face and my heart contracted in my chest. "Roland!"

"Rhiannon!" He hopped rapidly toward me as the others scattered, propelling himself wildly on his one leg. His prosthetic was nowhere in sight, and one of his eyes seemed oddly swollen.

In the mere seconds it took for him to reach me, I was

certain that I was about to see my only love shot down before my eyes. But he kept coming, somehow dodging the bullets that hit the earth all around him, and then he was stumbling into me, holding me, his arms crushing me to him, my face buried against his chest. "My love, my love, my love," he said, one hand in my hair.

Tipping my head up, I kissed his face, chin, jaw, neck. "Thank the gods I've got you back. I was so afraid—but Roland, the children are—"

Before I finished, they were there beside us, crowding in and wriggling their way between my beloved and me. Nikki had lost her grip on the spell, so they were once again visible. She was telling Roland excitedly how she and her brothers had managed to stow away in the belly of Roxanne's small yellow airplane to get here, and how she'd blocked their energy from me the whole time.

So very proud of herself, the willful little thing.

I adored her.

A cessation of gunfire, followed by wild clattering sounds drew my attention, and I looked around the sign to see rifles flying from the rooftop, landing in the grass, flipping and bouncing, one after another.

"It's Sheena!" Ramses cried, pointing the opposite direction, toward the perimeter fence.

Turning, I saw the seventeen-year-old Offspring we'd named Sheena standing just outside the fence and moving her hands as if she was grabbing each rifle and flinging it herself. And she was, I realized. But not by actually touching them. Her brother Wolf was beside her.

Relief washed over me so powerfully that my knees weakened with it. The two had jumped overboard to try to follow Devlin when he'd left *The Anemone* and until that very moment, I'd had no idea whether they'd even survived. Devlin was here, so apparently, the twins were with him. And I would let him know, very soon, what I thought of him dragging the teens into harm's way. But that would have to wait until we were all safe again.

"We have to get out of here," I said, whispering harshly. "This is our chance. Everyone join hands."

The children obeyed. Roland smiled, his right eye barely open and watering as he slung one arm around me, and reached out with his other hand to clasp Ramses'. Gareth held my other hand, and Nikki climbed up onto my back, wrapping her legs around my waist and her arms around my neck to ride along.

"By the power of three times three, I now evoke *the Glamourie*," I said in a tone that I used only for magic. It was deeper and more resonant, my magical voice. And powerful, incredibly powerful.

I felt it when we vanished, although because we were together within the spell, we could still see each other. It wasn't so much a spell of invisibility, but one of camouflage. We simply blended into our surroundings, chameleon-like.

"Run, and when we reach the fence jump it and keep on running," I said. "Now!"

We burst out of the shelter of the sign, running as fast as we could, which wasn't very fast, since Roland could only hop on one leg. Still, we made it to the fence. A few shots were fired as we ran, presumably by men who still had hold of their rifles, but none were aimed at us, since they couldn't even see us, and soon we were sailing over the barrier and dashing into the nearby woods.

I released the spell as we moved deeper and deeper into the forest, and soon Lucas and Pandora came crashing out of the trees and straight into our path. Pandora lunged at Roland, hitting his chest with her paws so hard she knocked him flat on his back on the ground, then stood there upon his chest, touching his face repeatedly with her nose as if kissing him.

"I will never get used to that," Lucas said with a shake of his head. "Is everyone all ri—What the hell are you *kids* doing here?"

Nikki shrugged innocently. The boys ignored him to fall

into the pile of vampire and black leopard currently tussling on the ground. It was as close to an emotional hug as I had seen them come, though disguised as playful wrestling.

"They stowed away in the cargo hold," I told Lucas. "Have you heard from Maxine and Lou?"

He nodded. "There's a barn ten miles north on Highgrave Road. It's safe, they said."

I nodded, then relayed the information mentally to Devlin. *We have the Sevens and we're clear. Get yourselves and the twins out of there. There's a barn ten miles north on Highgrave Road. Meet us there. Do not be followed.*

Then I turned and reached out a hand for my love, who was lying on his back, accepting a welcome from an overly enthused big cat and two little boys.

He reached through them all to let me help him up. "We have to go, children. It's not safe here." He glanced over his shoulder. "And yet, I sense no pursuit."

"Roland," Lucas said, and when I looked his way, he was holding a long straight limb that had been stripped of its bark. It had a natural rounded knot on the top. Lucas held it out and said, "I had time to kill while waiting for you all, and I thought you could use a staff."

Roland took it, thumping it on the ground to test its strength. "This is going to make my ten-mile trek much easier. Thank you, Lucas."

For the first time, I started to believe in the young man in a way I hadn't before. Maybe he truly was sorry for his misguided choices in the past. Maybe he was genuinely on our side.

Time, I supposed, would tell.

"What's up with your eye?" Lucas asked, then.

"No idea. Let's get out of here," Roland said. He used the staff, walked up beside me, and put his free arm around my shoulders. My side pressed to his, I relished the feel of him, his nearness, and more than anything, the life force still burning within him. He was alive. And besides the painful looking eye, he seemed well, I thought, as I examined him both with my vision, and with my inner knowing. He seemed well. Almost. There was something...a shadow over his essence that gave me pause, but I refused to entertain the notion that anything was seriously wrong.

Thank the gods.

We walked away with our little troop, leaving DPI behind.

I wished I could believe it would be forever.

CHAPTER SEVEN

Slowly, due to Roland's impediment, we made our way to the abandoned barn Maxine and Lou Malone had located for us. It was lopsided and its boards were gray with age. Great patches of bare roof were exposed to the elements, where shingles had been blown away by storms or simply rotted with time. The door was made of wood planks, suspended by rollers from a track nailed to the barn itself. When I tugged it open it squealed in protest, and my hands came away with a few slivers.

"Inside, children. We'll be safe here for a little while. Hurry up now."

My three darlings ran past me into the barn, Lucas right behind them. My poor dear Roland brought up the rear, struggling a bit now, with his one leg and makeshift crutch. It had been a long walk.

Only, it shouldn't have been. Not for a vampire.

Pandora was beside him. She'd been staying close to him, watching his every move. I wasn't certain if she was worried for him or perhaps could smell the evil of DPI clinging to him in some way. She acted almost as if she didn't trust him anymore.

He met my eyes, and I could see his shame, his humiliation at being so weak, so slow. I pressed my hand to his cheek and said, "Don't despair, my love. You're free and we're together again. Everything will come around as it should. Including your leg."

He nodded, but didn't reply, and hobbled past me into the barn. Pandora looked up at me.

"What is it, girl?" I would give a great deal if only my cat could talk to me, or if I could read her thoughts. I couldn't. But we'd been together long enough that I could make a very good guess most of the time. I knew she was uneasy. Troubled.

"Everything's all right, my girl," I told her, stroking her head.

She sighed heavily, turned and went into the barn, her paws making no sound on the earth nor on the aging floorboards within.

I gave a last look around with all of my senses, but I still felt no sign of pursuit. And that concerned me quite gravely. DPI should be chasing us, flattening the forest with their jack booted thugs and automatic weapons and tranquilizer darts.

I looked to the sky as if it would send me an answer. But there was nothing. With one last sweep of the dark forest and winding dirt road, I went into the barn and closed the door.

Max and Lou were standing on either side of Roland, clapping his shoulders and talking to him eagerly and too loudly, and then Maxine met my eyes over his shoulder, and came to me. "You did it!" The perky redhead had a gift for stating the obvious.

"Did you truly doubt I would?"

"Nope, not a bit." Then she sent a worried look Roland's way. "Is he all right?" she whispered, as if that might stop a vampire thirty feet away from hearing.

"As all right as anyone could be after spending time in the

hands of those beasts," I told her. "And his hearing is as good as ever," I added.

"But his eye looks like hell." She gave a sheepish grin. "We heard from Roxy. Those kids of yours are a handful."

"I haven't addressed that particular offense yet," I said. "I suppose they should be punished in some way...."

"You think?"

I shrugged. "If someone had tried to keep me from helping Roland, I'd have done the same. Or worse."

She rolled her eyes, shaking her head. "Are you sure they're not genetically yours?"

"Quite sure. Spiritually, though, I believe they were always meant to come to us."

She seemed touched by that, gazing at the children, who had discovered a mountain of hay in the rear of the barn and were climbing all over it like mountain goats. "So," Max said, shifting her focus back to me, "if we're going to get home before sunrise, we'll need transportation back to the plane. It will take too long on foot."

"And do you have a suggestion for that?"

"Wouldn't've brought it up if I didn't," she said. "Lou and I are going to hike into town and rent a van. Won't take us more than a couple of hours, which is a lot faster than we can all walk back to the plane."

"All right," I said. "If you insist on doing so, you must use false names. I don't want you and Lou implicated in any of this. DPI can make your lives hell."

"They tried to hire us, you know," she said, a mischievous gleam in her eyes. "To help track down vampires. Even suggested we inform them of any clients we suspected were in cahoots with you."

In cahoots? She was entirely too cute. "And what did you tell them?"

"That we had too much private work to accept any government contracts. But we were flattered by their offer. The dirty bastards." Then she turned away, our conversation over. "Lou, we've gotta make tracks."

Lou clapped Roland on the shoulder and said he'd see him later, and then the two of them headed out of the barn together, and to my surprise, Lucas got up to go with them. As he passed me, he said, "I know you trust them, and I know they're good, but I just want to make sure no one spots them, follows them, nothing like that."

"I appreciate your vigilance," I told him.

With a nod, he left as well. I went to Roland, led him deeper into the barn, and urged him to sit on a bale of hay at the bottom of the mountain. "You need to rest," I said. "You're in pain. Is it your leg?"

"My head, actually." He gazed lovingly into my eyes. "It's been throbbing incessantly. And I can't see a thing from my right eye."

"The gods only know what they did to you while you rested. Your eye should've healed with the day sleep. Here, let me try to help with the headache, at least." I worked myself around behind him and sat down on a bale a bit higher than his. My legs were on either side of him, my feet on the bale on which he sat. Sliding closer, so that my front pressed to his back, I began to massage his temples, calling up the healing magic I'd learned as a child.

He sighed, leaning back against me. "I'm sorry my mood isn't better. There were others there, captive vampires. I'm afraid I wasn't as much help as I would've liked to have been in freeing them. Devlin did most of it, including rescuing a barely alive, possibly mad vampiress from the furthest cell." He gazed toward the door. "I hope we hear from them soon. We shouldn't have left them."

"Please. You were arrested without cause, held prisoner, torn from your family. Besides, we had to get the children out of there. Devlin can handle himself."

He nodded in agreement. "I should be elated, not short-tempered. I'm free. It's over." He sighed deeply, and I felt the tension easing from him beneath my gentle massage. "It's finally sinking in, I think."

"Good. We'll be out of here within a couple of hours and Lucas will fly us all back to Maine." He groaned at the word "fly" but I only kissed the top of his head and kept on speaking. "We can stay with Maxine and Lou for a few days while we search for our new home. The place where we will raise Ramses and Gareth and Nikki." I smiled at the thought. "I'm actually excited about the prospect of motherhood."

He nodded. "We'll raise them to be good people, strong people, people who do not judge others based on their differences, but rather search for common ground."

"Hmm."

He twisted his neck to look up at me. "Go on. Say it."

"I'm hardly going to argue with you on our first night together again," I told him.

"But...?"

I shrugged, turned his head forward again, then moved my thumbs just above his ears and spread my fingers over the top of his skull to rub small circles there. "I was rather thinking we would raise them to be strong. To know their own worth. To never allow themselves to be mistreated or wronged, and to be warriors in their own defense when necessary."

"I suppose we'll find a compromise," he said.

I moved my hands to the back of his neck and the upper parts of his shoulders, driving a sigh of appreciation from his chest. "No compromise. You teach them diplomacy and tolerance, and I'll teach them pride and empowerment. They'll be very well-balanced children."

"I love the way your mind works," he said softly.

Then he sat up a little, and looking the children's way, called them to him. The three had been tumbling from the top of the hay to the bottom like circus monkeys, but they came quickly when he called and stood before him, curious and attentive.

Roland said, "I want you to know how grateful I am for your devotion, little ones. It means the world to me that you would risk your lives to come here and try to help free me."

"We didn't risk anything," Ramses said. "We're stronger than they are."

"And we're not little," Nikki added.

Gareth said, "We were afraid of what would happen if Rhiannon couldn't save you by herself."

"I did have other help," I reminded them.

"Humans." Ramses said it as if the very notion that they could help us had been ludicrous.

"Nonetheless," Roland went on. "You made some very bad decisions. If you're going to have good lives for yourselves, you're going to need to understand the difference between good decisions and bad ones. So I want to talk to you about that."

Gareth lowered his head and said, "I told you we shouldn't have stuck those needles into Roxy and Christian."

"They wouldn't have let us go if we hadn't!" Nikki countered.

Roland studied them one by one. "That doesn't make it right, Nikki. Those tranquilizers you used on them could have killed them. The doses were intended for vampires, not humans. How would you have felt if they'd died?"

Ramses shrugged. Nikki frowned and said, "I would miss Christian most, I think. He plays with us. Roxy mostly tries to tell us what to do. She's not as fun."

Her tone was matter-of-fact and emotionless. I looked at Roland, speaking mentally. *It's as if they don't have empathy.*

How can they have? Raised in cages like animals. We'll take it slowly.

Gareth said, "I don't think we're supposed to hurt people who are our friends, are we?" He looked to Roland as if looking to a god, and reminding me that he'd probably heard our silent exchange.

"No, Gareth. We're not supposed to hurt people who are our friends. We're not supposed to hurt people who've done us no harm. In fact, we are only permitted to hurt those who are trying to harm us. That's a hard and fast rule among most of mankind, and all of vampire kind."

"It's not a rule among *our* kind," Ramses said.

"Your kind are rather new," I told him. "You've been raised under the control of others, so you haven't had a chance to develop a set of rules by which you want to live. I would like for you to adopt ours for now, and as you grow, you can begin to think about your own. What you feel is right and what is wrong, and what rules you feel you want to live by."

"I already know what rules I want to live by," Ramses said. "None. I want to do what I want, whenever I want, and in whatever way I want."

Roland stood up from his bale of hay, tall and proud, despite the missing leg. "For the most part, you can. We all do. The only limitations on our personal freedom come into play when our actions affect others. Do you understand?"

"But I don't care about others," Ramses said.

"You care about me, Ramses. Why else would you have come to try to help me?"

"I didn't want you to be kept in a cage."

"Why not?" Roland asked.

"Because then you wouldn't be with us anymore." Ramses said it as if it should be obvious.

"And why do you want me to be with you?" Roland pressed.

Ramses frowned. Nikki, though, tilted her head and said, "Oh," drawing the syllable out. "*That's* what it is."

"That's what it is, Nikki," I said, getting up to go and stroke her hair. "When you care about someone, when you love someone, you feel hurt when you know they are hurting. You feel pain when you know they are in trouble. You feel compelled to help them, just the way the three of you felt compelled to help Roland. That's what caring is. That's what love is."

"That and so much more," Roland said.

Nikki was nodding slowly, and Gareth had moisture gathering in his eyes. Ramses, however, was still frowning.

"So no more harming Roxy or Christian, or anyone who is our friend, all right?"

Roland asked.

"And no more putting yourselves in harm's way for us," I told them. "We'd rather die ourselves than see you put back into cages again."

"Well that doesn't make any sense at all!" Nikki burst out.

I knelt and pressed my palms to her cheeks. "Yes, it does little one. Yes, it does. That's how much we love you."

Nikki frowned at me, and when I lowered my hands again, she looked left at Gareth, then right at Ramses.

"If you would die for us, then maybe you would do something else for us," she said.

Ramses clamped a hand to her shoulder as if in warning. Nikki shrugged it off and glared at him briefly before swinging her big eyes right back to mine again.

"There used to be four of us," Nikki said. "I want to know what happened to our sister."

I met Roland's eyes. He nodded. And I said, "Then we shall find out. What do you remember about her?"

"Almost nothing. Sheena says it's because we were only two years old when she went away. But I know she used to be with us. She had the most beautiful hair, all silvery white and soft. And she was smaller than the rest of us. Sheena remembers more. You can ask her when she gets here."

I lifted my brows. "When she gets here?"

Nikki nodded. "She and Wolf are on their way. And they're bringing someone with them."

* * *

I didn't think to doubt my little girl, so I was not surprised when, a half hour later, I sensed the nearness of the two seventeen-year-old Offspring we'd named Sheena and Wolf, along with the very weak energy of a vampiress I'd never known, probably the one Roland had mentioned, and a human, of all things! I hoped the two teens were not being marched here at the point of a DPI rifle. But if they were in trouble, Nikki and the boys would sense it. That much, they'd confided in me.

I met the newcomers at the door, and I couldn't help but embrace the teens. They both reacted in exactly the same manner, just stood stiff and awkward, neither returning my embrace, nor shying away from it.

Stepping back I said, "I am so glad to see you. I feared the worst when you jumped overboard to go after Devlin."

Sheena said, "We didn't know how hard it would be. But we survived." Then she turned. "This is Emma's father. Emma is the vampiress who was with Devlin back at The Sentinel. Her father was also a prisoner of DPI, that is why they were there. They also found a vampiress there, but I don't think she will live."

I looked past her at the human man, who seemed exhausted. His face was damp with perspiration, a shock of thick dark hair stuck to his forehead, and his eyes were slightly unfocused.

"Professor Oliver Benatar," he said as I examined him.

"I'm Rhiannon," I told him. And I saw his eyes widen. He'd heard my name, then. "You look as if you're about to drop, Professor. Give her to me."

"I've been telling him that all the way here," Wolf said.

"If I could just find a place where she could lie down."

Nodding, I led them all inside. The children came running to greet their older siblings, but there were no hugs, no tears. And yet I sensed their immense relief at being reunited. As they all talked at once, I led Professor Benatar to the small room off the right side of the barn. It held a large sink and there was a big area of bare floor where there had obviously once been some sort of contraption. Perhaps a tank to hold milk. I'd gathered from a large metal stanchion lying on the floor in the main part of the barn, that this had once been the home of a dairy.

"This is perfect. Thank you."

"You'll be safe here, Professor Benatar," I told him. "I don't know what you've heard about our kind, but—"

"I have never believed the lies," he said. Then he looked at the woman. "She was kept in a concrete box for I don't know how long. Starved. Probably mad."

"I'll draw some of my own blood to help heal her. Roland will as well."

I left them then, closing the door. Then I called to Sheena, "What about Devlin and his Emma?"

"Devlin was shot in the leg," she said. "They told us to come without them, and said they would join us soon."

My brows went up and I sensed Roland's concern. Devlin had saved his life—twice now. "Are they in danger? How badly is he hurt?" he asked.

"Emma said he would live," Sheena told him. "And there was no one following us, so I think they will be all right."

"Good," I said. "Good. Well it seems we have a bit of time then." I took a seat on a bale of hay beside Roland and patted the next bale over. Sheena took my meaning and came to sit beside me. She was a beautiful girl, just blossoming into womanhood. Her skin was as dark as if she'd been raised in constant sunlight, but I knew that wasn't the case, and I wondered about her parentage. Had DPI bred the children from the DNA of only one or two of their BDXers, or had they combined the genes of many? Her hair was dark and tended to be wild, but she carried a comb in the back pocket of her jeans. It was the only thing she carried, so clearly it was important to her.

"Nikki has told me she would like to know what became of her sister. Will you tell me what you remember about her?"

Sheena shot a look at Wolf across the hay mountain. He shook his head as if in disgust. It was becoming clear to me that these children had, at some point in their captive lives, decided not to tell anyone anything about themselves for any reason. We still didn't know the full extent of their powers. And when Nikki had asked me about her sister, Ramses had much the same reaction that the teenage Wolf was having now.

When I brought my gaze back to Sheena's again, I found her staring at me. And she said, "We barely understand our powers ourselves, you know," she said softly.

I blinked. "Were you...can you hear my thoughts?"

"Not so much hear them. I feel them. We all do. Also, I can move things without touching them. But for a long time I thought everyone could. When we realized that we had... abilities that were different from the keepers, we decided never to tell them. And perhaps one day we would use our powers against them, to get free."

"That makes perfect sense, Sheena. In your position I'd have done much the same."

She nodded. "I no longer believe vampires are our enemies," she said. "Wolf is more stubborn, but deep down, I think he knows it too."

I looked his way. He wasn't missing a word, but he had joined the children atop the hay and was pretending to ignore us.

"What can you tell us about Nikki's sister?" I asked.

"She was so different from the other three," Sheena said. "She had pale skin. Violet eyes, sometimes pink if she was upset. She was smaller than the others. Very fragile. And her hair was even lighter than sunshine, and thin and soft."

Listening raptly, Roland covered my hand with his and squeezed. "What became of her?" I asked, my voice gone raspy.

"She died. One day she just stopped moving and breathing. No more thoughts came from her mind. After a while, the keepers came and took her away. She was, as close as I can guess, two years old."

My heart broke for the lost child. "I'm so sorry."

"I wish I knew what made her die," Sheena said. "Wolf and I were shot by those men Devlin calls Crows, with the weapons he calls rifles." She pressed a hand to the center of her chest. "Right here. It hurt, and then it didn't. There was just nothing. Devlin said he thought we were dead. Only, we woke up."

She looked up at Wolf and he met her eyes briefly, but even

that small glance seemed to convey myriad feelings. There was a powerful connection between the two of them. I'd never seen siblings so close.

"We do not know how we can die," Sheena said, returning her attention to me. "We only know we can. And we only know that because of what happened to the little pale one."

Roland said, "Unless of course, she woke up too."

CHAPTER EIGHT

"Devlin's coming," I said, rising all at once and rushing to the door, relieved that he was all right. Roland hopped to my side as I opened the door, and the sense of something *else* hit me like a foul odor.

Devlin and the beautiful blond-haired Emma, so recently turned that I could still smell the humanity in her, approached us eagerly. Devlin glanced at Roland's leg, and at the walking stick he held. Roland met his eyes and said, "Bastards stole my prosthetic."

"That's pretty low, even for them," Devlin said, clasping Roland's shoulder affectionately. "I'm glad to see you, my friend."

"Not as glad as I was to see you in that prison," Roland said. "That's twice now you've saved my life."

"I heard they blew up *The Anemone*," Devlin replied. "I've been sick to my soul ever since. Did everyone make it off the ship?"

"They did," Roland told him, but then he noticed what

I had already been keenly aware of. The two tawny-maned strangers emerging from the wood, a male carrying a female. They looked not much older than our own Wolf and Sheena, but the way their kind aged, they could be that plus a century or two.

"*Lycan*," I said, curling my lip.

The little blond vampiress Emma widened her brown eyes and said, "Lycan? You mean—"

"Werewolves. Where on earth did you find them?"

"We freed them when we freed Roland," Emma said. "Tara's been shot. I told them I thought you could help."

I glanced at Roland, because he'd had more experience with their kind than I. And he, being who he was, said, "The enemy of my enemy is my friend."

I squelched my objections and inclined my head. "Fine. Bring them inside, I'll see what I can do."

They all trooped into the barn, but I had not thought to prepare Pandora. She came slinking down from the haystacks where she'd been watching over the children, emitting a low growl, her eyes on the male.

Devlin's new mate Emma seemed alarmed, and then the male lycan growled at my cat, the deep threat of a wolf. I considered tearing his head from his shoulders, but the girl in his arms said, "Tomas, no."

Pandora moved nearer. Roland put his hand on my shoulder when I would've intervened, and the girl extended her arm rather weakly. Pandora inched forward, sniffed her hand delicately, and then allowed the girl to touch her silken coat. Then she sat down, glancing at me as if to give her approval to the newcomers.

I was still reserving judgement, myself. I'd never had much fondness for lycanthropes. They were wild and dirty things, living in the forests and embracing their animal nature as much as their humanity. Perhaps more.

Then the girl's arm fell limply, and I refocused on the matter at hand. "Lay her down here on the hay, quickly," I said.

The male, Tomas, obeyed, and then he stood too near, with Devlin and Emma crowding in as well. I examined the bullet wound in the girl's abdomen. It was a neat round hole that pulsed blood with each heartbeat. And I had no idea what damage the bullet might have done to her internal organs. But I did know it was still inside her.

"I can stop the bleeding," I said. "But healing the wound is beyond even my abilities."

And then little Gareth shouldered his way in close to the girl, looked at her belly, and then up at me. And he said, "I can do it."

"Gareth, I don't think–"

What can it hurt to let the boy try? Roland asked me, speaking mentally. *We have no idea what he's capable of. Let him show us what he can do.*

"Your name is Gareth?" Tomas asked.

My boy nodded. "Roland gave it to me."

"My grandfather's name was Gareth," he said.

I met Roland's eyes then, and I knew we were both thinking of the same thing. That time, that long, long ago time when he'd been human, just a boy himself. He'd come upon a younger boy being attacked by a wolf, and had saved the child's life. The boy's father, a knight named Sir Gareth, had taken young Roland as squire. He'd become almost like a part of their family.

But the boy had never been the same. He'd been turned. He had become Lycan.

Could this Tomas be a relative, a descendant?

Our Gareth was standing close beside Tara by then, and he looked up at me and said, "You better move back. Sometimes you might get burned."

Burned? Fascinating. I took a step back and watched the seven-year-old hold his hands over the bullet wound as if he were performing Reiki. He closed his eyes. I watched intently, but nothing happened.

Then he looked up suddenly and called, "Sheena, I need

your help."

"What for?" Sheena asked, rising lazily from her spot on the hay, and brushing pieces of it from her clothes.

"The bullet is inside her," he said. "You can pull it out."

She sighed heavily but came to Gareth's side all the same. Looking down at the girl's abdomen, she said, "I cannot move it if I cannot see it."

"It's right here," Gareth told her, pointing. "About this deep." He made space between his thumb and forefinger to illustrate. "Try to bring it out the same way it went in. And be careful."

Sheena nodded, and stared hard at the girl, concentrating perhaps. Then she mimicked pinching the bullet between her thumb and forefinger, and moved her hand up the girl's abdomen to the bullet hole. She pulled back, and the bullet emerged with a little gush of blood and lay there on Tara's belly.

"Perfect," Gareth said. Then he held his hands over the wound and within a few seconds there was a glow emitting from his palms, and heat, and power that I recognized. The light was yellow orange, like sunlight, and the wound began to burn, sealing itself over. The stench was unpleasant, the pain must've been worse, as the girl moaned with it. But it healed. Right before our eyes.

I looked at Roland and thought, *Now we know Gareth's special ability. He's a healer.*

Roland beamed with pride. He clasped Gareth's shoulders and said, "Well done, my boy. Very well done."

We all stood there, watching the patient to see how she would respond to the child's efforts. Soon her breathing seemed to deepen, to regulate itself. It was an improvement from the shallow panting of earlier. And moments after that, she opened her eyes, looked right into Gareth's and said, "I dreamed there was an angel."

"It was just me," Gareth replied.

I put my hand on Gareth's shoulder, and said, "Child, why

have you not tried to use this healing gift of yours on Roland's wounded eye and throbbing head?"

"It doesn't work on vampires," he said, as if it was something so obvious I should have known. And then he ran off to practice jumping and climbing with his siblings.

* * *

Roland sat with Devlin outside the barn, beneath the stars. They'd come out to surveil their surroundings and make sure they were still undiscovered. But that was only an excuse, truth be told, to get away from the others for a bit of man-to-man conversation.

Roland had respect for Devlin. It had begun as a grudging respect, but it had become full blown and heartfelt. He'd seen, firsthand, what the man would do to care for his own kind. And while his dislike of mortals, even the Chosen, was consistent and unapologetic, he was a good man. Roland sensed that his hardest edges had been softened a bit, and he could guess why. The love of a good woman had a way of easing a man's soul. And it was obvious that Devlin and Emma were in love quite completely.

The two men walked—Roland hobbled, really, using his tree limb staff in place of his missing leg—around the barn's perimeter. Devlin was limping as well, due to being shot in the leg earlier. They must make an interesting sight, Roland mused. Two gimpy vampires, staggering through the darkness, one of them half blind.

The night was a beautiful one, cloudless and star-spangled with a brisk autumnal chill. Every nocturnal creature in the forest around them seemed to be in the mood for singing. Frogs and grasshoppers and even an owl joined in the choir. It was soothing to Roland's senses.

"So what did they do to you in there, Roland?" Devlin asked.

Roland had expected the question. It was one Rhiannon had been deliberately not asking, but he'd heard it in her mind over and over. "The truth is, I don't know. But...." He sighed.

It was an expression of frustration, not a mechanism of breathing. He didn't have to breathe.

"But what?" Devlin prodded.

Roland looked at the forest around him, trying to capture its serenity for his own. "I don't know. But something happened. My head hasn't stopped aching. There's an incredible pressure behind my right eye and it's all but blind at the moment. I'm short-tempered and impatient, and–"

"You? Short-tempered and impatient?"

He met his friend's eyes, knew he was teasing just a little. Trying to lighten up Roland's dark mood. "Yes. Me. And there's something else. A presence. I have the constant feeling that if I should turn and look over my shoulder, I'll see someone there, right behind me, watching me. And yet, of course, there's not."

Devlin frowned very deeply. "Have you told Rhiannon about this?"

"No, and I don't intend to. I'm going to give it some time. It will probably pass. Perhaps it's some sort of post-traumatic stress."

"Post-traumatic stress. From a battle-seasoned knight, a thousand years old?"

"Eight hundred sixty-seven," Roland corrected. "And that is old enough for me to know the best course of action here. Rhiannon, the children...they need a rest from all the worry and strain and constant pursuit. I cannot put any more on them just now."

Devlin nodded as if he understood that.

"It was quite out of character, what you did back there," Roland said, trying to change the subject. He'd grown weary of focusing on his own problems. "Breaking into DPI's Sentinel to rescue an ordinary mortal man like Professor Benatar."

"And my little gang of rebels will never let me hear the end of it, when we get back to them and tell the tale." He shrugged. "What can I say? He's Emma's father. And I have fallen quite ridiculously in love with her."

"I can see that."

They walked in silence for a moment. Roland took in the platter-sized fungi growing on fallen logs, and the patches of mushrooms forming fairy circles on the forest floor.

"I don't sense anyone out there," Roland said at length. "Do you?"

"No. And I'm concerned, Roland. Why aren't the Crows combing these woods in search of us? Getting in and out of there was a little bit too easy, if you ask me."

"Easy? We had bullets raining down around our feet," he said, nodding down at Devlin's leg. "You were hit by one."

"I was near the shifters when I was hit," he said, glancing down at the tightly wrapped wound in his thigh. "I have to wonder if that bullet was meant for them. Because you and Rhiannon and the children, stood there in plain sight outside that building...until you pulled that disappearing act of yours. There were trained marksmen on the roof. Dozens of them. They couldn't have all missed you unless they were deliberately trying."

"And yet they shot at you?" Roland asked.

"At the lycans. I was just in the line of fire." He shrugged. "Of course, I can't be sure of any of that. Perhaps the great Rhiannon knows how to deflect bullets. I don't know."

"No. She doesn't." Roland was searching his mind. "But why would they deliberately let the vampires go?"

"That's the question, isn't it?" Devlin shrugged. "Just something to think about."

Roland nodded. They'd made a full circle and arrived back at the barn just as a moving van came speeding along the narrow road, slowing and pulling over near the barn. Before he even had time to go tense, Roland recognized the energy of its occupants. Maxine and Lou Malone and young Lucas Townsend, former DPI lieutenant.

He glanced at Devlin. *It's all right, they're with us.*

The larger man's shoulders relaxed.

"We're leaving now, Devlin. Apparently I'm to be conveyed

to Maine by means of a flying machine, though I freely admit, I'd prefer to hop the entire distance. We need to get underway soon if we're to make it by sunrise."

Devlin extended a hand and Roland clasped it firmly. "Be safe, Roland. And if you need anything, contact me."

"You're returning to the west coast?" Roland asked.

"Further, even. Regina Island," Devlin said. "But I can get back quickly if I'm needed, and I can bring reinforcements as well. Tavia, Bellamy—"

"I know, my friend. Thank you for that. I pray it won't be necessary." Roland glanced at the barn as Lucas opened its doors. He hadn't seen the two vampires lurking in the dark shadows outside. "I hope for peace. Peace and a home that is a haven, where Rhiannon and I can raise the Offspring to be decent beings. And teach them to master their powers and to temper them with kindness."

"Rhiannon's going to teach them that, is she?"

Roland heard the jest in Devlin's tone and smiled in amusement. "One can only hope." Then he grew serious again. "Sheena and Wolf are more than welcome to come with us—"

"I've talked to them already," Devlin said. They want to return to the island with Emma and Me. But uh...I think it's important that we facilitate regular visits. They're family, them and the Sevens. A strange, laboratory-generated family, but family all the same."

"Then that's what we'll do. Be well, Devlin."

"Be safe, Roland."

* * *

Only a few days after leaving our barn-hideout in New York, we were driving my new car, a sleek black crossover SUV made by Porsche–because if I were going to drive an SUV then what other kind would I be driving?–through a set of strong iron gates and onto the grounds of our new home. The gates closed behind us the moment we passed through them, and our tires crunched over a driveway lined in white gravel. It wound and twisted among perfectly groomed lawns. It was night, beautiful night, and I was bringing my beloved Roland and the three children we intended to raise together, to the place I had named Serenity.

I'd handled all the details from Maxine and Lou's home, which was forty miles north of us, in the space of a few days. After a night spent browsing the realty listings, the internet had turned up the perfect place, as I had known it would. It was in a rural area, surrounded by farmland and forest. We submitted an offer well above the asking price in exchange for immediate access to the place, and it was accepted eagerly. I made it clear we would not want to be bothered. At all. For any reason. Any documents in need of signing could be faxed to us or simply left in the mailbox. There was no reason for further contact.

We had long kept a safe deposit box in Bangor, since I loved Maine beyond any other state in the US. Maxine was kind enough to visit there during daytime hours and retrieve the items it held. Our false identities, credit cards, etcetera. Roxanne had provided birth certificates and Social Security cards for the children to match our current false names. She'd done so by means of some shady contact of hers, about whom, I knew nothing. But I trusted Roxanne.

Money had expedited the process of purchasing both the Porsche and the house, as only money could do. And now, as I drove slowly among the trees and lawns, I felt the sensation of an immense weight lifting from me. Reaching across, I put my hand over Roland's. "Do you feel it, my love? We've come home."

He glanced my way and smiled, but it didn't reach his eyes. The right one was still swollen and red, though it seemed to be improving. He was holding a warm, moist cloth to it as he had been doing frequently, to relieve the pain. We vampires feel pain more than mortals can imagine.

Something more than just this lingering eye problem was weighing on him. He hadn't even complained about the hour-long car ride. My gaze on him lingered only briefly. We would talk about it later, I decided. I would not let worry cloud my joy of this day.

I drove around another bend in the white snake of a driveway, and there was the house, broad and tall, built of stately red brick. Four white columns supported the portico above the massive red entry door, and concrete porch and steps. Black shutters flanking every window. Five thousand square feet, not including the guest house and four-car garage. It was a home worthy of us.

I stopped the car in front, shut it off, and opened the door to get out. And then I just stood there, staring at the place with my heart filling. This was where we would raise the children. This was where they would grow and learn and become adults. This was our haven.

The children climbed out of the car as well, and went running round the house to the backyard.

"Wait!" I called. "Wait until I've made certain it's safe!" I started after them, only to feel Roland's hand on my shoulder from behind.

"It's perfectly safe. It's fenced all the way around. There are alarms and motion sensors enough to protect the president. And on top of all of that, they have abilities we've only begun to understand. They're fine, Rhiannon."

I turned to face him, and saw just then, the Roland I'd been missing. Relief washed through me and I smiled at the rush of it. "You're probably right. But I must check all the same." I pressed the keys into his hand, and my lips to his mouth. "I'll be inside momentarily."

He nodded and, hating to leave him, I headed around the house to the backyard where a large swimming pool sparkled in the sunlight, just off a massive deck. Farther back, the giant wooden swing set I'd requested the seller install before our arrival was perfect in every way, and the children were already climbing its attached tower, then descending by way of its slide.

So odd, watching them. They used the swings methodically. There was no boisterous giggling, no laughter.

Spotting me, Nikki got off her swing and came to me. "We're really going to stay here?"

"This is our home now, Nikki," I promised, stroking her hair and loving the sparkle in her eyes and the genuine smile on her lips. Smiles were new to the children. Laughter would come, too, in time.

"When we go inside, we'll choose a bedroom just for you, and I will proceed to fill it with everything a little girl could want."

She blinked her eyes. "I can't think of anything to want," she said softly. "Thank you, Rhiannon."

My own throat was going tight. "You're welcome poppet." I heard another vehicle, and turning in alarm, saw Roland coming out through the large double doors onto the deck. He wore a new prosthetic, sent to him by the ingenious Killian. But for some reason, he'd kept the walking stick Lucas had made him. He'd packed it with the rest of the belongings we'd acquired since returning to Maine.

"It's Roxanne and Christian," he said when I met his eyes. Lucas had returned to his duties as a DPI Lieutenant on the West Coast. He intended to act as a spy for our side, and felt he could do the most good from the inside.

"You have to stop being so nervous, my love," he went on. "We're safe here."

"It's almost too hard to believe." I joined him on the deck, up the steps to its higher level, and then slid my arms around his waist and rested my head on his chest. "I love you so much, Roland. I don't know what happened to you back there, but I promise you—"

"I don't know either," he said.

Frowning, I lifted my head to stare into his eyes. "What do you mean, you don't know?"

He seemed to search for words, then quickly shook his head. "Nothing. I...I suppose I'm just acclimating."

Before I could question him further, I heard Christian's booming voice and thundering feet from just beyond the doors, and then he came bursting through them. "There's a pool! Roxy, there's a pool!" he shouted, then he ran past us and out to join the children.

Roxanne came behind him a bit more leisurely, shaking her head. "This is some place you picked, Rhiannon. Gotta hand it to you, you know how to live. Always have."

"I only know what I like." I hooked my arm through Roland's. "Shall we explore our new abode, love? I'm eager to see the master suite. *And perhaps to test out the bed*, I added silently. *It's been too long.*

I saw the spark of arousal in his eyes. It was his only reply as we walked into the house, leaving Christian and the children to their playing.

* * *

"It's working beautifully," Dr. Bouchard said.

"It's about freaking time," Colonel Patterson replied.

"I expected the day sleep would heal him completely," Dr. Bouchard said for the tenth time. "But the ongoing presence of the foreign object kept the irritation returning every night. His body seems to have adjusted to it now, though."

They were watching a large flat screen monitor in Patterson's office, and seeing everything Roland de Courtemanche saw, just as if his eyes were a camera. Because one of them was. "Look at that place," she said, feeling a little envious. "Living like royals, aren't they?"

"And yet we don't know where it is." Her ever-critical employer was true to form. "The camera didn't work all the way there. We should've inserted a tracking device."

"We don't need a tracking device, Colonel Patterson. We already know the Offspring can sense each other over long distances. Besides, Roland will do whatever we command him to do, when we're ready.

"An assumption that has not yet been put to the test."

"I'm just giving it some time to take," Bouchard said. "He's uneasy, sensing something wrong. If we tip him off, he'll bolt. Or worse." She returned her attention to the screen. Reaching down to her computer mouse, she moved the curser until it hovered over the redhead's face. With a click of a button the facial recognition feature spelled out her information.

Roxanne O'Malley

BD Positive

Age Unknown

Wanted for Crimes Against the State

Biological granddaughter: Charlotte O'Malley, vampire.

The underlined name was a clickable link to the files on Charlotte O'Malley, but Bouchard wasn't interested in her at the moment.

"Roxanne O'Malley." The colonel said the name as if it left a bad taste in his mouth. "That's one human who's got to go. She's been a thorn in our sides far too many times. Probably the best mortal friend a vampire could have. Who's the big guy playing with the mutants?"

Dr. Bouchard moved the mouse to the large blond man and clicked again.

Christian Svensen Slate

Age 25

BDX Subject

Euthanized at Conclusion of Experiment

"According to the computer, he's dead," she said, unnecessarily, because the colonel could read it for himself, and was leaning over her shoulder so closely she could smell his dinner on his breath.

"Yeah, well he's not," he said. "And he's not a vampire. Yet. Given his size it's probably better if he never becomes one, either."

"He had the full series of injections. The failsafe is in place. If a vampire drinks his blood to change him, they'll die."

"They managed to change the O'Mally bitch."

"O'Mally never received the full series of injections." Bouchard shrugged. "But Slate did, so they can't change him.

And if he's exposed to extreme stress, his heart will explode," Dr. Bouchard said.

"Then let's stress the bastard out."

"I'm not sure how you expect me to–"

"You just keep track of the Offpspring. I want to know everything those little mutants do. Clearly they were keeping the full extent of their abilities to themselves in captivity. Let's let 'em experience freedom for a while, see if they get comfortable enough to start flexing their muscles, so to speak."

"And what about Christian Slate?" she asked.

"I don't know yet. We need their location, that's our top priority. I consider the lack of a GPS implant a failure on your part, Bouchard. You figure out where they are. Pronto."

"Yes, sir."

"And don't spook them. We want 'em to feel safe. Secure. Stay put. They run again, we might not catch up."

"I understand, sir."

He nodded, but his cold gray eyes were glued to the screen. "How are the experiments on the albino going?"

"I can switch feeds, if you like. This is all being recorded. We won't miss anything."

He gave a nod, and she flipped a button. The screen flickered, and the images on it changed to a view of what looked like a little girl with shock white hair, seated in a chair in the center of a room. In front of it, there was a table littered with wooden building blocks in multiple shapes and colors. There were metal closures securing the subject's wrists to the chair's arms. Its eyes, usually a striking violet in color, were pale pink at the moment. They tended to lighten like that when it was angry. There were electrodes taped to its head for monitoring, and to its legs, for motivation. But so far, it had not revealed its powers, and Bouchard was beginning to wonder whether it actually had any.

The subject moved its lips and Dr. Bouchard quickly turned up the volume.

"I can't. I keep telling you, I can't move the blocks."

And then came the voice of the technician, who stood nearby with a clipboard in one hand and a remote control in the other. "Try again. Move the blocks. Use your powers."

"I told you, I can't!"

"Then I'm sorry." The tech moved his thumb on the remote, and the little albino mutant stiffened and screamed as a small electric shock was administered to its legs.

"Now, try again," the tech said.

The Offspring looked at him. Its pink eyes almost glowed. "No."

"Try again, or I'll have to hurt you."

"I'll have to hurt you," the subject said, in precisely the same voice the tech had used.

"That's the same skill the other one has!" Dr. Bouchard rose from her chair in alarm.

"I'll have to hurt you," it said again.

Bouchard felt a cold chill creep up her spine and reached out to a microphone that stood nearby. "Get out of there," she told the tech, who wore an earpiece and could hear her.

"Bullshit." Patterson yanked the mic off the desk and used it himself. "Administer the shock and turn up the juice. We can't tolerate disobedience."

"I'll have to hurt you," the mutant repeated, staring hard at the technician, its eyes glowing bright pink now. The tech backed toward the door and then his lab coat began to smoke. A hole opened up in it, its edges cherry red and black. And then it burst into flames.

"Hurt you, hurt you, hurt you!"

The tech fell down screaming, trying to roll. The remote he held went flying. The sprinklers came on. The fire alarm went off.

The door opened and guards swarmed into the room. One manned an extinguisher, blasting its white powder all over the suffering technician. Then they dragged him out and closed the door again.

The albino looked up at the camera that was mounted in a

high corner of the room. It felt to Sarah Bouchard as if it was looking right into her eyes. "I'll have to hurt you," it said again.

The colonel pressed the button on the mic and said. "Gas it. Then put it back in its cell. Make sure it's out first."

He let off the button and jets of mist shot from all four walls, slowly filling the room as the subject choked, coughed and gagged. Tears ran from its eyes, fluid from its nose. It fell to the floor, chair and all, and vomited, and then it finally passed out.

Bouchard pressed the button and said, "It's enough. Stop the gas."

The gas stopped. She couldn't look at the screen anymore as men came in to scoop the little mutant from the floor and carry it away.

"I told you enhanced methods would get results," the colonel said.

"That lab tech might not survive," she said. "Are those the results you were after?"

"We know what it can do. It gave it up, just as I said it would if we pushed hard enough. Now we just need to find out if that's *all* it can do."

Sara Bouchard lowered her eyes, almost afraid to ask, but knowing it was expected. Demanded. "What are your orders, sir?"

He said, "One, get the albino to locate the others for us. Do whatever it takes." He opened the door to go, not even turning to face her again. "Two, the first opportunity you get, try a command on de Courtemanche to see if it works. And three, find a way to stress Slate enough to blow his heart before they figure out a way to turn him. He'd make one hell of a strong vampire." He did turn then, looked her right in the eye. "Manage all three and I'll double your salary."

"D-double?"

He sent her a snappy salute and left the room with a spring in his step.

Bouchard clicked the monitor off, took off her glasses,

and laid her head down on her arms on the table. Torturing seven-year-olds, even non-human seven-year-olds, and killing oversized innocents was not what she had signed up to do. She didn't like it.

She hated it, in fact.

But she was fighting to prevent the extinction of humanity. Vampires would wipe them out. These experiments, the Offspring, would be the best weapon mankind had to defend itself. This was for the greater good.

But that didn't make it any less disgusting to her.

CHAPTER NINE

I lay beside my husband in our own bed for the first time since his rescue. Daylight was approaching. But we had a bit of time. I'd coaxed him upstairs far earlier than was necessary. We'd tacked blankets up over the windows for the time being. So the room would remain dark, even through the brightest part of the day.

Autumn was maturing in Maine. You could feel it in the chill bite of the nighttime air and see it on the vibrantly colored hillsides where some of the maples were already bare. Perhaps human eyes couldn't yet detect it, but vampire eyes had no problem there. The nights were growing longer. I loved long nights.

I rolled onto my side and caught Roland staring up at the ceiling, his expression troubled.

"It's time to tell me, my love."

He quickly schooled his expression into a more relaxed one, but the tension showed all the same. "Tell you what?" he asked.

"It's time to tell me what's happening to you." I stroked his cheek with my fingertips, gently turning his head toward me in the process. "Was it the captivity? You've never told me what happened to you, to your eye. Were you...were you tortured, darling?"

"No. No, it's…it's something else."

"Something else like what?"

He sighed, licked his lips nervously, then gave a nod as if he'd come to some vital conclusion. "Have you ever wondered if our minds are as immortal as our bodies?"

I blinked, not understanding the question. "Our minds?"

"Or do they age, do you think? Do they weaken as we get older?"

Lifting my brows, I sent him a fierce, but false glare. "I'm far older than you, Roland. Are you questioning the condition of my sanity?"

"No." He shook his head. "No. But then, some humans live to be a hundred or more. While others die in their seventies. Perhaps it's the same with the mental faculties of a vampire. Some may last longer than others."

I stopped playing with him because he seemed very serious and very troubled. "My love, are you concerned about your sanity?"

He looked at me, but did not answer.

"You are, aren't you?"

He rolled onto his back again, resumed staring at the ceiling. "I haven't felt right since The Sentinel. It's as if something is inside me, some consciousness that is not my own."

I sat up in the bed, letting the covers fall to my waist, naked, of course. I slept naked as often as possible. "Tell me more."

He nodded, seeming relieved to have finally shared his fears with me. "I'm not sure I can describe it accurately, but...I feel a presence. The way you would feel someone if they were in that closet over there. You'd know."

"Well of course I'd know, darling. I'm a vampire."

He nodded. "You'd feel them even if you weren't. Mere

mortals sense when they're being watched. It's that feeling. Only it's coming... from within."

I suppressed the feeling of ice water filling my spine and ran my hand through his hair from the front, down as far as his pillows would allow, and then down along the side of his head. He'd taken out the band, so his long dark hair was loose. I loved his hair. Loved touching it, stroking it. I loved the feeling of it brushing over my breasts when he made love to me.

I swung my leg over him, straddling his body, and feeling the stirring of arousal as his sword sensed the nearness of its scabbard.

Then leaning over him, I held my palms near his temples on either side, but did not touch. "May I?" I asked.

"I've nothing to hide from you, my love."

I pressed my hands to the sides of his head, closed my eyes and opened my senses. And the thoughts I felt swirling around inside his mind were of sex, and of love, and of worry, and then others came, dark whispers I wasn't even sure he could hear. Whispers about the children.

They're dangerous.

Do not trust them.

Watch them. Observe them. Learn their powers.

They're not normal. You don't know what they are capable of.

Learn their weaknesses. In case you need to exploit them to stay alive.

Keep them close, but don't let down your guard.

They could kill you in your sleep for all you know.

They aren't human. They aren't vampire. They aren't Chosen.

They're something else.

Monsters.

Dangerous, deadly, monsters

I took my hands away, averting my eyes and blinking rapidly. My heart seemed to contract in my chest, and my throat went tight. "Is that what you really think?"

"What? What did you hear?"

I looked back at him, stabbed his eyes with mine. "That the children can't be trusted, that they're monsters who might kill us in our sleep. Is that what you truly believe?"

Holding my gaze, lifting his head from the pillows, he said. "It's not what I believe. I'm telling you, those are not my thoughts. And certainly not what I was thinking about just now."

"And yet, those thoughts are there," I told him. I was truly stunned to have discovered it, but it was true. "They're in you, lurking deep in your mind."

He closed his eyes. "Yes. Those and worse. They surface once in a while, but so far I've managed to force them back down."

I drew a deep breath, nodding slowly as my mind raced in circles for an answer. "If it truly is another consciousness, then I can expel it. I can cast it out as I would a demon or ghost. Perhaps that's what it is. The Goddess only knows how many non-humans have died in that place where they kept you. Perhaps some unsettled spirit got inside you while you were there."

He opened his eyes slowly. "Do you really think that's what this is?"

"It has to be, hasn't it?" I grabbed hold of the theory, clung to it almost desperately. "It's certainly not you. It can't be you. You love the children as much as I."

He nodded. I thought I felt a hint of relief in him. "I want it out of me, Rhiannon. Whatever it is."

"At sundown, my love. At sundown, when we rise, the first thing I will do is to perform a rite to rid you of unwanted entities. An exorcism."

"All right." He sighed, and I sensed him allowing relief to finally flood him. "Why didn't I just tell you this from the start?" he asked. "I should've known you'd have a solution."

"That will teach you to keep things from me," I told him.

He reached for me, his hands caressing my breasts, then sliding around my waist to pull me down upon his chest. "Keeping any of me from you is the last thing I want to do."

"Some parts even less than others?" I asked.

"Some parts wish they could live in you, Rhiannon. And other parts already do."

I kissed his glorious chest over and over, my mouth moving back and forth and then down his ribcage, and across to his belly, and just below his navel, then back up again.

He caught my face in his hands when I reached his neck, pulled me in for a kiss that was deep and searching and hungry. I kissed him back. The passion between us had never waned, and never would. I was yearning and ready for him, and he for me when I reached my hand down between our bodies, and clasped him to guide him inside me. And I sat upright and lowered myself over him.

"You are so beautiful," he whispered, reaching up to fondle my breasts as I began to move atop him. "Like making love to the Goddess."

"If I am the Goddess, my love, then you are the storm on which I ride." I moved in a slow rhythm, arching my back and rocking forward, as if he were a stallion I would tame. Each time I did so, he thrust his hips upward, sinking himself more deeply into me, driving the breath from my lungs and replacing it with sheer delicious sensual pleasure.

"Roland," I whispered, rising up a little.

He clasped my hips and pulled me back down, holding me to receive him as he increased the pace of his hips and I, my undulations. I moaned, for he was driving me to climax without mercy. No slowness, no gentleness, not this time. This time he buried himself in me, seeking, I sensed, the solace our love had always been able to provide.

His fingertips drew together on my breasts as the waves of orgasm began crashing over me. I grabbed one of his hands and drew it to my mouth, raking an incisor across his palm, and lapping up the blood I drew. The taste of it, the power of it, drove my release even higher.

His other hand at the flat of my back, he pulled me down against him, and burying his face against my neck, he bit me, hard and fully and deeply, drinking me into him. The feeling of his fangs in my flesh set my body aflame, and I swallowed the cries of pleasure he was driving from me, as the release took hold, ravaging me.

He drove one last time, deeply, and then held me there to receive him. And then we clung, trembling in the aftermath, weak and in need of one another.

He held me there upon his chest for a long time, stroking my hair, my back, my shoulders as my body slowly recovered from the devastation of ultimate bliss. And after a while, he whispered, "Whatever happens, I want you to swear in the name of Isis that you will never let me harm the children. Or you, Rhiannon. Never let me harm you. Do whatever you have to, to prevent it. I'd rather be dead than to live with knowing I had brought you pain. You are my own heart. You know this. You know this."

"You would never hurt me, much less a child. Any child." I tried to sit up, to stare into his eyes and see what was there, but he clung to me, and I relented.

"Make the vow, Rhiannon. Please, before the dawn takes me into her embrace. Make the vow."

I pushed against his chest, and he released me this time. Easing myself from our bed, my bare feet sinking into the plush carpet of our bedroom, I faced east, knowing instinctively where that was. The direction of the morning star of Ishtar, of Innana, of Isis, and of Venus, their descendent. Standing with my legs shoulder width apart, raising my arms out to my sides and up high, I tipped my head back, assuming The Goddess pose. And I said, aloud, "In the name of Isis I vow that I will never allow you to harm me or the children, Roland de Courtemanche. I make this vow with my whole heart, my whole soul, my whole mind. It is a promise I shall not break. So mote it be."

"So mote it be," Roland repeated softly.

I lowered my arms and watched his eyes feasting on my body as I moved, catlike, back toward the bed and slid beneath the covers. Then I curled around him, resting my head on his chest, and I felt the sunrise kissing the eastern sky.

"I'll exorcise you when we wake, my love."

"Thank you, Rhiannon."

I brushed my lips across his chest. He stroked my hair with his strong hand. And my eyes fell closed.

* * *

That night when we rose, we joined the children, Roxanne and Christian for dinner at our elegant dining table. Just because we had very different dietary needs than they did, did not mean we should not spend time together around the table. Roxanne had cooked up a veritable feast, and the children were making fine progress with their table manners. As was Christian.

Roland seemed troubled. Or perhaps he was only worried for what was to come. It wasn't every day one was the subject of an exorcism, after all.

"Rhiannon, Roxanne said I should ask you to tell me about Halloween," Nikki said. And she did well, having chewed, swallowed, and even dabbed her mouth with a cloth napkin before speaking.

I smiled. "The Celts called it Samhain. In Egypt, it was the time of year when the Great Goddess Isis began searching for her husband Osirus, who had been murdered by his evil brother and hidden away from her. Always, in every culture, it has been a time to acknowledge the connection between this life, and the life that comes after, for it is the start of the darkest part of the year. It's customary to remember our dear ones who have died, and to reaffirm our belief that the soul lives on even after the body is dead."

Nikki frowned very deeply, then turned and shot an accusing look at Roxanne. "*You* said it was for dressing up in costumes and stealing candy from the neighbors!"

I felt my brows rise, and Roland pretended to cough to cover his laughter. He met my eyes, and we shared our amusement.

"Not stealing, little one," Roxanne said. "Trick-or-treating.

There's a very big difference."

She then glanced my way and Roland's. "You have to take them trick-or-treating. You realize that, right?"

I tilted my head to one side. "This is not our first experience with children, Roxanne. We had a large part in raising Jameson, after all."

"Just sayin," Roxanne went on. "It won't even be an effort. You can wear your normal attire and go as Gomez and Morticia."

Christian released a bark of laughter, then started pounding his own chest because he'd choked on his food. When he contained himself again, he looked at Roland and smiled. "If you're not too old for a costume, then I'm not either," he said.

"Certainly not," Roland agreed. "What will you be?"

"A scientist. Like Albert Einstein."

"Hmm," I said. "Or perhaps, Dr. Frankenstein."

"Or Frankie himself!" Christian said.

"And what Roxy said about the pumpkins?" Gareth asked. "Are we going to make faces in pumpkins and light them up at night, too?"

I felt my soul growing lighter. "Of course we are, darling. We'll do all of that and more."

The children smiled, even Ramses, and they launched into a discussion of costumes and what sorts they might want to wear. Still no laughter, but emotion. Yes, there was definite excitement in their voices, in their faces, in their hearts.

I looked at Roland, telling him with my eyes how wonderful this was. And without a word, he celebrated with me.

A couple of hours later, we were once again alone.

Roxanne and Christian had taken the children outside. I'd explained to Roxanne what had to be done, and she had assured me we wouldn't be disturbed. That was essential.

Roland lay on the carpeted floor in the center of the room I had chosen to be my temple. I kept a temple room in every house I owned. It was sacred space to me. My statues of Isis, Hathor, Osiris, Anubis, Bast, and the eye of Ra lined the room. My herbs in labeled jars and rows of semi-precious gemstones filled what had been intended as bookshelves. On an antique table in the east, lay my wand, my dagger, my mortar and pestle, my crystal ball, my Gypsy goblet, a gift from my friend Sarafina, and pink colored chunk of raw salt, mined from the earth herself. These items had been in storage since we'd fled the US several years ago, and I'd had them shipped to me here the moment I'd found the house. It was like reuniting with old friends to have them back again. My pendulums were here, my pentacles, my sword and my staff, my tarot cards and divination stones. And my cauldrons, all four of them.

A woman of magic could never have too many cauldrons.

I had lowered the lights. Roland was dressed in soft clothing, white, loose fitting cotton pants and shirt much like one would wear to practice the martial arts. Soft, music played. Mozart, his favorite. I had candles burning around the room, and the smell of rare and exotic incense I'd purchased on our last trip to India, filled the air with fragrance and purified the space.

"And are you relaxed?" I asked, speaking softly, my cadence slow and my tones deep.

"I am."

"Sink deeper, then. Deeper. Follow my voice into the depths of your soul. Swim through the velvet folds of night. Deeper. All is well. There is nothing to fear. You are at peace. And safe. And you trust me completely."

"I do."

"Then surrender, my love. Surrender and sleep."

I felt it when he let go. His resistance released like knots coming untied. He relaxed open, and I knew he was resting, barely conscious, and in a highly suggestible state.

"Good. Very good. Sleep and I will converse with the presence you sense within. Sleep, relax, and let it come to the fore."

He tensed a little.

I placed my hands on his shoulders, used my will just a little bit, to nudge him back into complete relaxation. "All is well. You are in my hands. You are safe."

Beneath my palms, his muscles loosened, softened.

"And now," I whispered. "I call upon any entity who lives in this body. Any soul, any being who is not Roland de Courtemanche. I call you forth. Come to the surface, and face me."

He lay still, very still. I watched him for a long moment, waiting expectantly, but nothing happened.

"Speak to me, spirit who inhabits this man. Speak to me now. I command you by the power of Isis."

And still, he lay there.

I was puzzled. The candlelight cast dancing shadows on the walls around us. Now and then one of the flames would stretch a little taller than the rest, but there was nothing in them to indicate an entity among us. No spirit. No ghost. No demon. I didn't feel any other presence at all.

"Roland, can you hear me?"

"I can," he said, his voice deep and lazy, almost drunk.

"You are completely safe my love. I want you to tell me what happened to you while you were held captive at The Sentinel."

"I...was asleep."

"You were asleep when?"

"When they did it."

"Did what, Roland?"

He began to pant, rapid, short little breaths he did not need to take. His head turned back and forth on the pillow.

"Calm," I said, tracing his forehead with my fingertip. "Calm, my love. You're not there now. You're here, with me, in our home, safe from all harm."

"No. Not safe. Not safe."

"Calm, my love. Calm, I command it." I sent my will into his mind to ease him back into a relaxed state.

It didn't work. He pressed his hands to either side of his skull and moaned, "My head, my head, my head."

"Are you in pain, Roland?"

The door opened, and I recognized the heavy steps even before Christian said, "What are you guys doing?"

And I heard a voice coming from Roland. Not from his lips, from his head, as if I were hearing his thoughts. But this was not him. It was a stranger, and it said, *Attack! He's come to kill you all!*

'What in the name of–"

Roland's eyes flew open wide and he came to his feet with a terrible growl, like a wounded bear. He shoved me aside so hard I stumbled, and barely caught myself on the altar, knocking several stones and tools to the floor. Roland ran at Christian, teeth bared, fangs gleaming, eyes glowing red.

Christian froze and emitted a strangled cry like a trapped rabbit. Roland gripped his shoulders. He was going to devour Christian! I lunged, grabbed my love from behind and flung him bodily across the room. He hit a bookshelf and it broke, pouring gemstones onto his head as he sank to the floor.

He tried to get up, but I flung out my arms and focused every ounce of power I possessed upon him. "Stay down!" I told him, commanding him with my mind, my will.

There was a very heavy thud behind me, and I turned. And there was poor Christian, fallen to his knees, clutching his chest, clawing at it, his fingers tearing the fabric of his shirt. By the gods, his heart was going to explode!

I went to him, gripped him under his arms and pulled him out of the room and into the hallway, quickly closing the door behind me.

Christian only had minutes, if that. He was gazing up at me, his eyes wide with terror and swimming with hurt, his heart pounding.

"Come, darling, let me help you. You trust me, don't you?"

"Wh-wh-why is Roland mad at m-me?" He let me help him to his feet, but he was trembling, and I could hear his heart hammering rapidly. This was bad. I had minutes. Seconds, perhaps.

"He's sick, something's wrong with his head. They did something to him when he was a prisoner." He was walking beside me, limping, panting as I tried to hurry him along.

"Christian, do you trust me?"

He met my eyes, nodded.

"I'm going to save you. All right?"

Again, he nodded. His pupils were pinpricks, his pulse like the beat of a hummingbird's wings. "W-will it h-h-hurt?"

"No, love. Not one bit, I promise." I got him through the doorway into his own bedroom, closed the door and cast a magical lock upon it—one that I hoped would keep Roland out, should he manage to escape the containment spell I'd hastily conjured around him there in the temple room. Then, taking hold of Christian's arms, I pulled him into his adjoining bathroom, and urged him to kneel on the floor beside his giant tub. We'd chosen this room for him because it had a bathtub that would accommodate his size.

He knelt and I knelt beside him. "Come here, Christian." I opened my arms.

The big man leaned against me, knowing just as I did what had to be done. I exerted my will over him, knowing he didn't have the capacity to block or to resist me.

Sleep, my friend, and feel no pain. No pain.

As his eyes fell heavily, I sank my fangs into his throat, my mind soothing him the entire time, my fingers stroking his hair gently.

A sigh stuttered out of him as I tore a larger hole in his jugular, and then I pulled back, and tipped his body sideways, leaning him over the tub as the blood pulsed from him. I could not drink his blood as I should. DPI had poisoned it, a trap for any vampire who might try to help him. His heartbeat sped even faster. I held his chest hard against mine so I could feel its pace. We were out of time. I could feel that powerful organ expanding in his chest. Seconds, only seconds. I watched the blood flow, and prayed it would be fast enough.

And finally, his heartbeat began to slow. I nearly sagged

in relief. But the big man had a lot of blood in him. I sensed Roland trying to get up onto his feet in the temple room, and without taking my arms from around Christian, I hammered him hard with my will. I heard him hit the floor, or perhaps the wall, and hoped I hadn't hurt him too badly.

But I had no time to check, for this task must be completed right now, or there was a risk I might lose this innocent, childlike man. My children would lose him, and I would not permit them to feel the pain of that. He was like an older brother to them.

And so I held him to me as his pulse slowed, and his heart calmed and settled, and the force of the flow became a trickle. Christian's heart skipped, paused, beat once more, and then.... silence. I laid him gently on the floor.

Roland was on his feet again and nearer than was safe. I realized it, turned away from Christian only to hear the bedroom door burst open, and even before I leapt to my feet, the bathroom door did the same.

The man who stood there was not my Roland. He was a monster, his eyes glowing more fiercely than I had ever seen them. He stared at me as if he did not know me, and then his gaze fell on Christian and he took a single step forward. I reacted in the only way I could. I balled up my fist and swung, putting my entire body into the blow. My knuckles hit Roland's jaw, and he sailed back into the bedroom, hitting the wall, and then the floor. I stomped out after him, and bending, grabbed him by his collar and lifted him, dragging him out of the bedroom into the hall. And then I swung my arm like a bowler and sent him skidding back through the temple room door.

"Stay down, Roland!" I slammed the door, locked it, and raced back to Christian. He would not come back if too many minutes ticked by. Quickly, I nicked a vein in my wrist with one of my incisors and pressed it to Christian's mouth. No response.

"Drink, Christian. Drink, damn you!" I sent my will into his mind, into his soul if need be.

His lips moved. Thank the gods! He swallowed. And then, at last, latched onto my arm and drank wholeheartedly.

When he'd had enough, which was a lot, I pulled free, tugged a sash from my bloodstained dress, and wrapped my wrist tightly. And then I picked up the giant of a man. We must have made quite the picture—me, carrying him out of the bathroom, across his bedroom, placing him gently upon his bed.

It was night. He would sleep through it, and through tomorrow as well, waking tomorrow night to a new life he wasn't yet ready to live, as a being he wasn't yet ready to be.

Never again would he have to worry about his heart exploding from his big chest.

Weak now, and in desperate need of sustenance myself, I left him, closed his door, stepped into the hallway and walked back to my temple room. For a moment, I stood there, facing its door and wondering what had happened to my beloved Roland. What had they done to make him into this cruel being who would frighten a boy like Christian almost to death?

* * *

Roland's head was pounding as if it would explode. He forced his eyes open, though he anticipated it would make the pain worse. Then squinting against the pain, he looked around the room where he found himself, realizing that he was on the floor, and that the room was in shambles.

Rhiannon's temple room, he realized, getting slowly to his feet. Sacred space. There were books, broken jars and spilled herbs on the floor all around him, and he turned to see the shelf they'd once occupied split in half. Frowning, he took in the rest: the toppled chair, the spilled candles, and the wax they'd dripped onto the carpet, hardened now.

Something bad had happened here. Why couldn't he remember?

He pressed the heel of his hand to his forehead, and stumbled toward the door, calling out mentally, *Rhiannon, where are you? Are you all right? Where are the children? What happened here?*

He reached for the doorknob, only to see it turn before he could touch it. And then it opened, and his beloved came inside. And there was something off about her— the way she looked at him, her eyes wary and searching, her entire being on guard. Almost as if...as if she were afraid of him.

His stomach convulsed. "Rhiannon? Tell me what happened here. Was it DPI?"

She stared deeply into his eyes. "You don't remember?"

He frowned, searching inwardly, thinking back. "You brought me here to try to exorcise whatever spirit or demon might to be inhabiting my brain." He swayed a little. She reached out, quick as a cobra, caught him, steadied him, then righting a nearby chair, she eased him into it.

"I took you into a very deep state of relaxation, but I couldn't make contact with the entity. Then Christian interrupted us, and I heard it. I heard it very clearly, as if I were hearing your thoughts. But it wasn't you. The energy of the message was female and hostile."

He looked at her, his gaze roaming her beautiful face, flawless skin, those full lips like ripe berries whose juice he required to survive. "What did it say?"

"It said Christian would kill us all and commanded you to attack him."

He felt his eyes widen, jumped to his feet, knocking the chair over and nearly falling over with it. But he caught himself on the edge of the wooden table that served as his priestess's altar. "Did I...is he...?"

He couldn't bear to complete the question.

"He's all right. I intervened."

Roland looked around the room again with fresh eyes. The way the bookshelf was split down its center, he could see how his body might have hit it there and caused that exact damage. Then he sought out Rhiannon's eyes again. "I'm sorry, my love. I'm so sorry. Christian, is he–"

"I had to turn him, Roland. His heart was too near the

breaking point. He'd have died if I hadn't."

"But...how?"

"Drained him into his tub. Fed him from my veins." She sighed heavily, seeming both heartbroken and exhausted. "I've fed, but not enough. And I cleaned up the mess. so the children wouldn't see and become frightened." As she said it, she looked around her wrecked room, sorrow in her eyes.

He let his head fall forward, bracing both hands on the table. The remorse that rose up in him was almost too much to bear.

"It wasn't you," Rhiannon said. She came close to him, but he noticed she did not touch him. "It wasn't you, it was something else."

"Something you could neither summon, nor evict," he said. Then shaking his head slowly, he went on. "I cannot be around you and the children. It's not safe."

"It wasn't you, Roland." She went to a small mini-fridge disguised to look like a wooden stand, and removed a decanter. Its scarlet fluid glinted in the light of the one candle that was still burning low. She poured a glassful and handed it to him. "You were in a deep state of hypnosis, open and extremely vulnerable to suggestion." He drank deeply from the glass. "I took a huge risk by putting you into such a state. It made you susceptible to this...this whatever it is. In your normal state, you would never have obeyed its command."

He drained the glass, held it out to her, and she refilled it, then put the decanter away. He drank again, relishing the feel of the blood filling his body, electrifying his cells, infusing him with strength. His head cleared, the headache eased. His body stopped sagging.

"Roland, I will not let you leave us. You're no danger to any of us. This only happened because of what I did."

"Do not try to take the blame for this travesty, my love."

"I will not let you leave us."

"The children...."

"You would never hurt them. If you hadn't been under—"

"Rhiannon, if I'm not sure of that, then how in the names of the gods can you be?" He set his glass down hard, noticed that his hand was trembling. "I cannot stay here."

She gripped his wrist fiercely. "We face things together, Roland. We do *not* go our separate ways when times are difficult. We will find an answer to this. We *will.* But only together."

"I can't risk—"

"I have help now. Christian, that giant of a man is one of us now. He can help me."

"A fledgling is going to control a vampire as old as I?" He shook his head. "I'd break him like a toothpick, and you know it."

"Perhaps. But you couldn't break me, Roland."

"I could. And it would kill me." He went quiet then, looking her up and down more carefully as his blood seemed to turn to ice in his veins. "Did I? Did I hurt you?"

"Pssh. *You*… hurt *me*? You flatter yourself, my love."

He grabbed her then, pulling her against him, snapping his arms around her and holding her, rocking her, kissing her hair. "If I hurt you, gods, if I hurt you, Rhiannon–"

"You didn't. And you won't."

"I can't trust in that."

She took a breath she didn't need to take. A stuttering, tear-laden breath. Then she said, "I'll get us more help." And it was but a choked whisper. "I'll get the one you trust above all others. I'll get Eric here, darling. He'll come if we inform him of what's happening. And he would be the first to tell you if he thought you were a danger to the children and me."

"It will take time."

"A day, a night, perhaps. The blink of an eye in the grand scheme of things."

"Long enough for me to hurt you. To hurt the children."

"They heal, Roland. They heal faster than we do. You know this from what Devlin told us about Sheena and Wolf. They don't die."

"Everything dies," he said softly. "Sooner or later...even us." He lifted his head, met her eyes. "I'm so sorry, Rhiannon. I'm so sorry for this."

She pushed her hands through his hair over and over, cradling the back of his head, her face close to his, her eyes pouring her plea into his. "You've nothing to apologize for. It wasn't you. It was something else." She kissed his face, his nose, his chin. "Hear me now, my love, and doubt me not. I will find her, whoever she is, and I will make her pay."

He closed his eyes, his pain almost unbearable. To think he had attacked Christian, an innocent. The most innocent being Roland had ever known, and the kindest as well. To think he could have killed that gem of a man, and that his own Rhiannon had to physically restrain him—it was beyond enduring.

He clasped her nape, his forehead resting against hers. "There's no spirit haunting me, no demon possessing my soul. I fear I'm losing my mind, my love."

"You are not losing anything. This is not coming *from* you, but rather it's being done *to* you, by someone else. We will solve this, Roland. One way or another, we will solve this. And we'll do it together."

He let his eyes fall closed. "If you have to kill me—"

"Roland!" She pulled free of him, as if those words hit her like a blow. Staring at nothing, she blinked her eyes repeatedly, as if she'd been beaten about the head.

And yet, it had to be said. So he said it. "If you have to kill me, don't hesitate. Do not allow me to hurt you or those children or Roxy. Or Christian, assuming I could hurt him more than I already have." She started to argue but he held up a hand. "Promise me you will take my life if necessary to protect the others. If you love me, Rhiannon, you will say it. And you will do it."

She stood very still, her gaze still affixed to some invisible spot in mid-air. But then she lifted her chin, turned her head and met his eyes. Her entire body trembled. "You know I will. I will always do what's best for you, Roland. And allowing some devil to use your body to do harm to those you love would not be best for you. It would destroy you. I know this. You don't have to explain it. I would feel the same if our situations were reversed. I would ask the same of you. This should not have to be affirmed out loud, Roland. You know this in your heart. And I know in my heart you would do the same for me."

His love for her expanded inside him until he thought his chest would burst with it. She was right. He hadn't needed to ask for her promise. It went without saying. They knew each other so deeply, it was as if they were one soul.

"I'm sorry. I insulted our sacred bond by asking."

"I would probably want it reaffirmed if I were in your shoes," she said.

He drank in her beautiful face, her dark eyes, more expressive than a gilded marquee. "I'll stay until Eric arrives. He should leave Tamara behind. It's too dangerous."

"Of course, he'll try," she said.

He nodded, too heartsick to smile. "Where are the children? Do they know what I—"

"They've been playing in the backyard with Roxanne for the past few hours. They don't know a thing."

He sighed in relief. "And Christian?"

"In his room, sleeping as my blood transforms him."

"Your blood," he said, nodding slowly. "He already had enhanced strength and power, due to the BDX. With his size and your blood, he's going to be a formidable vampire."

"Yes, he is." Rhiannon frowned, titling her head slightly to one side. "Perhaps that is why the voice in your head wanted his heart to explode before he could become one. And if that's the case, Roland, then this has to be some kind of DPI plot. They *did* something to you there. That has to be the answer. There's no demon, no spirit possessing you. This is them."

CHAPTER TEN

I was troubled, traumatized, and murderously furious over what had been done to my love. But those emotions troubled me less than the one that was all but foreign to me. Fear. I was afraid. Not for myself, of course. My Roland couldn't harm me, and even if he could, I was as strong as he. But I feared for the children. As much as I denied it, there was a cold terror in my heart for what the intruder living inside my husband might attempt to do to them.

I had meant what I had promised my love. I would take his life if it came to that. And if it did, I would cross that dark valley with him. I would not stay in this world without him. We were one. There was no Rhiannon without Roland. I would never allow there to be. The pain of losing him was simply not something I was willing to suffer.

Eric Marquand, one time French aristocrat whom Roland had saved from the guillotine, was my husband's closest friend. His bride Tamara, a product of the modern age, was sweet, insufferably cheerful, and beloved by us both. And when the two of them arrived at our home within hours of Roland's call, I felt the most immense rush of relief I had ever felt.

I even hugged the little chit, with her long frizzy curls and her big innocent eyes. Eric, I embraced even harder. "Thank the gods for you both," I said, and I meant it. Their very presence seemed to relieve a tremendous weight from my shoulders.

Eric looked past me, though, even before our embrace was complete. I knew why. My Roland sat in a chair, before the fireplace, watching the flames devour the wood in a macabre dance of destruction. I believe he saw in that dance a reflection of his darkest fears. Fears he seemed to believe were manifesting in his mind even now.

My tormented love! My heart bled for his pain, and it was worse that I could do nothing about it. If there were villains to be eviscerated, cities to be razed, I would've been fine. But to sit helpless while he was tortured by an unseen enemy... It was not my way.

Eric lowered his head, seemed to gather himself, then surged across the room with a full voiced and confident "Hello, old friend."

Roland rose only, I knew, because it was the polite thing to do, and Eric clasped his hand hard, pulled him in close and clapped him on the back. "You look like hell." It sounded almost lighthearted.

"I feel worse," Roland said. Their eyes met and locked. Tamara clasped my hand in her smaller one and gave a squeeze that I supposed was meant to be reassuring. It was a good thing she was a vampire, I thought. Otherwise, her bird-sized bones would break like fine china. I caught her eyes, huge and heartsick for Roland and for me.

Then Roxanne came in, the children trailing behind her like the fractious, noisy tails of a comet.

"Roxy!" Tamara cried, opening her arms. "Oh, it's been too long." She embraced the redhead wholeheartedly, looking her up and down, and paying close attention to her face.

She wondered, as we all did, why Roxanne was still alive. She was one of the Chosen. They died by forty, as a rule. She'd seen forty at least a decade ago. Possibly two. Perhaps more. It was impossible to tell and she guarded her age like an ancient divine secret. She was as healthy as she had ever been. Not a single symptom of the weakening and waning of a Chosen one's lifetime had troubled her, and I had my doubts they ever would.

"Good to see you both," Roxanne said. "We've got some catching up to do."

I moved to the children, my chin lifting a bit in pride. "Eric, Tamara, may I present our three children, Ramses, Nikki, and Gareth."

Smiling, Eric came to us and dropped into a crouch, forearms resting across his thighs, bringing himself to their level. "I've heard a bit about you three. I'm Eric. Roland and I have been friends for..." he shot Roland a smile. "Well, for a long time."

"Centuries," Roland said softly.

Eric nodded. "And this is my bride, Tamara."

"Very nice to meet you," Nikki said, just as I had instructed her. Then she beamed up at me, and I nodded my approval.

"She looks enough like you to be yours by blood, Rhiannon," Tamara said.

"You don't suppose it's the haircut, do you?" Roxy asked with a wink in my direction. "Get in here and sit down. Just leave your bags by the stairs for now. I'd have Christian get them, but he's still sleeping in his room."

"Christian?" Tam sent me a questioning look.

"He was one of the BDXers. Those Chosen who were given the chemical cocktail dubbed BDX."

"Right, the super soldiers," Tam said, nodding as Eric carried two cases to the stairway and set them down.

"He wasn't ready for the change. But I had no choice," I said. I did not elaborate. I would fill in the details later. No doubt Eric, a physician, a surgeon, and a scientist who'd had centuries to perfect his skills, would want every detail.

Eric lifted his brows. "He's one of us now?"

I nodded.

"I'd like to meet him when he's ready," Eric said.

"But in the meantime," Tamara was rubbing her palms together and looking at the room around her. "This place you've found is wonderful, and I'm ready for the grand tour."

Roland got up slowly, and then he took charge of his thoughts. I saw the moment it happened. He lifted his head first, straightened his spine, and a determined look came into his eyes. He led the way with a strong, even stride, thanks to the new prosthetic leg Killian had sent to him. My admiration for my husband grew. I hadn't known it still could.

We went through the entire house with the children providing commentary the whole time. Then we went outside, into the beauty of the night. The sky was a deep blue, backlit by a pregnant moon. It was warm for an October night in Maine, and the scent of the decaying leaves seemed to fill the air with the very essence of fall. Gray-blue squashes and orange and yellow pumpkins lined every dying field, and many such fields surrounded us. Sunflowers were just passing the peak of their lives, with gaps in their pedals like missing teeth in the face of a smiling old man.

Roxanne had enlisted the children to help her make our secluded home more seasonal, as she had put it. Bright orange pumpkins lined the front steps, and a pair of scarecrows, made of burlap bags and old clothing stuffed with straw, stood on either side, like sentries guarding the door.

As we walked together, Eric and Tamara filled us in on some of the other friends we'd lost contact with. Jameson, the first child Roland and I had taken a hand in raising many decades ago, and his wife Angelica were living an idyllic existence in the Canadian wilderness. This news came as a great relief to me, and to Roland, who loved Jameson like a son.

As the night wore on, the children grew tired and Roxanne took them off to their beds. As soon as they vanished up the stairs, we went to the pool area and sat beneath the stars in the teak lawn chairs that had been left in the storage shed behind the house. Roxy and Christian had discovered them and spent an afternoon reclaiming them from the dust of time. We sat in the four chairs, their square matching table between us. Tamara waited, knowing it was time to broach the reason for our call.

I looked at Roland. It was his tale to tell, after all.

He said, "There's something inside me that is foreign."

Eric frowned, leaning forward in his seat. "Explain," he said.

Nodding Roland said, "I was held by DPI for a very brief time."

"He was taken while trying to distract them," I interrupted, "in order to allow me to escape with the children."

"I did what any man would've done," he said.

"You sell yourself short, my friend." The admiration in Eric's eyes was genuine. "But go on. What did those bastards do to you?"

"I don't remember them doing *anything* to me, but since I've been free, I've been experiencing...a presence. I've been feeling watched. All the time."

I nodded. "I put him under, hoping to call forth the entity and expel it," I said.

"Entity?" Tamara tipped her head sideways. "You think it's a spirit or something?"

"I did at first. What else would I think?"

"Gee, I don't know. Anything?" Tamara's skepticism was not lost on me. Eric nudged her and she said, "What? I don't believe in demonic possession. I'm a modern woman."

"Most modern women didn't believe in vampires either," I told her. "Until recently, that is."

"You two can argue this later, if you don't mind." Eric shifted his attention to Roland, listening with his entire being. "So you tried to exorcise the intruder. And what happened?"

"I don't remember," Roland said, but he nodded at me as

he lowered his forehead into his hand, making small circles in his temples with his thumb and middle finger.

"Christian interrupted us." I slid my hand onto Roland's thigh, and he brought his free one up to cover it. "And I clearly sensed a feminine energy commanding Roland to attack him."

Eric's eyes widened. "To attack Christian?" And then he seemed to see the rest in his mind. "And you did, didn't you?" he asked his best friend. "That's why Rhiannon had to change the poor lad."

Roland nodded, regret in his entire demeanor.

"Where did this woman's voice come from, Rhiannon?" Tamara asked.

"Not voice," I said. "Thought. Energy, if you prefer. I heard her the way we can hear each other. And her thoughts came to me from *inside* Roland's mind. As if *he* were the one thinking them. And yet, it was clearly not his energy. Clearly female."

Eric looked extremely troubled as he stared at Roland's face. "Did it feel to you like a spirit, Rhiannon? When you were working on exorcising it?"

I shook my head slowly. "No. It felt like nothing was there at all, until there was." I leaned back in my seat, tipping my head up to stare at the night sky. The stars glittered above us like diamonds on velvet.

"Rhiannon had to physically restrain me, Eric. She had to drag Christian from the room, change him, cast a spell to keep me contained...." Roland was shaking his head. "I could've hurt her. And I *did* hurt Christian."

"You did not hurt him," I argued. "I stopped you before you even got close."

"I frightened him. And that fear caused the time bomb that was his heart to start ticking. Racing. I made it necessary for him to take the Dark Gift long before he was ready. That's harm."

"He had to come over anyway, my love," I told him for the thousandth time. "It was something we would have had to do very soon or risk losing him to some random fright or close call. A mouse running across the kitchen floor could've done as much harm as you did."

"That doesn't excuse—"

"All right." Eric rose to his feet, holding up his hands and looking from one of us to the other. Tamara too was wide-eyed.

I understood. We were arguing. It was something few had ever seen. Certainly we engaged in good natured bickering from time to time, but for the most part, only in fun. This was different. I was arguing with passion. I felt I was fighting for his life. And it frustrated me to feel as if he was my opponent in that battle.

"Tell me you have an idea, Eric. I'm too close to this to think clearly and Roland's mind has been compromised. We need that genius brain of yours to help us fix this before...." I let my words trail off there. But he knew what I was going to say. *Before it's too late.*

Tamara thumped a small fist onto her palm and said, "We need to figure out which scientists are in charge over there at DPI Central, and go get them. We need to put them into a room with one of us and get some answers. That's what I think."

I tilted my head sideways and noted the anger on her face. She was so small and so soft that it was touching and a bit amusing to see her this infuriated.

"We *could* do that," Eric said, speaking slowly and watching his wife the way he would watch a lit fuse burning its way toward a barrel of fuel. "*Or* we could begin by getting Roland's head examined." Roland shot him a look that said this was no time for jokes, but Eric went on. "I'm talking about an X-Ray, my friend."

"An X-ray?" Roland's brows lifted, his eyes suddenly alert, the gears behind them turning. "You think they put something *physical* into my brain? Some kind of gadget capable of controlling my actions, rather than a spell or some sort of powerful post-hypnotic suggestion?"

"I'm a man of science, my friend. And therefore, yes. That's what I think."

Roland shook his head in doubt, but in his eyes I saw the desire to be convinced. "Don't you think I would know if I had undergone brain surgery, Eric?"

"No, Roland, I don't. If they did it by day, you would have been completely oblivious. And the incision would've healed before you woke again. You know the healing power of the day sleep."

"I thought I did." Roland said it with a longing look at his leg. Then, refusing to indulge in even a moment of self-pity, he looked at me, silently asking my opinion. I stared back at him, communicating only with a look. It was all we needed after so long together.

"Would an X-ray even work on our kind, Eric?" Roland asked, and for the first time, I heard hope in his voice.

"I don't know. I've never performed one on a vampire. But I do know how to operate the apparatus. I can run a CT Scanner too, if needs be."

"Of course you can," Roland said, a hint of sarcasm in his tone. That he could tease his friend, even that little bit, made my heart lighter.

Eric grinned and gave a nod of self-deprecating concession, then turned serious once again. "Even if *you* don't show up on X-ray film, any foreign object inside you would."

Roland's eyes lit. "Yes," he said, nodding harder. Then he repeated the word, smacked his hand on the table and bounded to his feet. "*Yes*, by the Gods, that's what I'll do. I'll get an X-Ray!" Then he frowned for a second. "But...if they put something into my head, then they might be able to track me here. Surely whatever it might be, it would've included that."

Alarm rippled through me, but I pressed my hand to my chest, quieted my fears, and allowed logic to speak above their clamor. "If they could track you, my love, they would have by now. We've been here long enough."

"True," he said. "But we cannot be sure. It might be malfunctioning, or perhaps they have some reason for waiting."

Eric nodded. "Let's begin with the X-ray. Perhaps we can find out whether some kind of device is even what we're dealing with. And I hope to the gods it is, my friend."

"You prefer fighting technology over demons, Eric?" I asked. For frankly, I'd have preferred the latter. Demons, I could handle.

"I don't believe in demons. I believe in science. And I'd rather fight a technological demon than one as irrational and illogical as madness." He held Roland's eyes for a long moment, and said, "Especially in my closest friend." There was a catch in his voice.

My chest clenched as if to block the tide of emotion rushing through me, but of course, it could not. "There are still a few hours of darkness remaining," I said. "If at all possible, I'd like you to do this now, tonight."

Eric pursed his lips, nodded three times, and turned to Tamara. "We'll need to know the names of nearby medical imaging facilities."

"No prob," she said, turning to me. "How fast is your internet?"

* * *

"I am more grateful to you, my friend, than I can possibly express," Roland said as Eric drove him in the wretched motor vehicle over winding, heaving roads at sickening speeds. He couldn't bring himself to watch the passing scenery. It made his stomach heave to see landscapes speeding past. One of the things he hated most about automobiles was that no one seemed capable of driving them *slowly*. As a rule, when traveling in motorized vehicles, Roland kept his head down, and his eyes on his companions.

"I'm only going forty," Eric said to his friend, having heard every bit of that inner dialogue. "You look green around the gills, Roland. I'm sorry you're not enjoying the ride. It's not far, I promise."

"I'll survive it. How much farther is this clinic your bride found for us?

He shook his head as he gazed at the panel on the dash, with its miniature television screen showing a map, and a car shaped icon that represented Eric's car. Although it was the wrong shape and the wrong color. Eric's car was red.

"Just a few more miles. Ten minutes at most. Try to relax."

Roland did not try to relax. He knew he never would, anyway. Leaning his head back against the seat, he closed his eyes. "What if the X-ray shows nothing?" he asked.

"Stop borrowing trouble, Roland."

"I need to know. What's our next option?"

Eric lowered his head, made a right turn so quickly it caused Roland's body to lean left, and then picked up even more speed than before. A pair of vampires racing through the rural Maine countryside at four in the morning in search of an X-ray machine. They were ridiculous, the two of them.

Soon enough, homes with small yards took the place of rolling farmland, and soon after that, Eric brought the car to a stop.

Roland dared to look up at last. They were parked in a lot behind a donut shop that wouldn't open for business for two more hours, according to its sign, which looked exactly like the sign on every other donut shop in the chain. Roland preferred independently owned businesses. There was too much cookie-cutter to the world today.

They opened their doors simultaneously and closed them without a sound. Then in a burst of speed, they moved to the clinic's doors. Eric opened the alarm system's panel, pulled a tiny tool kit from a deep pocket, and within a few seconds, the doors were wafting open for them.

Roland gave his friend a nod of approval, and they headed inside, moving quickly through the place's square waiting area and into the rear, where a hallway with two right angles moved amid treatment rooms. The fourth door on the right had a yellow and black radioactivity symbol on it, so that was the one they chose.

Roland stood there feeling less than useless while Eric examined machines, turned dials, caused screens to light up. He seemed almost gleeful.

"You're having too much fun at my expense, Eric."

"If I were miserable, would your problem magically vanish?" Eric asked. "Come here, now. Stand right here." He stood Roland where he wanted him, then adjusted a machine's lens higher until it was aimed directly at his head.

"Eric, are you sure this won't...well, incinerate me, to put it bluntly?"

"X-rays are waves of electromagnetic energy," Eric said slowly. "They behave like light, but they're not light, Roland. Their wavelengths are a thousand times shorter."

"In layman's terms....?"

"Those were layman's terms. But to state it succinctly, no, it shouldn't burn you. Now stand perfectly still."

"Shouldn't?"

He put a weighted vest on Roland, and then pressed small pods over his eyes to cover them. "Just in case," he said. Which did nothing for Roland's confidence. Then Eric walked away to the control panel on the other side of a transparent wall. "Be very still now," he said. And then something buzzed, and there was a snap, and then it was over. "All right, come here."

Roland took the pods from his eyes and removed the vest. Then he went to the other side of the wall to look at an image of his own skull on the screen.

Eric pointed at some shapes that clearly didn't belong. "There," he said. "There's definitely something electronic. And here, look at this, behind your right eye."

Leaning closer, Roland tried to see what his friend was pointing at.

"By God, that could be a camera," Eric said. "In fact I think it is."

A wave of nauseating disbelief washed through Roland,

and he stumbled, reaching for the chair behind him. "Are there–" He stopped himself there, continued the thought mentally. *Are there microphones near my eardrums as well?*

"I don't see any. Keep your right eye covered my friend. And let's get a couple more shots so I can make sure."

Nodding, Roland returned to his former position, turning sideways this time, as Eric readjusted the apparatus.

CHAPTER ELEVEN

It was only an hour before dawn, and still no sign of Eric and Roland. The children were asleep. Roxanne, too, had retired. Tamara and I were waiting in the living room, with a clear view through the foyer to the front entrance. She was sitting near the fire, trying to keep from wringing her hands. I was pacing.

"They should've been back by now," I said, not for the first time. "A simple X-ray at a clinic five miles away should not have taken this much time." And again I focused my thoughts on my love. *Where are you? Why is it taking so long?*

I received no reply, but then I felt his nearness and rushed to the door, flinging it open just in time to see Eric's sleek red car come to a stop in the drive. The two of them got out and I ran down the steps and across the gravel. "Where on earth have you been? Why haven't you answered my—Good Lord, Roland, why are you wearing a—?"

Eric put a finger to his lips, and Roland pulled me into his arms as if he were very tired. "I need to be alone for a bit, my love. I think I'll walk the perimeter of the grounds, just to be sure all is well."

"But...."

Eric met my eyes and there was a message in his. Why he didn't just speak it to me, orally or mentally, I could not fathom. I frowned and searched Roland's face as well, and read his message quite clearly. He wanted me to go along with things, and it was important.

"All right," I said, leaning up to press my lips to his cheek. "Go on, take your evening constitutional. I'll be waiting."

His lips pulled upward at the corners, and he bent to kiss mine. "Thank you, love. All is well, I promise." And then he turned and walked off, moving quite admirably in his new prosthetic. Barely a limp. As he vanished onto the path that wound along between the thicker fruit trees and the wrought iron fence, I turned to Eric. "An explanation, please?"

"Once we're inside," he said very softly, and taking my elbow, turned me toward the house. Tamara stood in the doorway, leaning there, awaiting her man like a devoted wife. But even her welcoming smile didn't hide the worry in her eyes.

Eric hurried me inside, embraced his bride while I closed the door behind us. Then he took her by the hand and headed into the living room where the fireplace snapped, filling the place with the delicious scent of burning apple wood.

"I was correct," he said, going directly to the darkly stained hardwood cabinet that concealed a mini-fridge behind it, and pouring himself a glass of sustenance. "There's a device, a complicated one, implanted inside Roland's head."

Relief washed over me. "Thank the gods," I said. "He's not losing his mind."

"No, he's not, but he probably feels as if he is."

"Why the eye patch, Eric? And why all this silence?"

"The device is complex," he said. "I couldn't tell as much as I wanted from the X-ray so we headed into Bangor to the Diagnostic Imaging Center and I made use of the CT Scanner.

State of the art equipment they have there, I must say. Highly impressive."

Tamara touched his shoulder before he could wax on. "Eric, if you don't stay on topic, Rhiannon's head is going to explode. And mine won't be far behind."

"Of course." He looked at me. "Sorry. All right, so from what I could tell, this device has some kind of camera feature that is positioned behind his visual cortex. Theoretically, whoever is on the receiving end of its signal can see whatever Roland sees. Now, we've fixed that, albeit temporarily with the eye patch. I do not believe there is any audio component to this. Nothing seems to be out of the ordinary in or near the auditory centers. But we can't be sure he's not bugged in some way. That's why I wanted him out of reach when we had this discussion."

"So DPI has been watching us all this time?" I asked, suddenly feeling unsafe in my own home. And angry, very angry. "Perhaps listening as well?"

"Not watching you, per se," he said. "We don't show up on cameras. They can see everything Roland sees, except for other vampires."

"The children," Tamara whispered, her eyes widening.

"Indeed." Eric nodded. "And then there is the mental aspect. Somehow, part of this implant allowed someone at DPI to give Roland a direct command, which he was compelled to obey."

"He was under hypnosis. Highly suggestive." I paced to the mantle, bracing a hand on the cool stone and staring into the flames. "I don't think he would have obeyed otherwise."

"But you can't be sure. Just as I can't be sure there aren't other aspects to this device. There is definitely more." The word "more" sounded dire. I was afraid to ask what else he thought there might be, and then he went on before I could. "Perhaps they can monitor his thoughts, mental communications, and possibly location as well. We won't know until we get the thing out of him. If we can remove it. And that is one of our top priorities."

I lifted my gaze to meet Eric's. "It's our only priority."

"There's one other," Eric said softly. He came across the room to me, setting his now empty glass on a table as he passed, and put his hands upon my shoulders. "Rhiannon, I have to believe the DPI's true goal here is to retake the children. If they'd wanted Roland, they would have made it much more difficult for you to rescue him."

I nodded slowly. "I knew our escape was too easy. They didn't even give chase. Now we know why. They wanted Roland with us, so that they could use him to monitor the children." I backed away, shaking my head. "But then why haven't they moved on us yet? Why are they waiting?"

"There are other children, aren't there?" Tamara asked.

I looked at her swiftly. She shrugged and said, "Maybe they're hoping to get you all together."

"Or perhaps they wanted to observe for a while. See how the children act in a different setting, test their skills from a distance," Eric said. "Scientifically, it would make sense."

I nodded. "The children knew intuitively not to reveal their powers to their captors," I said, recalling what the children themselves had told me. "They were too cautious to even test their own limits while in captivity. They felt they needed to keep their secrets to themselves." Then I lifted my head, looking from one of my dear friends to the other. "What are we going to do?"

Tamara and Eric exchanged a knowing look. Eric sighed heavily and said, "You're not going to like it, Rhiannon, but I do not believe the children are safe here."

"He would *never* hurt the children."

"He hurt Christian."

"I'm telling you, Eric, that would not have happened if he hadn't been under hypnosis! How can you doubt him this way? He's your best friend. You *know* him."

"Wait, wait," Tamara said, moving between us and holding up her palms. "I don't believe for one second Roland would be capable of harming a child. Any child, under any circumstances. But Rhiannon, DPI is keeping tabs on those kids through him. Watching them through his eye, maybe listening to them through his ears. Maybe even through his thoughts. We don't know if there's a GPS component to this thing. They could be on your front lawn with tanks and guns at any moment."

Everything in me rose up like a cobra, ready to strike down her arguments. Except that she was right and I knew it. The children would not be safe with us until we removed the device from Roland's head.

"You're not safe here, either, Rhiannon."

I shot the well-meaning and gallant Eric a glare. "My Roland and I will be together even when all that remains of us is dust." I turned away, paced to the window and parting a heavy drapery, gazed out at the night. "But you're right. We need to send the children away."

Tamara said, "Maybe you can have Roxy and Christian take them–"

"The last time I left them with Roxanne and Christian, the children stuck them with DPI tranquilizer darts and ran away. They need...stronger hands." I thought of Roxanne's granddaughter, Charlotte, and her husband Killian, who, along with Charlotte's mother, had taken the eleven-year-olds DPI had referred to as the Betas to Portland. But they already had four Offspring to contend with.

"I imagine Maxine and Lou Malone know how to reach Vlad and Stormy," Tamara said softly. "I can't imagine a better pair to keep track of the children."

"You want me to hire Dracula and his bride as babysitters?" I'd have laughed at the irony, but if I had, it would have sounded maniacal. "The children don't even know them."

"But Christian and Roxy will be with them too," Tam said. "They're not going to like it, but until we get this thing out of Roland's head..."

"If they could see through Roland's eye, then they must

know Maxine and Lou helped us. They're human and would show up on camera. Not to mention that DPI is familiar with them, has tried to hire them to help hunt down the Undead."

Eric frowned. "If that's the case, one wonders why Max and Lou haven't been arrested already."

Tipping my head to one side, I thought back, and then it came to me. "His eye was swollen and watering for days after we rescued him. It didn't heal with the day sleep. He complained he couldn't even see from it."

Nodding slowly, Eric said, "If he couldn't see through his eye, then the camera couldn't either. When did his vision begin to clear?"

"Not until after we'd settled in here. And he hasn't been anywhere since, until you took him last night."

"He kept his head down most of the way, complaining about my speed and his hatred of motor cars," he said. "It was dark, as well. Perhaps they still haven't figured out our location." He was clearly deep in thought for a moment, then he said, "I honestly don't recall any signs we might have passed or seen on our way into the clinic that could've given them a clue."

"Unless there's a GPS," Tamara said.

Eric nodded hard. "Yes, but as investigators, our friends the Malones are apt to be in possession of a device that can easily detect the presence of a GPS. I'll borrow it when we take the children there, use it, and then we'll know for sure."

I felt my heart twist into a knot in my chest. I did not want to be separated from my precious Nikki, nor from sweet natured Gareth or his stubborn and aptly named brother Ramses. I loved them.

"I'm so sorry, Rhiannon. I'm so, so sorry," Tamara said. "I'll stay with the children myself, if it makes you feel better."

The children had warmed to Tamara right away. She was that kind of an individual. In fact, seeing her with them, a young modern woman, made me feel a bit jealous. She related to them in a way I could not equal. I nodded, holding up a hand because her sympathy made me feel worse. "Once we've secured the children, then what is our next step?" I asked, needing desperately to change the subject.

Eric said, "The pieces in his head are in extremely delicate areas. We need a skilled surgeon to remove them. Preferably, the one who put them into his head in the first place."

"Are you saying you can't do it yourself? You've been a physician, a surgeon, for two hundred years." He nodded, and again, I sensed something dire in his demeanor. "Just tell me. What do you suspect, Eric?"

He met my eyes, then closed his slowly and when he opened them again, I saw resignation in them. "There's something attached, something that doesn't seem to serve any purpose. It's a vial of some kind of liquid with apparent sensors attached to it from every other piece of hardware in his head."

"A vial of liquid. With sensors."

He nodded.

I looked from him to Tamara and back again, but she seemed as confused as I.

And then Eric said, "It appears that if any of the other components are removed, a signal is sent to the vial."

"A signal?" I frowned.

Tamara gasped and whispered, "You mean this device is booby trapped, Eric?"

"I can't be sure," he said, "But I can't think of another reason for that kind of engineering. There is a chance that if we try to remove any part of this device from Roland's brain, it could set off some type of a reaction."

"What type of reaction?" I asked, my entire body going cold.

"We can't know that unless we know what's in that vial. That's why we need the surgeon who installed it before we can risk trying to take it out."

I pushed my devastation down, squared my shoulders, lifted my chin and felt my eyes flash with determination. After all, the sort of action we needed to take was my specialty. "Then that is precisely who we shall have."

* * *

Roland returned and I rushed into his arms, holding him tightly, kissing his face and neck. Dawn was approaching, and all of this was more than I could bear. Not talking to him, not even exchanging thoughts just in case DPI was somehow listening, that was all too much.

And yet, he was there with me. He was not losing his mind. There was a solution in sight. We might have to walk barefoot over burning coals to reach it, but reach it we would. Together. No matter what. I tried to convey all of that with my eyes, and the love he sent back into mine was powerful and needed no words, nor even thoughts. I felt it. I basked in it. It was as powerful, as essential to me as the sun to the planet.

"I believe you're turning into a pirate my love." I glanced at his prosthetic leg, and then at his eye patch. "All you need is a parrot for your shoulder."

He smiled at me, and I saw the relief in his eyes, the hope. He hadn't had that before when he'd believed his sanity had reached its end. He was much better than he had been when he'd left my side earlier. Even knowing now how difficult removing this device might be, at least we knew it was possible. We had a plan of action, we knew what to do. Calling Eric Marquand was surely the right move.

"Dawn approaches, my wench. And I'm quite eager to take you to bed."

I smiled slowly, took his hand and drew him up the stairs.

* * *

At sunset, after waking, after showering and dressing for the night ahead, I went to Christian's room, tapped the door, and then went inside. "Hello my dear friend. How are you feeling?"

He was up. Dressed. I saw the empty pitcher, tinted red, on the nightstand and knew by the scent it was fresh. Roxanne was spoiling him, and I was glad of that. He deserved it.

He didn't answer me, so I went to his bed and sat down, patting a spot beside me. He only stood there, near his dressing table, looking at me. "I wasn't ready."

"You would have died."

"Not if Roland hadn't...hadn't...." His eyes welled up.

"Yes, even if Roland hadn't done what he did, you would have died. You know that. A spider on your arm in the bath could have startled you enough. Or a snake, slithering through the grass and across your bare toes. Anything could have trigged your heart to explode, Christian. At any time. Waiting was risking your life. It had to be done."

He lowered his head. "So it's okay with you, what he did?"

"I threw him bodily across the room so hard that he hit the bookcase and split it in half."

His eyebrows rose first, then slowly his head followed, baby blue eyes widening in surprise. "You did?"

"I did. But I want you to know, it wasn't his fault, what he did."

He nodded. "That's what Roxy said. She told me something's wrong with him."

I nodded. "The good news is, we now know what. DPI put some kind of machine into his brain while they held him captive. They can give him commands, and they can see what he sees. We're not sure what else it can do, but we do know we have to get it out of him. And until we do, the children are not safe here."

Christian blinked. "You want me and Roxy to take them back to Max and Lou's place?"

"Yes. Yes, I do." We were still unsure whether DPI might have tracked us to that location, but since they'd seen no sign of anyone watching the place it seemed a safe enough first step. I'd spoken to Maxine, who told me she did, indeed, have a device that could tell us within a few seconds whether there was a GPS hidden inside my husband's brain.

"But last time–" Christian began.

"You'll have more help this time. You, my friend, are going

to get to meet a very important vampire, and Roland's best friend. Eric Marquand. He's come to help us."

"He has?"

"Um-hm. His wife is here too. Her name is Tamara and you're going to love her. She's going to help you with the children."

He nodded slowly, but still looked like a broken man. I ran a hand over his hair and said, "I'm so very sorry for what Roland did to you, Christian. But he was not in control of himself. DPI was pulling his strings as if he were a puppet. And he feels terrible."

"Worse than terrible." Roland's voice came from the hall. I'd left the door open, and he stood there now, his face a picture of remorse aside from the patch on his eye, which to me, looked sexy and vaguely menacing. "Christian, I am more sorry for attacking you, for frightening you that way, than I've ever been for anything in recent memory. I can't apologize deeply enough. But I'm going to make it up to you, somehow. I promise, I will."

Christian looked at Roland for a long moment, and then he said, "Are you going to be okay?"

"I hope so," he said. "But either way, what happened between us will never ever happen again. I can guarantee you that." Roland came further into the room, approached Christian, offered his hand. "Can you ever forgive me?"

Christian stared at his hand for a moment, then his lips quivering, he swung his big arms around Roland and hugged him hard enough to break him in two.

"I'll take that as a yes," Roland grunted, wobbling a bit.

When Christian finally released him, he was smiling. "I'm ready to do whatever you guys need me to. Whatever you need. I want to help."

"Thank you, Christian," Roland told him. "You are a part of this, you know. A part of our family. I hope you realize that."

Christian blinked as if stunned. "I didn't. But..." Then his lips split into a huge smile. "But I do now." And he hugged Roland again.

If he squeezed my husband any harder, I thought the device might simply pop out of his brain.

I left the two to continue their conversation and went to place a telephone call to Lucas on the cell phone that was supposed to be a secure line. He didn't answer, so I left a message. "I need the name of the surgeon who operated on my husband during our brief separation." I said no more. It would be enough.

Lucas was back in the military by now, reassuming his position as a lieutenant in the DPI. He would have access to information that we did not.

If he kept his word. *If* he wasn't lying when he said he intended to work from within as a spy for our kind. *If* he wasn't truly waiting for a chance to march us at gunpoint into a blazing sunrise.

Only time would tell.

* * *

The hardest part of the entire night was breaking the news to the children. I had so wanted to give them a normal life.

No, not a *normal* life, exactly. We were not normal people, nor were they normal children. But I wanted to give them a home, stability, security, and love. I wanted them to have a childhood filled with fun and wonder and spoiling now and then. And now, no sooner had they settled in and begun to feel secure, than we had to uproot them yet again.

Furthermore, I had no reason to expect them to cooperate with us any more than they had the last time I'd left them in the care of others to help my Roland.

As Maxine and Lou Malone waited in the driveway in a large van with their company logo on the side, Nikki cried and wrapped herself around me. She begged and pleaded with me not to send her away.

I set her down, dried her tears, and crouched low. Her brothers stood on either side of her, trying to be stoic. "Look at you, all three of you. You're feeling emotions. You're feeling sad, and that is such a good thing. Not a good feeling, I know that. I'm feeling it too, and not enjoying it at all. But it's good to be able to feel. It's very good."

"It doesn't feel good," Gareth said softly.

"I know. I'm going to be honest with you now. So I want you to listen. Those DPI people put something inside Roland's head. They've been watching us through his eyes, and they could come at any time and find you here. That's what they wanted the whole time. That's why they didn't chase us when we broke him out. Because they wanted him to be with you, so they could watch you, and learn your secrets, and when they are ready, they will come and try to take you back. You must agree, none of us want that."

"I could fix Roland," Gareth said. "I could fix him if only he wasn't a vampire."

"I know you would help him if you could, darling." I put my hands on his shoulders, met his eyes. "The things are in his brain. They have to come out very carefully. Even if you could fix him yourself, we would need a surgeon or we could do more damage, and we've learned the hard way that not every injury a vampire suffers, repairs itself during the day sleep. Haven't we?"

He sighed, lowered his head.

"We won't be apart for very long, darlings. Two nights, perhaps three. We need to find the surgeon and make him perform the operation, and then we'll be together again. All right?"

"I don't want to go. I love my room." Nikki stomped a foot.

"Roxy and Christian have packed piles of your things to go with you. You'll have a room at Maxine and Lou's, all your own, and you can fill it with your own things. It's only for a few days at most. I promise."

Then I hooked a finger under her chin and made her look at me. "And you must not run away. No matter what, you must not run away. We are doing all of this to protect you, to make sure you never return to those cages you hated so much."

"I know," she said, sighing heavily.

"And I want you, all three of you, to remember the talk we had about hurting people who are our friends."

She nodded. The boys did as well.

"I'm putting you in the safest place I can think of. I need to know you will be all right, or I cannot help Roland. And I'll report in every day to tell you how things are going. All right?"

"Where is this doctor?" Ramses asked. "Where is Roland?"

"Roland is going to come downstairs to see you before you leave. But we don't know if DPI can hear what he hears, or even read his thoughts. So you have to settle for a hug, and not say any words that might give it away. We don't want to give them a clue where you are going. Or even that you're leaving at all."

I would not tell them any more. If they knew we were heading back to The Sentinel, they would be there with us. Especially Ramses. Of all of them, he was the most like me, despite that everyone thought it was Nikki. It was Ramses. He was furious right now. And I saw through his questions. "Two days, Ramses. Give me two days to make this right. And we can resume our lives together."

His jaw was clenched in a hard line, but it softened when I whispered, "You can take Pandora with you."

He and my cat had bonded quite thoroughly. In fact, she was sitting beside the children in a way that seemed to state emphatically that she was on their side, not mine, in whatever conflict we might be having.

Still, I felt Ramses surrender and my muscles seemed to unclench.

"Roland?" I called.

He came down the stairs, limping a bit more than he had been the night before, his eye patch in place.

Gareth broke free of the other two and ran to him, and Roland scooped him up and held him close. The other two went to join them, wrapping their arms around his legs until they all fell over, hitting the floor in a tangle of limbs and one prosthetic. He hugged them and said, "Two nights from now we are going to carve those pumpkins into fine Halloween Jack-o-Lanterns."

"To scare the demons away?" Nikki asked.

Roland sat up, holding the children close. Nikki was on his lap, and he had an arm around Gareth on one side and Ramses on the other. "To scare anything and everything away. We'll light them with candles, and set them on the front porch to frighten anyone who happens by."

"Who would be scared of a pumpkin?" Ramses asked.

"That's just the beginning," Roland went on. "We'll put on costumes. Disguise ourselves as ghosts or goblins or ghouls... or even vampires." He bared his fangs and the kids grinned. "And then on All Hallow's Eve, we, all of us, will prowl the nearest village, visiting one house after another, knocking on doors. And when those doors open, do you know what happens?"

"We bite them!" Nikki shouted.

Roland laughed, a deep chuckle. "We say the magic words. 'Trick-or-treat.'"

"I knew that," Gareth said. "Roxy told us."

"Did Roxy mention the bags? We carry bags or buckets with us. The bigger the better. And as we say the magic words... what were they again?"

"Trick-or-treat!" they all shouted at once.

"Yes. Trick-or-treat. As we say them, we hold up our bags or buckets. And people put treats into them."

"That's what Roxy said." Nikki frowned. "But she didn't say what treats are."

"Treats," Roland said, "are candy."

Her brows lifted. "Candy? Like chocolate?"

"Chocolate bars and candy corn, and popcorn balls all coated in caramel. Lollipops and chewing gum. Sweets and confections galore."

"Wow," Gareth whispered. "Why haven't we done this before?"

"Because it only works on one special night of the year. Halloween night. And do you know when Halloween night is?" He pulled out a phone, tapped its screen to show them the calendar. "It's in two weeks."

"How many nights is that?" Gareth asked.

"Fourteen nights."

"That's too long," Nikki said.

"It's just long enough. It takes time to come up with the perfect costume, after all. For the next couple of nights, I would like you to give some thought to what you would like to wear. You can dress up as anything you want to be on Halloween. Anything at all. A gorilla or a princess. An angel or a devil. So give it some thought. I found you this, to give you some ideas." Reaching behind him, he pulled a rolled up catalogue from where he'd tucked it into the back of his trousers. It was a two-inch thick book of Halloween costumes for children.

"And in a couple of days, when you've decided, we'll start creating your costumes. All right?"

"All right," Nikki said.

"Okay," Gareth said.

Ramses shrugged, but took the catalogue and began leafing through it.

Roxy and Christian were outside, waiting with Max and Lou in the van. Roland hugged each of the children tenderly, and then turned to go back up the stairs. When he was behind a closed door, I sniffled, stiffened my spine, and said, "All right my loves. It's time to go. Be good children. We'll be together again very soon."

And then I gathered them together and led them out to the waiting car, though it broke my heart to do so.

CHAPTER TWELVE

Sarah Bouchard had been awakened by a phone call an hour before her alarm would've gone off. Muttering under her breath, she rolled over in her bed, and looked at the caller ID. Colonel Patterson. Of course it was. There wasn't anyone else likely to phone her before sunrise. She brought the phone to her ear, and he spoke before she could even say hello.

"We have a problem. Are you near your computer?"

"I don't sleep with it, sir." Damn, that was insubordinate. She cleared her throat and added. "Sorry, sir. Half asleep. Give me a minute." She slid out of bed and winced at the chill. Nights were getting colder and she figured it was time to turn up the heat. It had probably been time for a few weeks now, she just hadn't remembered to do it. Too much else going on.

She yanked a heavy robe around her, a spa robe in a French vanilla kind of color. It was heavy and like new after five years of wear. She'd bought it from the hotel spa during her last vacation.

Shoving her bare feet into a pair slippers, she headed into

the living room to take her heavy duty, military-grade laptop out of the locked gun safe where she kept it. Her ID was in a lock box in the den and she went after that next. She had to insert the card to activate the computer, so she didn't keep them in the same place.

She didn't mind the extraordinary precautions. The projects she worked on for DPI were sensitive and extremely classified. She had the highest security level the government issued. Higher than the president's. She wasn't even sure the president knew it existed. But her work was important. She was trying to save the human race. No matter what all the bleeding heart liberals out there called it. They didn't have a clue. And they didn't need one, either. They just needed their government to keep them in the dark, feed them a lot of shit, and let them grow like mushrooms in blissful ignorance.

They didn't know that's what they needed, but that's what they needed. Idiots.

Setting the laptop on the kitchen counter and turning it on, she put a K-cup on to brew. The phone tucked between her ear and shoulder, she fixed her coffee while the computer booted up and connected.

"Okay I'm online. What am I looking for?"

"Last night's surveillance," he said.

She lifted her brow. The surveillance was by way of a remote camera implanted behind the vampire Roland de Courtemanche's eye. She quickly pulled up the feed, which was silent. A microphone would've been too easily discovered. Put it near another mic or a speaker and the vampire would get that screeching feedback noise, which was hard to mistake for anything else. Even for an antique like de Courtemanche.

Watching the night's surveillance feed was like watching an old horror flick. Vampires didn't show up in video, so there were a lot of shots of doors opening and closing by themselves, furniture sinking beneath the weight of an invisible backside, wine glasses full of blood rising in unseen hands. The wine glass would pour itself into empty space, and the contents would vanish. Like a magic trick.

"What am I looking for, boss?" she asked.

"Go to oh-three-hundred. About ten after, actually."

She sped to that point, then stopped, leaned forward, stared at the screen. "Is that a…is that a medical clinic?" She was seeing through the vampire's eyes, but what she saw looked an awful lot like…. "Is he having an *X-ray*?" She was about to point out that there was no one behind the glass partition to run the machine but she bit off the stupid comment. There was someone there all right. Someone who didn't show up on video. And she seriously doubted it was his wife. The self-proclaimed queen of the Undead—bitch-queen if you asked Sarah—was a product of a time and culture that no longer existed.

There was a lot of nothing after that. The view of the clinic's hallway as de Courtemanche walked through it, the view of a dashboard as he rode in a car's passenger side. Occasional glimpses of the empty driver's seat and a steering wheel that moved as if all by itself. He hardly ever looked up to give her a hint of the scenery outside the car. But she kept watching, praying he would.

Then there was the front of an all-night drug store. And finally, an eye patch, floating toward her from within the monitor screen, growing larger until it blocked everything. Complete blackout.

She blinked in shock. "The son of a bitch knows about the implant. He found the camera."

"And we've seen nothing since," Patterson said. "Bastard's negated our best technology with a fucking eye patch."

"Look, Colonel, I'm sure we can–"

"We can do nothing. I've been all over this. Now we can't even observe the Offspring as planned. How are we going to know what they can do, much less catch sight of the others if they should come together, with a complete blackout?"

Sarah had a backup plan. Patterson had been certain it would never be needed, but now it was, just as she had predicted it would be. One of the things in life she knew for sure, was that she was quite a bit smarter than her boss.

"I can find them," she said. "More easily now than before, actually. This is the first time he's left their freaking mansion since the camera started working." She scrolled back through the video that had been recorded overnight, backed it all the way up to the car ride. She let the recording play out again in slow motion, then paused as the flashy red sports car pulled into the drugstore parking lot. There were only three other vehicles there. But all of them had the same plates. "They're in Maine," she said. Then she moved the recording forward again, and strained her eyes as an invisible man took an eye patch from a white plastic bag. She backed up, and then moved forward again, frame by frame, until the words on the plastic bag were readable. "Cornucopia Village Market. They're in Cornucopia, Maine. Or near it."

Colonel Patterson was quiet for a moment. Then he said, "You've impressed me Bouchard."

"It's still not quite enough. They might move. I think it's time we put our secret weapon into use," she said.

"Yes, I agree. Initiate it today."

"Yes sir. I'll do the groundwork first, deploy it tonight after hours."

"I'll see to it everything goes smoothly," he said. "But remember, not a word to anyone else in the Division. This is eyes only, right?"

"Absolutely," she said. "And don't worry, sir. I'm sure I'll be able to get close enough to retake the Offspring. I can still command de Courtemanche directly from inside his own brain."

"Unless they find some vamp-sympathizer surgeon to take the device out first. You'd better believe that's their next move."

"If they try to remove it, they'll blow his head off, boss," she reminded him.

"I know that, Bouchard. The fail-safe was my idea." It was

not. "But if that happens, we still lose our connection to those Offspring. And we must get them back. I want that to be your top priority. Get those mutants back into their cages where they belong."

"Yes, sir."

"I'm counting on you, Bouchard. Don't let me down."

Sarah promised she wouldn't and hung up the telephone. Then she used her secure computer to find a realtor near Cornucopia, Maine. She jotted the number on a paper napkin, then went to shower, change and pack for her trip. She would have to wait until business hours to make the phone call. And after that, she'd have a lot of shopping to do.

But that was fine. She had all day. Her plan couldn't be executed until nightfall anyway.

* * *

With the children gone, the house I'd named Serenity seemed to have lost its soul. I rose at sundown, slipped out of bed before Roland had yet roused. My thin silk gown puddling around my bare feet, I went into the hallway, down the stairs and across the gleaming marble floors all the way to the back, to the kitchen. That was where everyone would usually be gathered when Roland and I rose. Either in the kitchen or the backyard. But the patio and pool and lawns beyond were deserted and seemed as bereft as my heart.

I felt my love coming behind me, sliding his hands over my shoulders, bending to kiss my neck. "I've brought you nothing but grief lately. And I'm more sorry for that than I can ever express."

I tipped my head further, rubbing my cheek against his. "In my very worst times, you've stood by my side. You've loved me at my darkest, fought in my defense, saved my life. You know if our situations were reversed, you would stay by my side no matter what. And I love you every bit as much as you love me. Remember that, the next time you're tempted to indulge yourself in guilt."

I felt him smile, and his hand trailed over my buttocks,

squeezed and turned me toward him. His left eye blazed into mine, and I lifted my brows and regretted leaving our bed too soon.

"Oh, sorry!"

"Sorry!" Eric and Tamara spoke at once, stumbling into each other in the kitchen doorway. They'd spent the day here, but the plan was for them to head over to Maxine and Lou's as soon as we had established our plan of action for the evening.

"We were looking for—"

"Breakfast?" I asked, not moving my eyes from Roland's. I found the eye-patch ridiculously sexy. It suited him. And we *had* committed piracy, after all, according to the US Government. "It's in the refrigerator, dear. Help yourself."

Tamara rattled around our kitchen. "I'll heat some for everyone," she said.

"I'll help," Eric said.

I was still gazing up at my husband. "Ironic, isn't it, that in the weeks surrounding our actual pirating of *The Anemone*, you lost a leg and took to wearing…that," I nodded at the eyepatch.

"Bitterly ironic," he agreed.

I shifted closer, my entire body pressing to his. "My sexy buccaneer."

I saw his amusement, the teasing curve of his delicious lips. "Get me a–a pint o' grog or something. Wench."

"Ah…careful now." I kissed his chin and restrained myself from pulling him on top of me on the kitchen table, but only for the sake of our guests.

Tamara was stirring a pot over a burner, and the scent it emitted made my mouth water. "We *do* have a microwave, you know," I said, and I pointed to the device, which was directly in front of her. She could hardly have missed it.

"Oh, no. We don't use *that* anymore. Eric has found that heating blood in that thing, or even water, changes it on a molecular level. And not in a good way."

"It's true," Eric said, nodding. "I've sworn off the thing."

"I do that with most modern contraptions," Roland said. "And frankly, having one inside my head is damned disturbing."

"Roland…." My tone held a warning.

"They must know by now that we've discovered the implant, love. Besides, the Malones' handy device found no sign of any kind of microphone or GPS inside my head, so we can assume it's safe to speak aloud."

"Yes, and I find it difficult to imagine even DPI has developed technology advanced enough to read our thoughts," Eric said. "But at this point, it doesn't really matter."

"We'll find out, once we get our hands on the surgeon who put it there," Roland said. "Speaking of which, have we heard from Lucas?"

"I haven't checked," I replied.

We took our evening beverages and headed back through the house and into the library. The emptiness of the place hit me anew. I supposed it would continue to do so until we had the children back.

How had I become so attached in so short a time?

I went around behind the corner desk, where the largest iMac computer to be had, held court. I had taught myself to use the things, though Roland refused to even try. I opened the email program to see if Lucas had sent anything in response to the call I'd placed to him before bed.

"Yes, here's something," I said. Lucas had sent an email, and I read it aloud. "'Dr. Sarah Bouchard. 1979 Cherry Street, White Plains." I blinked, looking up at the men. "This is it? This is the surgeon who put that thing inside you? Just like that?"

"I told you Lucas was trustworthy," Roland said. Amazing that he could sound so smugly self-satisfied when his life was on the line.

"And you trust this?" I asked. "How do you know it's not an ambush?"

"We'll know," he said, setting down his mug on the desk, "when we get there. Where's my cloak?" He seemed almost excited. Eager.

I found his optimism contagious. "Perhaps," I said, "you should take the time to get dressed first. Though I hate to give you any reason to cover up that delicious chest of yours."

He looked down at his shirtless torso and baggy pajama pants, then smiled up at me. Yes, he was optimistic. Even hopeful.

"If we must," he said. And he headed back through the house and upstairs.

* * *

Dr. Sarah Bouchard carefully reinforced the blocks around her mind, as she had been trained to do by her employers, before she tapped on the door, then opened it and walked carefully inside. Gamma F-2, the albino Offspring who'd died at the age of two only to revive on the autopsy table just as the first incision began, lay in the bed, sleeping, and Sarah didn't want to startle it and end up like that poor lab tech. He was in a burn unit, and still listed as critical.

"It's Dr. B," Sarah whispered from the open door. She didn't step inside. She might need to pull it closed in a hurry. "I need you to wake up."

The Offspring rolled onto its side and opened its eyes. Creepy violet eyes. Sometimes they were purple, like amethyst stones, deep and sparkling. But other times, they lightened, first to lilac and then to pink. That was when it was truly dangerous, when those eyes went pink.

"Please, don't hurt me anymore," it said. "I don't want to burn you, too."

"I'm not going to hurt you, Gamma. And I'm not going to let anyone else hurt you either. I'm going to take you out of here. Right now."

The childlike creature blinked, white blond lashes almost angelic. It was so easy sometimes to forget it wasn't an adorable, frightened little girl. "You're taking me away from here?"

"Yes, but we have to hurry. Come on."

"No." It shook its head and cringed beneath the covers,

crowding as close to the wall as it could. "No, it's a trick."

"It's not a trick. I can't let them hurt you the way they're doing. I have a nice place, one they don't even know about. Come with me. I promise, you won't regret it."

The mutant lay there, thinking, mulling with its sharp mind. They were smart. Smarter than they had let on, smarter than Sarah had known. She'd been with them from the beginning, but had left the research vessel *Anemone* for a briefing with Colonel Patterson just in time. The Coast Guard cutter had picked her up only hours before the vampires had taken the ship.

"Look, it can't be worse than staying here, can it?" she asked, trying to sound kind and caring. "There's a world out there you have never seen, a world where...children," she had to force the word out, "have good, happy lives. You've been here since you were just a baby. But you can live differently."

That bit of logic seemed to tip the scale. It nodded hard and threw back the covers. "All right. I'll come with you."

"Good. Hurry now. We have to be careful."

It hurried across the room to stand beside Sarah in the doorway. Bouchard caught herself almost reaching down to take its hand. So easy. So easy to forget.

"What about the cameras?" It asked and it looked up toward the camera mounted high in the far corner of the room.

"I disabled them, but they'll come back on in a few minutes. Come on. Hurry now."

The Offspring thinned its lips and followed Bouchard out of the room and down the hall. It was obedient all the way down the hall, and on the elevator, which it had ridden before as the lab where its daily testing happened was one level down. This time, though, the elevator took them all the way to the ground floor where the exit doors were unlocked and the guards on break. Bouchard led the creature through the front doors, and outside into the dark night.

It stopped there as a stray breeze blew its platinum blond

hair into motion. It touched its own face as if unsure what that feeling was. Bouchard realized it had never before been outdoors, except perhaps, when they'd taken its lifeless body from *The Anemone*. It had revived, but it had been sick, terribly sick, for a long time.

Sarah waited only a second or two before reaching for its hand. Tiny and warm in her own. It was a necessary evil. "Come along, now, before we get caught. My car is right—"

"What is car?"

"I'll show you. Come on, now. Come on." Bouchard clicked her keyring to unlock her Mercedes, opened its passenger door. "You sit here, and I sit there," she said, touching the respective leather seats. "This machine carries us to where we want to go. It moves much more quickly than we can move on foot."

Gamma F-2 blinked and said, "I can move very fast, you know."

"Yes, I know. But this can move even faster. Go ahead, sit down."

Gamma did so, hopping up onto the seat, then inspecting the entire dashboard with curious purple eyes. "Good, very good. I need to buckle this around you, now. In case we have to stop quickly, it will protect you. I will be wearing one too."

It was examining the seatbelt, turning it in impossibly small hands. Its eyes were wide with fear, but still dark. It nodded twice. "All right."

Sarah buckled the seatbelt around it, and thought it probably ought to be in a safety seat. That went by size, didn't it? Or weight? Or was it age? She wouldn't know. She had no experience with children. "Now I need to close this door. And I'm going to go to the other side and get in from there. You see?"

It nodded twice, but slowly.

"Don't be afraid," Sarah said, and then she closed the door slowly, giving only a slight push at the end so it would latch without making a loud sound that might startle the little beast. She hurried around to the driver's side, pulled her door open, and got behind the wheel.

So far, so good, she thought. As least her dress wasn't smoldering yet. She started the engine, put the car into gear. "All right," she said. "Here we go."

The Offspring's eyes went very wide and their purple lightened to lilac. It clutched the arm rest on one side and the console on the other as Sarah drove the car through The Sentinel's parking lot and out through the front gate, which opened at her approach, and finally she was on the road and the gates were closing behind her.

From here on, she was off the books. Off the record. And the only person in DPI who knew anything about her mission, where she would be or who with, was Colonel Patterson.

She truly wished she trusted him more than she did.

CHAPTER ONE

Roland and I left immediately, taking my car and heading for White Plains while Eric and Tamara drove to join the children at Maxine and Lou Malone's place, 40 miles away. It was the second time I'd made this ridiculous trip of late, and I resented it. But Dr. Sarah Bouchard and I had some words to exchange. And I was eager to get started.

For once, my beloved Roland didn't complain about the drive.

Eric and Tamara had argued that they ought to come with us, but I had refused. I wanted them with the children, protecting them, no matter what.

On the way, I used my phone's bluetooth connection to phone Maxine and Lou on the private line they'd told me to use, and Maxine answered on the first ring, not even bothering with a greeting. "How is Roland? How is everything going?" she asked.

I glanced at the dashboard, from whence her voice seemed to emit, automatically, and shook my head. She was always running on high speed, that one. "Roland is fine at the moment," I said. "We're well on our way to White Plains to see the surgeon who put this thing inside him. I expect it to be a good time."

"I really didn't need to hear that. Try to restrain yourself, Rhiannon. Tam asked me to remind you that you need her alive to help Roland."

"Believe me, I am well aware of that."

"You know she might be expecting this, right? She might've already gone into hiding."

"If so, we'll find her. Maxine, I need to talk to my children."

"All right, but first, listen, if all else fails, check the garbage."

"I'm sorry, what?"

"If things fall through, if you hit a dead end—don't overlook Dr. Evil's wastebasket or trash cans. Check them." Then she said, "Here are the kids. Hang on, I'll put you on speaker."

Gareth's voice came over the line. "Rhiannon?" he asked. "Where is Roland?"

"I'm right here, son," Roland said. "I'm right here. And I'm all right. Can you call the others around?"

"We're here," Nikki said. "When can we come back home?"

"For Pete's sake," I heard Tamara call from somewhere in the background. "We haven't even got started on our learning to have fun marathon! Lesson One, Hide and Seek, as soon as you get off the phone."

I nodded to myself, knowing Tamara's childlike spirit would soothe the children. I was very glad she was with them. "You'll be able to come home soon, love," I replied. "Very soon. We've found the doctor who can fix Roland's head. We're on our way to get her now."

"Good," Ramses said.

"Tell me what you've been doing so far, children."

Nikki said, "Eric has been teaching Christian how to be a vampire," she said. "They practiced in the backyard, and we got to help."

"Eric says comp-competion–compe*titi*on–makes it more

fun," Gareth said.

"We can jump as high as they can," Ramses said proudly. "But Eric can run faster."

"You'll get faster as you get older, you know," Roland said. "Taking that into account, you might be faster than all of us by the time you're grown."

"And we're already better at jumping from tree to tree," Ramses bragged.

"You're more coordinated than we are," I observed. "More graceful. That's beautiful, children. I had thought the vampire the most graceful creature in existence."

"I'm not graceful at all," Christian said, and I heard laughter. Not the children's, of course. I'd not yet seen them laugh. But I heard the musical emotion flow from Maxine and Roxanne, from Lou Malone and Christian.

We spoke a bit longer, the children telling us of Christian's progress and of their indecision about Halloween costumes, before I wished them all good night and promised we would be together again soon. And yet, as I ended the call, I felt the cold breath of mortality on the back of my neck. Death hovered near, and one misstep on our parts would allow Her to sweep us into the dark folds of Her cloak, and carry us away across the River Styx.

All too soon, we were exiting the car. Sarah Bouchard's house was a two story brick structure at least a hundred and fifty years old, in a suburban neighborhood that held many like it. Victorians and Georgians were the majority. Here and there, an odd home of more modern design looked out of place and ugly by comparison. Unimaginative and dull.

We circled the place and I opened my senses. I would feel her fear, should she discover our presence. And I would relish it.

But then my excitement ebbed. We were behind the house now, at the back door. I looked up and met Roland's eyes. "I don't feel anyone inside."

"Wait, there's a security system," Roland said. He pulled a

small pouch from a pocket, a gift from Eric that had included a brief demonstration of how to use it. He removed tools from the kit and tinkered with the panel near the door. When he finished, he twisted the doorknob and slammed his shoulder against the door. It opened, the wood splintering around the lock. Either Bouchard was too stupid to install a steel door, or too smart to think even that precaution would keep out a vampire who wanted to get in.

This was too important.

By the time we'd crossed the kitchen, there was no longer any doubt in our minds that the place was completely empty. "She could be at The Sentinel," I said. "That is where she works."

I headed off in one direction, Roland in another, to search the place as thoroughly and as quickly as possible. We returned to the kitchen at the same time. "There are clothes on the bed," Roland said. "Things scattered on the dresser, drawers left open."

"Are you saying she's a slob, or that someone has ransacked the place before us?" I asked.

Roland crooked a brow. "I am saying her bedroom looks the way ours looks right now, the way it looks any time we are forced to pack in a hurry."

His meaning came to me like a flash of light. "She's gone on a trip."

"The bathroom is in the same condition," Roland said. Then he frowned. "But there's no clue where she's gone. I'm not certain what to do next."

I looked at the wastebasket and made a face. Roland followed my gaze.

"Right. Maxine said to check the garbage." As he spoke, he yanked the lid from the wastebasket and looked down into it. "It's a fresh bag, completely empty," he said. Then looking up again, he went into the living room and opened the drapes to look outside. "Trash cans on the curb. I hope they haven't been emptied yet. Come on, love."

"I'll...just wait here," I said.

Roland went out through the front door, across the lawn to the curb. I watched through the window as my beloved removed the lids from trash cans and smiled at the putrid refuse he found inside. Pulling my cell phone out, I texted Maxine and hoped she was standing by.

Besides the garbage, what else might provide a clue?

She responded instantly. Clearly she was following our progress with genuine interest. She cared about us.

She have a landline by any chance?

Landline? I typed back.

A telephone. The kind that plugs into a jack in the wall. As in not a cell phone.

I looked around the kitchen and spotted a telephone mounted to the wall.

Yes, there's a phone.

Before I could ask for further instructions, my cell rang. Maxine spoke as soon as I picked up. "Easier to talk than text," she said. "Click Re-dial to see who she called last. Oh, and after that, key in star-sixty-nine to see the last number that called in. I'll hold on."

Where did she learn these things? I picked the telephone set from the wall and pressed redial. The number rang a few times, and when someone picked up, I moved the cell phone closer, allowing Maxine to listen in. She did this sort of thing for a living, after all.

"You've reached Pine Tree Realty. We can't come to the phone right now. Our regular business hours are weekdays, eight to five. For more information on current listings, please visit our website, Pine Tree Realty dot com."

I hung up when the message tone sounded and pulled the cell back to my ear. "She's looking for real estate, Maxine," I said. "But where?"

"Hang on, Rhi, I'm looking up the website." I could hear the soft padding of computer keys as Maxine's fingers raced over them. "Got it. Let's see, location is…oh, hell, Rhiannon."

"What? What is it?"

"That realtor is in Cornucopia. She's…she's here, Rhiannon. She's in Maine, and not far from your place." She was still talking as I raced outside to find my husband looking almost as stricken as I felt, a mosaic of what looked like retail price tags dangling from his palms.

"Dr. Sarah Bouchard is in Maine, right in Cornucopia, the nearest town to us," I blurted. "We're here, and she's there!" My entire being wanted to burst free of my skin. I held up the phone, Maxine's voice squawking from it as Roland pulled me into his arms. "She can't know where the children are," he said. "They're safe at Maxine and Lou's."

"Of course they're safe," Max said, as Roland shoved the tags into a deep pocket. He took the cell phone from me, and spoke to Maxine, telling her to put everyone on alert, keep the doors bolted, curtains closed, children indoors, just in case." Then he disconnected and said, "We should go. We need to get back before dawn."

"And what good will we do?" I cried. "We'll be unconscious. As good as dead and useless to the children. All of us."

"Not all. There are Roxy, Maxine and Lou," Roland said, trying not to let his fear make his voice quiver the way mine was doing. And yet I felt his fear.

"Yes, three mere mortals, exceptional though they are," I said. "All by themselves all day tomorrow, facing off against Dr. Bouchard and whatever DPI thugs she has at her disposal."

We were moving toward the car. We hadn't re-locked the doors of that mad doctor's home, but I did not care. I reached the car first, then turning around, held out my hand to Roland, my palm up. "Show me what you found in the trash."

He sighed, and I knew he didn't want to comply, but he shoved his hand into his pocket all the same, and handed me the crumbled mess of tags. I opened my palm, picking a tag to unfold and read.

Girls Size 6X.

My head snapped up and I met Roland's eyes.

"They're all the same, my love. Tags from children's clothing she must have purchased very recently. Right on the top of the trash, not wet, no smudged ink."

"She's found a place to live in Maine, near us, and she's stocked up on children's clothing. She's coming for the children, Roland."

"Perhaps. But all the tags are from girls' clothing. None suggest they're for boys."

"We need to be back there. Now." I got into the car, Roland beside me. Soon we were heading north at speeds that were probably unsafe and certainly illegal. Thank the gods that it was fall and the nights, a bit longer. We would have time to make it back. Barely.

"Five more hours," Roland said, looking at the navigation system in the dash. I was surprised he would make use of it at all. "We'll get there just before dawn.

"Roland, what about the drug Eric created, years ago? When Jameson was just a boy and he needed our protection by day. Remember? What did he call it?"

"Diurnal," Roland said with a grimace. "And you of all people should remember the side effects. Increased aggression, lack of impulse control, outbursts of temper, violence. I could've killed you when I used that formula."

"If one could die of pleasure," I said softly.

He met my eyes, and we shared a brief moment of intimacy, or shared memory, of passion. We'd had so many of them. And I cherished each one.

"Do you think Eric has access to the drug on short notice?" I asked him.

Roland sighed, lowered his head briefly, but brought it back up again. "In his emergency kit, yes. He has everything you could imagine in there. I'd be shocked if his selection did not include Diurnal."

"Then I shall not sleep today. I'll simply warn everyone to…give me a wide berth."

* * *

Sarah Bouchard had been a Marine back in her younger days, had been in the middle of firefights and missile attacks. She'd got a top notch education on the GI bill, and had earned three Ph.D's. She was a skilled neurosurgeon and one of the top geneticists in the country.

This was the most afraid she had ever been. This little creature she was babysitting could burn her alive just as easily as look at her. It was dangerous. It was deadly.

Sarah had to tread with extreme caution here.

"What do you think, Gamma?" she asked.

They were standing in front of a yellow cottage with white trim. Beyond the cottage lay the rocky Atlantic shore, with patches of sand here and there, all of it being rhythmically massaged and caressed by the ocean.

It just stood there, looking at the sea.

Sarah broke off her own thought there and corrected herself. *She*, not *it*. If Sarah was going to convince the creature she was on its side, she had to try to think of it as a little girl. So...*she* just stood there gazing at the sea, and then at the sky, and then at the little house. Then finally, blinking, she looked at Sarah. "Is my cell in there?"

"No, Gamma. You don't have to live in the cell anymore. Come on, I'll show you inside, then we can go down to the water for a while before we unpack."

Sarah started toward the house, but the little Offspring remained planted right where she was. Sarah thought she might be trembling.

Yes, she supposed it must be overwhelming to see nothing but four windowless walls and a locked door your entire life, and then suddenly to be outside, beneath the endless sky, beside the endless sea.

Sarah went back to her, hunkered down in front of her. "I can't keep calling you Gamma, can I?"

"Why not?"

"Well, because it's not a proper name, that's why not. I'll tell you what, let's go inside and talk about it. I'll tell you lots of names and you can pick the one you want."

"Can a name be a color?"

Sarah blinked, thinking it was creepy how little emotion the thing showed. But then again, where would it learn such things? She shrugged. "Maybe a name can be a color. What color?"

"Blue. Like that." She pointed at the sky. "And sometimes, like that." She lowered her arm and pointed at the sea.

"I think Blue is a very nice name," Sarah said. Then she turned. "You and I are going to live here together, Blue. You'll have your own room, but not like your room at the old place. You'll like this. And we're going to play in the sand and the water—"

"What means play?" she asked.

Sarah blinked. An unfamiliar fingertip plucked at her heartstrings. She would have to be careful about that. Still, one would have to be made of stone not to feel a little something when what looked like an innocent angel child did not know what the word "play" meant.

"I'm going to have to show you. But rest assured, it's a good thing. Come on, let's get our things inside, and then we can get started. There's so much to do. You know, your siblings live around here somewhere, or so I was led to understand." It was the first time she'd broached the subject, which was, after all, her reason for being here.

"What means siblings?"

"Well, Blue, you have a sister and two brothers. Your sister is a little girl just your age, who was born at the same time you were. And your brothers are little boys. They're like you. They escaped from the cages where they were kept, and now they live in the real world. Except...." She lowered her head. "Well, I don't want to ruin our day."

"Except what?" she asked.

"Well, all right. Except that they live with vampires."

"Vampires?"

"Yes. The vampires took them prisoner. If only I knew

where they were, we could find them and rescue them. You know, like I rescued you. We could all live here together."

"They are like me?" she asked, staring back in the direction they'd come from.

"Very much like you," Sarah said.

"If they are like me, then they will kill the vampires and get away."

"I wish they could. But I fear they're outnumbered. When I knew them, they could sense when each other were near. Hey, I wonder if you could do that? Maybe if we drove around up here, we could get close enough for you to sense them. Do you think?"

The pale, silvery haired child stared at Sarah for a long moment. Then she shrugged and walked toward the little cottage, apparently ready now to see inside.

Not a hint of emotion about her long lost siblings, Sarah thought. This might make things just a bit more difficult. But she would get it done. And by the time she finished, she hoped to have four of the escaped Offspring back in her lab where they belonged.

* * *

Roland and I kissed passionately in front of our home, where I left him behind. He still insisted he not be around the children, in case DPI could command him to commit violence again. Eric met us there, feeling that Roland shouldn't be alone.

I didn't believe he would hurt anyone. I didn't believe he could, but there was no arguing him out of it.

I helped myself to the emergency kit in the trunk of Eric Marquand's little red sports car after he and Roland went inside. The Diurnal was clearly labeled, its dose spelled out on its face. I filled a syringe and injected myself, then sped to Maxine and Lou's, arriving just before dawn. I dashed inside as the sun began to rise. The heat of it touched me. I felt my hair begin to singe just as I pulled the front door closed behind me.

Maxine Malone saw me and jumped to her feet, sloshing

coffee over the rim of her cup. “Rhiannon? Holy, Moses, woman, how are you...what did you...?”

“There’s a drug. I took it. I’ll be dangerously short tempered, but–”

“More than usual, you mean?” Roxanne called.

I turned as she spoke to see her coming in from Maxine and Lou’s kitchen, carrying her own mug cupped between her palms as if for warmth.

“But,” I continued, irritated, “at least I can help protect the children throughout the day today.”

“That’s good, Rhiannon,” Maxine said. “We can use all the help we can get. Lou stocked us up on donations from the local Red Cross. It’s in the fridge. Help yourself.”

“Right after I see them,” I said.

Maxine smiled, and nodded toward the staircase. “They’re all in the same room. They didn’t want to be apart. Right at the top, third door down.”

Nodding, I hurried up the stairs, moving silently, so not to wake them, but aching to touch their little faces and to look into their eyes. I turned the knob, opened the door quietly, and stepped inside to see the large barrel of a handgun pointing at my face.

Almost as quickly as I saw it, it lowered, revealing the face of its owner, Lou Malone, and my own cat, standing beside him, looking lazily up at me. Lou frowned at me, then looked at the window, where the sunlight streamed through, and then back at me again.

“I appreciate your vigilance,” I said in a soft whisper. “But you can go.”

Nodding, he moved toward the windows, which flanked the bed, quickly drawing the shades, and then leaving me alone with my children. Pandora came to rub her head against my thigh, and I stroked her and told her I’d missed her without a word, as I gazed at my angels, lying sound asleep. My little girl’s hair had been braided, each pigtail sporting a pink bow at the end, and a doll was tucked into her arm.

I moved a chair nearer the bed and sank into it. Pandora lay down too, right on top of my feet. For a long time, I just sat there, looking at the children, relieved that they were all right, grateful to be with them again, and yet aching for my Roland. I hated being apart from him. But the children needed me right then.

My gaze skimmed the room, seeing their familiar things, and some new ones— toys and dolls and brightly colored Lego blocks scattered about. On the nightstand, a "coloring and activity" book lay open. It showed a picture of a woman and a little girl. They both had long, curly hair that had been colored purple, and they appeared to be holding hands. Underneath the figures were names, written painstakingly in a childish hand. "Nikki" was printed underneath the little girl. And beneath the woman, "Tamara."

Frowning, I flipped the pages, and saw many others pages that had been used as well. There were pages with letters of the alphabet, which had been copied with care by young hands. There were pages with simple three letter words with pictures depicting the objects they represented. There were dot-to-dot games and find the difference puzzles.

Tamara had been teaching my children basic things like the alphabet and how to print their names, I realized. I had not yet thought to do anything like that.

For a long time, I stayed there, looking at them as they slept peacefully. But my body was too twitchy to stay still for very long, a condition that seemed to grow worse as Eric's drug apparently took hold. Eventually, I had to get up and go downstairs, or risk waking the children. When I did, Pandora came with me, and Maxine took my place watching the little ones sleep.

* * *

I was as high as a manic, and Pandora knew it. It seemed she was picking up on my agitated state, pacing and chuffing and looking at me as if to say, "This isn't right. You're supposed to be sleeping."

But I didn't feel as if I would ever sleep again. My eyes felt wider than usual, and my gait, as I paced, was rapid. I knew it, was aware of it, but could do nothing to control it. Time seemed to be moving at a snail's pace while my mind was moving at the speed of light. Scenarios played out, one after the other, in my imagination. What if DPI raided this place today, with weapons and tanks and men? How would I fight them all and protect the children?

"We should have an escape route, like at your cabin, Roxanne," I said, shouting the idea out of the blue as I had been doing at intervals all day through.

After jumping out of her skin, Roxy took a deep breath and said, "Way ahead of you, hon. Maxie told me she has a car parked in a storage unit a mile away. Keys are under the wheel well and the plates are...borrowed."

"Where?" I asked.

"Cross the road out front and go through the woods, due west. It's EZ Store And More, 240 Euclid. Unit ten. The car's a green Ford Escape. Your friend *Mad Maxie* thought it was funny as hell to have an Escape as an escape vehicle." She lowered her head, shook it slowly. "That gal's got an odd sense of humor."

I assumed there had been a joke in her remarks somewhere but I had no idea what it was. I was already thinking about which door to exit with the children. How fast I could cast the *Glamourie* over all of us, and whether we should have a rehearsal. Yes, that was it. We should have a rehearsal. A–what do they call them?–a drill.

Small feet on the staircase alerted me. At last, my children were awake.

"It's awful now that Christian has to sleep all day like the rest of them," Gareth complained as they came down the stairs at midday. I was glad to see Roxanne had kept them to our routine, up till midnight, in bed till midday, or whenever they felt like waking.

They would never have alarm clocks, my children. They

would rise according to their bodies' dictates, and sleep when they felt tired, within reason.

"It won't be that long till Christian wakes up, though," Nikki said. They reached the bottom of the stairs and headed our way. Roxanne and I were in the large sitting room. They had to cross through to get to the kitchen, where I sensed they were heading, if their grumbling stomachs were any indication.

They were wearing pajamas Maxine and Lou must have purchased for them, for I'd never seen them before. Super heroes decorated my children's chests. Iron Man for Ramses. The Black Widow for Nikki. And Gareth wore the Hulk, though I suspected he identified more with the fictional creature's alter ego, the mild-mannered healer, Bruce Banner.

Yes, I had watched every film about each of the super heroes with the children during our brief time together thus far. They loved them. Identified with them, I supposed having super powers of a sort themselves. Roland felt it was good to expose them to role models who used their gifts for the cause of good.

The children spotted me, stopped walking, stopped talking, and just stared.

"How....?" Nikki began.

"She took a drug that keeps vampires awake by day," Roxy told the kids. "It's not good for her, and she knows it."

"I believe Nikki was speaking to me, Roxanne."

"Makes them grumpy as hell too," Roxanne added. "Tiptoe around her today."

Nikki came closer, tipping her head sideways to inspect my face. "Your eyes are *huge*."

"The better to watch over you with, my dear," I said, and she smiled, recognizing the line from a storybook I had read to her.

She wrapped her arms around my neck. "I'm very glad you're back," she said.

I hugged her, buried my face in her hair and inhaled her scent. I had missed her terribly. And when she stepped away,

I went and hugged the boys too, giving them no choice in the matter.

"Where is Roland?" Gareth asked.

"He has to stay away a bit longer. We haven't got him fixed yet, but we're closer than before. He asked me to tell you that he loves you and misses you very much and that we'll all be together again very soon."

Ramses sighed heavily, and I felt the disappointment in him. It was a good sign and yet I hated seeing it. "Don't be sad, Ramses. We've made good progress."

"I'm not sad, I'm hungry. Where's breakfast?" Though he tried to sound stern, I thought he might be kidding a little bit.

"Breakfast is in the kitchen, kids," Roxanne said, "because God forbid you should miss twelve hundred or so calories every four hours on the dot. You must burn through 'em like hummingbirds."

Roxanne herded the children toward the kitchen, and I went too. I wanted to observe her cooking methods. It had been a great many years since I'd had to feed a human. Pandora, yes, but raw meat, and the occasional human villain, required very little preparation.

Roxanne put bacon into a pan to sizzle. Then she cracked a dozen eggs into a large bowl, splashed in some milk, added salt and pepper, and whipped it with a wiry contraption.

"Where are Maxine and Lou?" Nikki asked, taking a seat at the kitchen's center island.

"They're going to try to get a look at the files in a real estate office," I explained as Roxanne poured the egg mixture into a hot skillet and sent me a look of censure. "I must tell them the truth, Roxanne. I know it's not the way mortals raise their young. But perhaps it should be. They need to know." Then I put my hands on Nikki's shoulders, standing behind her. She was sitting at the kitchen's center island on a stool. "Dr. Sarah Bouchard has come to town."

"Dr. Bouchard?" Nikki asked, twisting her head around to stare up at me with wide eyes. "I know her from the ship. She's here because of us, isn't she? She's come to take us back."

"Perhaps. But I'm not going to let her have you."

"That's why you stayed awake today. In case she comes."

I nodded. "And if she tries to take you, children, it's all right to kill her. This person is a dangerous, deadly, evil being who should not be allowed to live. She has harmed many vampires. Many humans, as well."

Nikki looked at the boys. Silent messages were exchanged. Messages I could not hear.

"I think this would be a good time for you to tell me what your powers are, children. I know you can all run fast and jump high. You have reflexes and flexibility and grace such as I have never seen. I know you can sense each other and read the thoughts of others. Nikki, I know you have the ability to mimic any magical act you see me perform. And Gareth, I know you have the power to heal. Do you have any other abilities that you've discovered since you've been free?"

Roxanne was putting out plates, setting them down rather hard to express her disapproval of my mothering skills. I didn't care. I would train these children for combat if it would keep them out of DPI's clutches.

"No," Nikki said.

"No," Gareth agreed. And they both looked at Ramses.

Roxanne paused with a bowl of the fluffy yellow eggs in one hand and a platter of bacon in the other, looking from Ramses to me and back again.

Ramses looked uncomfortable, then stood up and took the bowl and platter from Roxanne, setting them on the table. "I'm starving." He sat again and started filling his plate.

He didn't want to tell me. He still didn't trust me, I realized. And it hurt.

"Ramses, darling, it's time for you to tell me. It's time for you to trust me."

"Dr. Bouchard told us never to trust a vampire," he said. He lifted his eyes and locked them onto mine.

"Then look into my mind, child. Look into my heart when

I tell you, I would give my life to protect you. This woman is coming for you."

"She is our mother," Ramses blurted.

"No!" Nikki stood up, angry. "Rhiannon is my mother. Dr. Bouchard hurt us. Made us hurt them—" this with an angry jab in my direction.

"But she's the one who *made* us, Nikki," Ramses said. "You know the story as well as I. She took pieces from super-humans and put them together to make us. We wouldn't be alive without her."

I knew just by the way the words were put together, that they were not coming from Ramses. They had been taught to him by someone else. Indoctrination, seven years of it, would take time to overcome. I tried not to allow my feelings to be hurt, but they were hurt all the same.

I held up a hand when Nikki would have responded.

"You're right, Ramses," I said. "That's exactly how you came to be. What you do not know is that the super-humans Dr. Bouchard told you about were The Chosen."

"I don't know what that is," he said. But he was listening. I could see he wanted me to convince him.

"The Chosen are people who have a very rare kind of blood. When we vampires were human, we all had it too. All vampires did. Only The Chosen can become vampires. If they don't, they die very young."

"Well, not all of them," Roxanne said. Then she eyed the children and said, "She's telling you the truth of it, kids. You and the vampires—you're family. You're blood relatives. That Dr. Bouchard, she only wants to use you as weapons to kill people she doesn't like or understand. She'd have you back in those cages so fast your little heads would spin, if she had her way. And I'll tell you something else, Rhiannon and the others, all of us, we're bound and determined to protect you from her. So Ramses, if you can do something to help, it's high time you told us."

Ramses looked at his siblings, first Gareth, who nodded,

then Nikki, who said, "Tell them."

He closed his eyes. "Come outside. You don't want me to do it in here."

CHAPTER FOURTEEN

"I cannot go outside. It's daylight, my child."

Roxanne said, "Never mind, I've got you covered. You can watch from the computer screen. I'll take my phone and Facetime you." She nodded at the kids. "Eat your breakfast, so we can see what your brother's got in store for us."

The children gobbled their breakfasts with abandon, including cinnamon rolls I had smelled but not seen that Roxanne must have baked earlier. I noticed the way Pandora, who was on the children's heels everywhere they went, positioned herself beside Nikki. Nikki gave the cat a bite for nearly every one she took herself. My sleek panther was, I noticed for the first time, developing a bit of a paunch.

When they finished their breakfast, I sat at the computer and Roxanne opened the proper program for me, then used her cell phone to connect to the computer. I could see her face on the screen.

"Are you there?" she asked. "I can't tell from my end. Screen's just showing me an empty desk chair."

"Yes, I see you."

"Good. Wait there." She and the children trooped back across the house and out the glass rear doors, with Pandora trotting alongside. The sun flashed onto the screen, and I backed away from the computer, instinctively shielding my face with my arm. But no, I was indoors with only artificial light.

As I watched, the view broadened to include the three children standing near the gardens on the grassy back lawn of Maxine and Lou's home. There was a bubbling fountain amid the late fall flowers, mums, black-eyed Susans and miniature sunflowers.

"Okay," Ramses said. "Watch the water." He took a deep breath, seemed to focus, then lifted his hands skyward, and swept them in circles. I saw his hair moving in the sudden breeze, and heard Roxanne say, "Wait, is he doing that?"

"Doing what?" I whispered as my boy pulled an invisible something down, then shoved it toward the bubbling fountain.

"The wind–hell look, look."

The camera panned to the fountain as a spiral of water took shape and then rose, forming a spout that stood spinning all on its own.

"Well I'll be dipped," Roxy said.

Then the vortex whirled faster, and then, all at once, the water stilled, and I realized as I blinked at the screen, that it was frozen. Suspended in the air, a glittering ice crystal sculpture of a whirlpool defied gravity. And then Ramses pulled his hands down, and the thing fell into the fountain, breaking into ice chunks. Ramses relaxed, looking proud.

I wanted to run outside and hug him, so filled with pride I nearly burst. And then I heard Nikki saying, "Do me! Do me!"

"Put the phone near him, Roxanne," I said. Then as she did, I said, "Ramses, can you do what you did to the water, to people?"

He nodded at the screen. "I can make the wind pick them up and move them wherever I want. I've done it to Nikki and

Gareth. I did it with Sheena once, and she's as big as a grown-up. But I've never tried to turn humans to ice before."

"What about with...with vampires?" I asked. I knew it wasn't a question he would want to answer. "It's not your fault, and I won't be angry. But I know Gareth's power will not work on vampires, and I want to know if yours does."

He lowered his head. "They break into pieces, just like the water did," he said.

"It's all right, darling. It's all right. I'm so impressed with you, Ramses. I've never known anyone who could truly command the north wind with enough precision to freeze things. You are gifted, and that's the truth, my child. It's a gift, what you can do."

As I said the words and watched Ramses flush with pleasure and pride, I sensed the return of Maxine and Lou, and said, "Best come inside now, Children. We need to be careful."

"Okay, Rhiannon," Ramses said, and I heard him tell the others to come inside as he disconnected. He saw himself as the leader among them. I'd named him well.

Maxine entered the front door as the children entered the back. She handed me a sheet of paper, and said, "You're welcome."

I arched my brows. "For…?" And then I looked at the paper in my hand. There were three addresses written on its face, and I felt excitement rush into me. "Bouchard?"

"Those are all of the places that real estate agency has handed over to customers in the last three days. All of them rentals, and the first two are apartments. I'm betting on the beach house."

"You truly are a brilliant snoop, Maxine."

"Hey, what am I, chopped liver?" Lou asked.

I smiled at him. "You are the genius who is going to work out how to get me there in daylight without roasting me in the process."

He blinked twice, then shook his head. "Um, no. Look, sundown's in five hours. You're just gonna have to wait."

"Waiting is not my strong suit," I told him, rising as did my temper.

"Rhiannon," Maxine said, "Come on, what good would it do you to go there? It's a beach house. The view is the whole point. It'll be entirely windows. Even inside, you'd be exposed to sunlight. Wait for night, when you'll have the advantage."

"Why you mortals insist on thwarting my every effort is beyond—"

"You were right, Roxy," Nikki said from behind me. "That daytime drug *does* make them grouchy."

I bit back any further remarks, though it was like holding back an angry panther, "My Nikki is right, it is the drug. I'm sorry. Thank you for bringing me this information. At sundown, we go. That will be soon enough."

"Good."

"Good," I said. "Come children, we're going to the basement where there's room to work."

"What are we working on," Nikki asked.

"Hand to hand combat," I said. Then I pointed a long forefinger at her, my nail just touching the middle of her forehead. "Do *not* hurt me."

She smiled. "I'll try really hard not to." Then she raced ahead of us to the basement.

* * *

By the time Tamara and Christian rose, I was feeling as sensitive as an exposed nerve, but I tried to squelch that as Tamara greeted me with an awkward hug, all of her usual warmth and no small amount of concern.

You look haggard. Are you all right? She asked, her words for me alone.

No. I admitted it for the first time, and as soon as I thought the word, a rush of emotion seemed to flood out of me. My throat tightened, and my back bent with the power of the sobs I fought to hold inside.

Tamara rubbed my back rapidly, as if she could brush my grief away. *We will find a solution. Somehow.*

I nodded and straightened, blinking my eyes dry. "Come," I said. "We have much to do. While you rested, Maxine and Lou brilliantly found Dr. Bouchard's most likely location."

"Yes, we did," Max said. "Here, we can take a look." She gathered us around a computer and with a few clicks, pulled up a satellite image showing the beach house where we suspected Dr. Sarah Bouchard was staying while in town. I stared at the thing until my eyes watered, but could see no sign of human presence. The curtains were drawn. No movement came from behind them.

"I do not believe she's there," I said, disappointment heavy in my tone.

"Could be sleeping," Tamara said. "It's nighttime and she's human."

"The only way to be sure is to pay her a visit," Maxine said. "And yet we can't all go and leave the children unattended. They are her target, after all."

"You're right, Maxine. If Bouchard is not there, she's most likely on her way here."

"She doesn't know where here is," Lou Malone said firmly. "And I'd just as soon keep it that way."

I was dying to get my hands on the so-called doctor. But as eager and restless as I had been today, now that the time had arrived, I felt an intuitive and overwhelming sense that I should remain right there. Close to my children.

"I'll go," Tamara said. "You should stay behind to protect the children."

I shot the brave young thing a look. "Not alone, Tamara. It's too dangerous. We should always be in pairs when DPI is involved."

She nodded, and closing her eyes, called out to her husband mentally. *Eric? Are you awake? How are things with Roland?*

I awaited a reply, and when none came, I wondered whether Eric had spoken to Tamara privately, directing his thoughts only to her.

But then I saw the worried frown marring her pretty brow,

and realized she'd had no response.

"Tamara?" I began.

"Something's wrong." She swept her gaze around the room, turning in a full circle. "Rhiannon, I think we should move the children."

"Move them? That's exactly the opposite of what we should do. They're safe here."

"Eric isn't responding. What if something's happened? What if Roland is under DPI's control again? He knows the children are here."

"My Roland would never–"

"Then why isn't Eric responding to me?"

She all but shouted it, and there was a part of me that recognized her fear for her husband, empathized with it, even. But the rest of me rose up and struck back like a cobra. "Roland would never hurt Eric, either. How dare you suggest he would?"

"How dare I? He almost killed Christian, you told us so yourself. That's how I dare! The children–"

"You think you're a better mother than I am, don't you?" I accused, advancing on her. "That's what this is about. You think you could do a better job of raising them than I!"

Roxanne stepped right in front of me, clasped my shoulders in her hands, and said, very loudly, "It's the drug, Rhiannon. Don't bite your friend's head off over a chemical side-effect."

My eyes, I realized, had heated, as fury raged through my body. I caught hold of myself, lowered my head, tried to get hold of my temper, but it was whipping like a broken power line, sending sparks everywhere.

"What drug?" Tamara asked. "Rhiannon, what did you–?"

"Diurnal. I'm afraid I violated your husband's emergency kit and helped myself to a dose just before sunrise."

She stepped out from behind Roxanne, shook her head at me like a disapproving parent. "No wonder you're so bristly."

"I didn't feel there was a choice."

Tam nodded. Maxine, who had been standing aside with

her husband Lou, and looking from me to Tamara and back again, her eyes betraying her nervousness, said, "Rhiannon, Tam has a point. If we can't pinpoint Roland's location or Bouchard's...we should probably move the children. Just in case they're on their way here."

I closed my eyes, lowering my head. Just as I did, I sensed Eric's approach. He was speeding toward us and there was panic in his energy. Tamara's head came up fast, and she ran to the front door, yanking it open just as he appeared on the other side.

"Eric! What is it, what's wrong?"

He looked stricken. "Roland is gone. He was gone when I woke. I have no idea where. Are the children–"

"Upstairs, playing with Christian and Pandora," I said, having moved to the entryway to stand behind Tamara.

"We should move them," Eric said.

I closed my eyes and bit my lip to keep from snapping at him. "That seems to be the consensus." I wished for help. But Maxine had been unable to reach Vlad and Stormy and no other vampires were close enough to get here in time. None that I knew of, at least.

"We'll move them," I said.

"Good," Tamara replied. "Eric and I will go check out that beach house."

"I would like to observe as you do." I recalled Ramses' demonstration by day, which I'd seen on the very computer screen I'd just been looking at. "Roxanne, how did you do that earlier? Showing me what happened outside on this screen?"

"Pretty simply," Roxanne said.

Christian was the only vampire not in the room. He was upstairs playing Hide and Seek with the children in the vastness of the Malone home. "I can show you how to do it right from your cell phone," Roxanne said. She looked at me, and then at Eric, and then she said, "Scratch that. I can show *her*." This with a nod indicating Tamara.

I stood taller, my eyes going narrow. "Are you implying–"

"I'm implying that it might go easier with someone born in this century, Princess. Nothing more." Then she turned to Tamara. "Got a cellphone?"

Tamara nodded, then followed Roxanne into the living room where they sat together on the antique chintz sofa leaning over the phone's electronic glow. I turned to Eric. "When you find Bouchard, bring her to me. Alive."

"To torture?" he asked.

"To do whatever is required to make her tell us about the device she implanted inside my husband's brain," I said. "What it is, what it does, and how to safely get it out of him."

Eric nodded, but looked a bit reluctant still.

Not wanting to leave my husband's best friend with any doubt about my intentions, I added, "And then I am going kill her."

* * *

After Eric and Tamara left, taking Eric's red car, and spitting gravel in their wake, I called the children and Christian downstairs. Pandora came hurrying behind. My cat met my eyes, and I knew she was agitated. She'd picked up on the energy of fear that permeated us all, I was sure of it as her tail switched to convey her displeasure.

"We have to leave for a little while," I told them. "But this all going to be over very soon now."

Maxine and Lou came in from a back room. Lou carried a duffle bag and I could smell the gun oil and sulphur scent of bullets inside. Weapons. Maxine had the laptop, open and running. "Just get into the van, guys. It's a rolling hotspot. We can watch everything from anyplace we want."

I nodded, but as I took Nikki's hand to lead her through the door, she yanked it free. "I don't want to go. We were just getting good at the game."

And then Gareth said, "She knows where we are, doesn't she?"

I met his frightened eyes, wondered just how much of our conversations and thoughts he had heard. I still didn't know if

I could effectively block them out, though I had been trying. "We don't know for sure. But there's a chance she might, and if she does, and if she's coming here, we want to be gone before she arrives."

"How would she know?" Ramses asked. And then, pointedly, "Where is Roland?"

I held his gaze and tried to exert all my power, all my arrogance, all my exalted age and wisdom into that stare as I said, "I don't know that either. What I do know is that it's safer to leave and so that's what we are doing."

He was not intimidated by my haughtiest demeanor. In fact, his eyes held a veiled accusation. And yet I had no idea what he was accusing me of.

Lou pulled the van right around the house and into the back yard, flattening the lawn beneath its tires and positioning it near the patio in back. When he got out, he carried a handgun, and when he arrived at the rear door, he tugged two more from the back of his trousers, and handed them to Maxine and Roxanne. "We surround the kids, and on my word, make a beeline for the van," Lou said. He'd left its doors open. "All right?"

I nodded, stepped in front of the children, and called my cat to my side with a flick of my finger. Maxine and Lou positioned themselves on either side of them, and Christian and Roxanne brought up the rear. We made a tight little huddle of beings, with the children all but invisible in our center.

"Go ahead, move," Lou said.

I swept the surroundings with the power of my mind, even knowing DPI agents were often trained to block themselves from my kind. Not all of them were, and not all of them had the strength of mind to maintain such a mental barricade. I had to try. Sensing no one, I moved quickly forward, but not too quickly. I didn't want to leave the mortals in our wake, leaving the children exposed. Pandora kept pace, but like me, her focus was on the children.

The distance of perhaps fifteen feet felt like a mile, and

when we reached the van, I did not get in, but rather stepped aside to let the children rush past me, and through the open side door, Pandora leaping right in behind them. They scrambled into their seats in the center row, and Pandora sat upright on the floor in front of them. Christian and Roxanne wriggled their way into the third row seats behind the children. I got in and wedged myself onto the only bit of available seating, tugging the door closed. Maxine and Lou dove into the front, Lou behind the wheel, and we were in motion. The entire operation took mere seconds.

"Head south, Lou," Maxine said. She was already punching keys on her computer. "We want out of the way, but we also want top notch 4G."

"I know just the place."

* * *

Parked on a wooded hilltop, on a dirt road, in a pull-off we hoped was concealed by pines, we waited in the van.

I had all but affixed myself to Maxine's computer screen, gazing at it over her shoulder. Roxanne was observing by means of her cellphone in the back, and had turned its volume down, as we only needed one audio feed in the confined space. She had tapped into Tamara's signal as well.

The children were bored and restless, and seemed unable or unwilling to comprehend the danger we faced.

Now, tonight. Whatever would happen, would happen before sunrise. I felt it to my bones. And I felt exposed, as well, not safe as I had felt in the Malones' home, nor our own. We were out in the open, only the thin sheet metal of this van between the children and whatever lay outside.

"We'll get through this, Rhi," Maxine said. I detested when she called me "Rhi." "Eric and Tamara are gonna find this Bouchard bitch so you can put an end to her bullshit once and for all."

I missed my Roland so much it was an ache in my chest. It was difficult to focus on anything else, but I did note the passion in her tone.

I tried to smile, because seeing this small but spunky mortal, angry enough to condone violence amused me, but I couldn't even work up a convincing smirk.

And then the computer screen on her lap came to life. Naturally, Eric and Tamara were invisible to us, but Tam held the camera's eye away from her, allowing us to see what she was seeing.

"We're here," she said. "We're moving up to the beach house now. It's as dark and silent as a crypt."

I nodded as if she could see me, and listened intently as the image on the screen moved up and down in time with Tamara's footsteps. The small yellow house in the distance grew larger, and I could hear the ocean's waves rushing over the beach beyond it, then hissing as they withdrew again.

The beach house loomed even nearer now, a quaint square of wood, with a four-sided roof and more windows than walls, all of them curtained, all of them dark.

And then one of those curtains moved, just a little, and I glimpsed something vaguely human shaped and palest white on the other side, just briefly. It was like seeing a ghost. A bolt of foreboding shot up my spine like icy lightning. I leaned closer. "Tamara, get away from there. Eric—!"

Tamara screamed then, shrieked really, and kept on shrieking as her phone apparently tumbled, then went still on an image of the starry night sky. I snatched the laptop from Maxine and dove out of the van, not wanting the children traumatized by whatever was happening to their friend, Tamara.

My hands trembled as I clung to the small computer.

And then I jumped backward in horror as a form rushed past on the screen, a form made entirely of fire in the shape of Tamara.

"By the Gods, she's on fire!" I cried. "Tamara!"

I heard Eric's voice. "I've got you, I've got you. I've got you, my love. Tam. Tamara?"

"Eric!" I cried, then silently. *Eric, tell us what's happening.*

She was on fire, his mind told mine. *Her hair just burst into flames and now she's....*

You need to get away from there. But get the phone. She dropped the phone and–

Yes, yes.

A split second, and the view on the screen flipped and darkened as Eric apparently scooped up the phone and tucked it away. His footsteps were rapid, then a steady vibration as he sped away from that place and whatever was inside. I had seen no fireball thrown from the cottage. No flaming torch nor rag-stuffed bottle. How had Bouchard done it to her?

I'm bringing her back. She needs help, Rhiannon. She has to survive long enough for the day sleep to heal her.

Get her to the Malones' as fast as you can, Eric.

I closed the laptop as its screen had gone black, and turned to see every other adult had exited the van and surrounded me now.

"We have to go back to the house. We'll need to cool her burns and attend to her pain. Cold water, sterile towels, ice. And she'll need blood. We should...." My words trailed off, because Roxanne wasn't there.

"She stayed in the van with the kids," Christian said.

And as I looked up at the van, I knew it was empty. I knew it, felt it, before I even opened the door, to see that the sliding door on the opposite side stood open, and the seats were vacant.

"Children! Roxanne!"

I went cold inside as I raced around the van, and saw nothing but thick forest, and then vaguely, footsteps outlined by the squashed spots in the autumn leaf carpet. I raced at top speeds, and I knew the others were trying to follow, but they couldn't possibly keep up. I was a solid mile into the forest when what I saw brought me to a sudden halt.

Roxanne O'Mally lay in a bed of fallen leaves and pine needles, her head tipped back, her eyes closed. There were two puncture wounds in her throat, and twin rivulets of blood trailing down her neck.

I fell to my knees and screamed, "Roxanne!"

She opened her eyes, gazed up at me weakly.

"Roland," she whispered. "The kids said....he was calling them. That he needed their help." She lifted one hand, and pointed in the direction I'd been running. And then her eyes fell closed, and there was no more.

Christian leaped to my side, the other humans still far behind. We'd made the run in no more than a minute or two. I looked up at him, emotion almost blinding me. "I'm going after the children. Take Roxy back to the Malones'. Tell the others to do whatever they can to save her. But Christian, you must not turn her. Roxy would not want it."

"But...but..."

"There's no time. Take her, get back to the house with the others. Hurry, before it's too late."

I ran then, through the forest at speeds a gazelle would struggle to match. And as I emerged from its far side onto a winding road, I saw a car speeding away, its red taillights vanishing in the distance, and my cat, Pandora, racing after it at speeds she was far too old to be attempting.

And then all that remained was a dark, cloaked figure, standing on the roadside staring sightlessly into space.

Roland.

I ran to him, gripped his shoulder and spun him around to face me. His blank stare and vacant eyes made me furious.

"What have you done?" I shouted. And when he didn't respond, I slapped him hard, rocking his head back but gripping his shoulders before he could fall. "What have you done?" I shrieked, shaking him.

Roland blinked, frowned at me, shook his head.

"Dammit, Roland, speak to me!"

His eyes widened, and the pain in them was more intense than any man should have to bear. "What have I done? What have I—the children," he said, looking in the direction the vehicle had gone. Then he shot a terrified look back toward the forest. "Roxy!"

"I'm going after the children," I shouted. "Get back to our house, Roland. Lock yourself in a room where you can't do anymore harm, or I swear to Isis I'll kill you myself."

"Rhiannon—" Roland leaned toward me, as if he would embrace me.

I pushed him away from me, and he stumbled. "Go!" I shouted, pointing angrily toward the forest. "Now." My heart seemed to be wearing an icy coat, but I had no time for kindness, not even for my love. And then I shot forward in a burst of speed such as I had never used before, after that car and my kidnapped children. I passed Pandora, and she poured on more effort, trying with all her might to keep up.

CHAPTER FIFTEEN

I sped after the departing vehicle, calling out to the children mentally. *Nikki! Ramses! Can you hear me? Gareth! You must not go with that woman. You must get away from her.*

And immediately, without any hesitation my Nikki replied. *We have to, Rhiannon. She's taking us to our sister!*

She's lying to you! You must get out of that car. Do it now.

She's not lying. Roland said so himself. He called to us to come fast, because our sister needs our help, and he told us to go with Dr. Bouchard, that she was good, after all.

She's not good, I cried. *Roland didn't know what he was saying.*

But we can feel her. Our sister. She's near. Dr. Bouchard says she's waiting for us at a house on the beach. And I know she's telling the truth, Rhiannon. I know it, because I can feel her.

I could have screamed in frustration. By the Gods, Tamara burned alive. Eric's rage would be without equal. Roxanne lying dead, or nearly so, at the hand of a man she trusted. Roland completely out of control. And our children in DPI hands once again. What had our lives become?

I poured on more speed, eventually drawing near enough to glimpse the car, and once I did, I never let it out of my sight again. I was a dark, furious blur on the streets of Maine. A vampire on a rampage, speeding over rural routes on a late autumn night. The few vehicles I encountered were driven by mortals, oblivious to my presence, or sensing something, but unsure what. Pandora bounded through woods and fields along the roadside, intelligent enough to stay out of sight. She fell behind, but I could not slow. And I knew she would catch up to me. It was inevitable.

Bouchard drove rapidly through the night, down the East Coast Highway. My children were willing participants in their own abduction. And then finally the car turned onto a side road and slowed. I was nearly upon it when it veered once again, into a curving drive, its headlights painting streaks of light upon the beach house I'd seen on Maxine's computer screen.

Something was inside. Something capable of setting a vampire ablaze from a distance. It wasn't Bouchard. Bouchard had been taking my children while I'd been witnessing the brutal attack on Tamara.

I wondered briefly whether she would survive, and my heart seemed to contract in my chest. The pain of losing her, and perhaps Roxanne, too…and only because they had tried to help us. Tried to protect the children. Tried to save my Roland for me.

But I couldn't let my devastation weaken me. It hurt, yes, and emotional pain could be as crippling to my kind as physical pain could be. But I couldn't allow it. Not with the children even now spilling from that car. They hung close to the vehicle's still open doors, staring warily at the harmless looking little beach house.

I wanted to shout a warning but I dared not give away my presence. I had cloaked myself as completely as I was capable of doing. I'd cast the *Glamourie* while I'd been speeding through the night. I'd sealed my mind with the impenetrable wall of my will now that the cottage was near, because that creature lurking inside could incinerate me with a glance if it caught a whiff of my presence.

I knew Bouchard wanted the children alive. To her they were lab rats that needed to be returned to their cages. Once they were again under lock and key, she could get back to her work—creating the perfect weapon to exterminate the Undead. She needed the children healthy and well for her experiments. And yes, they'd blown up *The Anemone* believing the children still aboard, but they must have known how difficult it was to kill the Offspring. The two older ones, Sheena and Wolf, had been shot point blank in the chest with high powered rifles by DPI forces, only to revive moments later, completely healed. Bouchard must know all of this and more.

I was going to kill that bitch. And I was going to enjoy it.

She smiled down at my children. Gareth darted a nervous glance my way. Did he sense me there? Did he know?

"Your sister is inside," Bouchard said. She got out more slowly than the children had, her mind completely blocked against mine. She was an ordinary looking, pear-shaped, middle-aged, false blond mortal. She did not look anything like the evil that must be her soul.

"But you should let me speak to her before you get too close. She's a nervous little thing."

Their *sister*? Could this be more than just a ploy to get the children to come to her? Could this sister be the one who was supposed to have died around her second birthday? Was *she* the fire breather, then?

Before Bouchard took a step toward the cabin, its door opened and a little girl stood within it. I was caught completely off guard. She was so pale, she almost seemed ethereal. Her skin so light it nearly glowed, or perhaps it did glow a little when seen through the supercharged lens of a vampire's eyes. A little cherub, she was, with fine white-blond hair that had never seen a scissor and rarely a comb. She still had a little bit of her baby cheeks, round and soft, and Cupid's bow lips of palest rose.

Her eyes were in shadow, but I thought they were violet. She stood in the doorway, and Bouchard held up her hands and said, "It's all right, Gamma…I mean, Blue." She laughed, a nervous little titter, and I knew she was very afraid of that little girl. She shot a look at the other children. "Your sister has named herself Blue. You three have names now, too, don't you?"

Nikki nodded hard and said to the child in the doorway, "Blue is a nice name. I'm called Nikki." And then she blinked and asked. "Are you really my sister?" And I heard the gruff evidence of emotion in her words.

"We are made of the same parents," the girl in the doorway said. "That means sister, yes?"

Nikki smiled and started to rush forward. Even as I lunged to stop her, Bouchard caught her shoulders and held her back, and so I relaxed into hiding again, awaiting my opportunity. "Easy now, Nikki. Blue hasn't been around anyone else in a very long time. She's–"

But Blue came toward Nikki, her steps short and rapid, but not quite running. She pushed past Bouchard, who seemed to try to block her way, and stood facing my sweet little girl. I leaned nearer, ready to intervene in a flash of speed if necessary, even if it got me incinerated.

And yet I sensed no ill intent from the little girl. She was frightened, she was alone, and she was extremely confused. Lifting a hand, she reached out, perhaps intending to touch Nikki's face, but Nikki's hand shot up too and met the pale child's hand in the air. They stood like that, pressing palm to palm, as if they'd planned it that way. As if it was just what one did when one met a long lost sibling.

Something was happening. Some kind of connection. I felt it crackling in the air, and saw it in the way their eyes met and locked. And then the two girls lifted their other hands as if they were sharing the same brain. They moved in tandem, those two tiny hands, up to chest level, and then they pressed together, palm to palm. The pale child's violet eyes lightened to near pink.

"All right, girls," Bouchard said nervously, moving behind them, one hand on little Blue's shoulder. "All right, that's enough. Let's get inside and we can, um...."

But the girls remained as they were, eyes intense, palms pressed together.

"What are you doing?" Bouchard demanded. She sounded alarmed now. She turned to the boys, "What are they doing?"

"I don't know," Ramses said. "And I wouldn't tell you if I did."

I lowered my shields the tiniest bit, enough to send a tendril of my consciousness outward, into my Nikki's mind. And there was the most intense energy there—rapid fire images, flashing at dizzying speeds. Images and words and feelings. Memories.

It's a data exchange, young Gareth told me mentally. *They're telling each other everything that's happened since they've been apart. Ramses and I can feel all of it, too. They've been very cruel to Blue. They hurt her.*

I was still processing that when, apparently having reached the same conclusion, Bouchard grabbed each girl's shoulder and shouted, "Enough!" wrenching them apart so forcefully that Nikki stumbled and fell to the ground.

I surged out of hiding and ran at her, my hands like claws, my fangs bared, a battle cry worthy of the *Bean Sidhe* mutilating the air. I flew at her, hit her hard, clasping her to me as my momentum carried us twenty feet further. We only just missed colliding with the little house.

I grabbed Bouchard by her neck, holding her between the children and me as I reached behind me for the doorknob. Blue, the pale child, was glaring at me, and one hand flashed upward, but Ramses moved his own hands, whipping up a whirlwind around the girl's feet. Sand and dust rose to surround her and she lowered her arms to shield her face.

Then Nikki elbowed him and the wind died. She touched

the pale child's cheek and shook her head side to side. "You mustn't hurt Rhiannon. She is our mother."

I wrenched the door open. "Hide yourselves in case more DPI troops arrive," I told the children. "I'll only be a moment." I saw Pandora arrive, breathing fast through a slightly open mouth, and told her, "Stay. Guard the children!" Then as she sat down right beside them, I backed into the house, dragging Bouchard with me and kicked the door closed with my booted foot.

My captive hadn't struggled. She knew enough about our kind to know it would've been useless. She'd gone still, not even fighting me.

"You've won the battle," she said to me. "But not the war. You'll never win the war."

"I'll settle for the battle. For now. Before I kill you, Dr. Bouchard, you will tell me exactly what you put inside my husband's head, and how to get it out.

The door opened, and I whirled, only to see my Roland limping through. "Sorry to interrupt. I didn't…I didn't trust myself out there, alone with the children." He shot a hateful look at Bouchard. "And I too would like the answer to Rhiannon's question."

Bouchard shrugged. "No harm in you knowing that," she said. "There's nothing you can do to change it anyway. There's a camera behind your eye, but you obviously figured that out on your own." This with a nod toward the patch he still wore.

"And what else? What is in the vial? The fluid in the vial?"

"A powerful drug that makes the brain extremely suggestible. Controlled by me, by remote. I push a button, you get a dose of the drug, and then I speak into a microphone and tell you what I want you to do."

"Where is this button?" His voice was soft. Dangerously soft. Her eyes darted left, and her mind's pathetic mortal blocks were weakening beneath her fear. Oh, yes, despite her bravado, she was very afraid of us, now that she was in our hands. Entirely at our mercy.

She should be.

"It's in her handbag," I said.

Roland approached the woman, and she cringed. His step, tap, step, tap approach was slow, building the woman's fear. He was angry. My Roland never treated anyone cruelly. Never.

Reaching out he snatched her bag from her shoulder, rummaged inside and located a small black device that looked much like a miniature television remote control.

He nodded, pocketed it, and said, "Who else has one?"

"No one."

He looked at me. "She's lying isn't she?"

"Yes, she is." I tilted my head. "Why don't we let Pandora toy with her for a while, the way a smaller cat would toy with a rat before killing it and eating it. And not necessarily in that order."

Roland nodded his head, walking away. "I'll get Pandora," he said.

"No, wait, wait....don't bring that animal in here." She drew a deep breath.

"Stop blocking us from your mind, Bouchard. Let me in," I told her. "Lower the blocks and let me in."

She shook her head. "I can't. I can't, I won't. You'll kill me anyway."

"Then we'll do this the old fashioned way." I slammed her bodily into a chair, then straddled her and pressed her forehead backward with the palm of my hand. Her neck arched. Her blood pulsed through her jugular even faster, making my mouth water in anticipation.

I opened my mouth and leaned in, deliberately blowing my cold breath onto her skin. She shook her head. "Kill me. I'm dead either way."

"Oh, I'm not going to kill you," I said. And I bit down.

Her blood rushed into me, and with it, the last of her defenses melted away. As I imbibed her, I scanned her mind, searching for everything she had tried to keep from me, from us. My mind was open wide to Roland's so that he could experience everything I did.

There was a drug that she could release into my husband's brain to make him susceptible to her commands. But there was also an explosive fluid that would go off if anyone tried to remove the device from his mind. As I drank from her, I got all of it, absorbing it as it shot rapid fire from her mind to mine. I saw the volatile chemical compound in a diagram that meant nothing to me. I saw the schematics of the device itself, the fuses and the triggers. I saw the ultra-classified documents and got that only she and her superior, one Colonel Patterson, whose face came clearly into my mind, knew about this project to find and recapture the children.

Roland's hand came to my shoulder. "It's enough my love. We might need her alive. For the children. She knows more about them than anyone, and if you keep drinking to learn it all, you'll kill her."

I withdrew my fangs, and lifted my head, swiping my chin with one hand and meeting my Roland's eyes. He stared back, his own darkening with despair such as I had never seen.

I nodded, then turning, I looked at the very pale, unconscious woman.

* * *

"Rhiannon."

Roland put his hand on his beautiful Rhiannon's shoulder.

"Come, my love. The children are waiting."

She blinked at him as if she'd never seen him before, and then the heartbreak that shaped her features almost made him join her in her tears. "My Roland, my Roland," she said, pressing a hand to his cheek.

"It'll be all right," he said. "Rhiannon, the children."

He took her arm and led her through the place, locating the bathroom easily enough. Then he cranked on the taps, adjusted the water warm, and taking Rhiannon's hands, ran them beneath it. Then he took a soft cloth and washed the blood from her chin and her lips.

Scarlet spirals whirled down the drain. He shut the taps off again, and then impulsively crushed her to his chest and kissed her hair. "I have loved you, my lady, and will love you, always. No matter what else happens. If any part of me goes on—"

"Don't say it."

"If any part of me goes on, then so does our love. Because nothing of me can exist without loving you."

"Roland, don't…."

He kissed her mouth to quiet her. He knew their time together was coming to an end. He felt it. The device in his brain would kill him if they tried to remove it. And he could not continue to exist while it remained. It made him a danger to all those he loved. And he would not live that way.

The knowledge was almost too painful to bear. But bear it he did, and led her back through the place, past Bouchard, who was going nowhere for the time being. She would linger for a few hours, and then die, unless they got her some transfusions.

For now, she would keep. He took Rhiannon's shoulder to lead her outside, but she pulled free.

"No, wait. First I must ensure this one gives us no more trouble." Then she went to Bouchard.

"Darling, you can't kill her."

"Oh, I'm not going to kill her," she whispered. "Not yet, anyway." She pricked her own forefinger on one of her razor sharp fangs, just a little, then squeezed it until a droplet of blood emerged. Moving back to Bouchard, she pressed that fingertip between the woman's lips.

"Rhiannon, what are you–"

"A little trick Sarafina taught me. That Shuvani vampiress has many of them."

Bouchard's eyes flew open wide, and she tried to grab hold of Rhiannon's wrist, but Rhiannon just pulled away. "A drop or two a day, and she'll be ours to command for as long as we wish it. A mindless drone. She'll be very useful in our ongoing battle against DPI. And of course, in the meantime...." She looked at Bouchard. "You will contact Colonel Patterson in your usual way."

"Text message," she muttered, her eyes unfocused and sleepy.

"Mmm." Rhiannon looked around the cottage, spotting Bouchard's handbag on the floor and took her phone from it. She handed it to her. "Tell him all is well. You've acquired the children, and you will be returning to The Sentinel in the morning."

"Yes," she said, and her fingers tapped out the message on the screen as Rhiannon looked over her shoulder, nodding, and then taking the phone from her.

"Do you have any other way to contact him?"

"No," she whispered.

"Good. Then you will remain here. You will not open your door or speak to anyone until we return for you. Understood?"

"Yes."

"Good."

Roland did not like what he saw, believed it immoral and indecent to make a mindless slave of a human being. And yet, how could he criticize? This woman had done so much evil. And he knew, too, that Rhiannon's precautions would keep Colonel Patterson from doing anything drastic, at least for what remained of the night.

He took Rhiannon's arm. She picked up the remote control device and added it to a deep pocket where she'd already dropped Bouchard's phone. They went outside to the four children who rose from where they'd been crouching behind a large dark boulder. Pandora was with them, so close she was always touching one or another of them. They stood together, a little group of four siblings, and the resemblance was obvious except for the coloring.

"Go on," Nikki said to Blue, nudging her forward.

Blue looked at Rhiannon and Roland. "I know….I know everything that has happened."

Rhiannon said, "Then you know we would never harm you, or your siblings. That we only want to give them a good life, and raise them to be good people, in freedom, never enslaved."

"Yes," she said softly.

Nikki nudged her again. "Say the rest, Blue."

Blue nodded. "I promise not to set you on fire. Not even if you make me mad. I would like….I'd like to stay with…with Nikki and Gareth and Ramses."

Roland looked to Rhiannon, and she understood his gaze and nodded. "We'll make sure the four of you remain together. I promise," she told them. But he heard the catch in her voice. The heartache. It might not be with them, that was what she was thinking. And it was killing her.

"But we must hurry now," Rhiannon said. "Our friends need us. Come on, get into the car, let's go."

"We should take Bouchard somewhere else and burn this place, Rhiannon," Roland said softly. "We must leave no trace that we were ever here."

"I can do that for you," the little girl said. And she waved her arm, like a television witch casting a spell. The window smashed, as if she'd thrown something physical through it and the beach house exploded into an instant conflagration. Bouchard didn't make a sound, not a scream, nothing. It must have been over very quickly for her.

"Hell," Rhiannon said. "I wasn't finished with her yet."

Sighing, she got behind the wheel of Bouchard's vehicle. "Buckle up, children. We need to go fast."

* * *

I filled the children in on the way, as gently as I could saying that Roxanne had been hurt very badly. I didn't tell them it was Roland who had done it to her. I just couldn't. It hadn't been him, not really. It had been Bouchard, and justice had been served sizzling hot.

I also told them that their dear Tamara had been burned.

Blue blinked, realizing that was her doing. "I did not know she was good. Dr. Bouchard told me to do it to any vampire who came close, or they would kill me. "

"It's all right, Blue," Roland told her. "We know you were

misled. All is forgiven."

I brought the car to a stop near the front door of the Malones' and we all piled out. "Nikki, I'd like you to take Blue upstairs to your guest room. You children have a lot to catch up on, after all."

I hustled the children inside. No one was downstairs. I called, "Eric! Tamara?"

"Upstairs!" Maxine bellowed, and we all rushed up there in an almost stampede, Roland hobbling rapidly, only a step or two behind. At the top we turned left, heading toward the sound of Maxine's voice, but stopping sooner, at Roxanne's bedroom. Its door stood open, and I gazed inside.

She lay in her bed, eyes closed, peaceful and beautiful. Sitting in a chair beside her was Lou Malone, his shirtsleeves rolled up past his elbow. A small plastic tube ran from his arm to hers, and blood filled the entire length of it.

I felt my brows draw together. "Is she…?"

"Alive," Lou said, and he lifted his arm. "Type O. Universal donor."

I swore my knees gave out in relief. I reached for the wall to support myself and found Roland's shoulder instead.

"Thank the gods," he whispered.

Then he walked past me, right up to Roxanne's bedside. Leaning over her, he pressed his palm to her face. "I am so sorry, Roxanne. I will never ever be able to put into words how–"

"Roland?" Roxy asked weakly.

"Yes, yes, I'm here." He leaned closer.

Roxanne's hand shot up from the bed, and she gripped the front of Roland's shirt. "When I'm strong enough...."

"Yes?"

"I'm gonna kick your ass." Then she let go and her hand dropped to the pillows again.

"This is my second round," Lou said. "We're gonna need another donor after that, but she's gonna be okay."

"I am greatly relieved to know that," I said.

Roxy looked my way and winked. "Takes more than one antiquated... addle-brained... vampire... to do in Roxanne O'Malley," she said.

I smiled. "I'll come visit you later, Roxanne," I backed into the hallway again, looking toward the closed door to the guest room where Eric and Tamara had been staying. I got a chill to my soul.

"Children, go on to your rooms now," I told them. "I need to focus on my friends. All right?"

They all nodded, and Gareth looked at his hands, thinned his lips in frustration. "I wish my power worked on vampires," he said.

"I wish mine didn't," said Blue, her voice soft.

I frowned and then crouched low to put myself at eye level with the child. "Gareth, how do you know your healing power doesn't work on vampires?"

"I've always known."

"Yes, but how? Have you ever tried?"

"No, I've never tried. Our keepers and Dr. Bouchard always said…." Then his brows lifted. "But they lie, don't they?"

"Yes. Yes, they do." I held out my hand and he took it. Together we walked to the bedroom door, and after a brief knock, I opened it and we went inside.

Eric sent me an irritated look, but then seeing it was me, the irritation vanished. He noticed the children beside me, nodded, his relief palpable. Then he returned his attention to the woman in the bed.

Tamara's face was burned very badly. One side of it looked like melted wax, with bright pink places alongside charred black ones. Thin ribbons of skin hung loose. Wet towels were draped over her head. I didn't see any hair beneath them.

"The children shouldn't be in here," Eric said.

I didn't reply right away, still stunned into speechlessness by the sight of my friend.

"She's in so much pain," Eric went on. "I've given her my own blood. It helped somewhat, but…not enough. How many hours till dawn?"

"We may not have to wait for dawn, Eric." Turning, I nodded at Gareth.

He moved up to the opposite side of the bed from Eric. Roland wrapped his arms around my shoulders and held me close. The other children gathered in front of us.

Gareth held his hands over Tamara's head. I watched for a long time as nothing happened, but then there was a faint green glow emanating from his palms, so slight that at first I wasn't certain whether it was real or whether I was conjuring it by wanting it so badly. And then, within seconds, there was no denying it. The glow beamed.

I remembered the heat of his healing touch from when he'd used it in the barn on that injured lycan girl, and I cringed as I realized more heat on already burned flesh was going to hurt far more than Tamara could bear.

"It's cold, Rhiannon," Ramses said, reading me in that uncanny way of his. "Can't you feel it? It's cold this time."

Lifting my brows, I stepped out of Roland's arms and moved closer, holding my hand out toward the glow and feeling for myself the coolness of that energy. Beneath it, the skin began to move, to uncurl, and turn to a soft healthy pink right before my eyes. The charred black bits fell away and the raw, red parts covered themselves in new skin.

Eric sat up, leaning over her to peel the towels from her head, looking on in amazement as the skin of her nearly bald scalp repaired itself in much the same way.

Eventually, Gareth's hands stopped glowing, and he opened his eyes.

Then he smiled broadly. "It worked!"

"It did!" Roland boomed. "Gareth, I'm so proud of you!" He hugged the boy impulsively, then held him close and patted his back a moment longer.

Gareth stepped back, but Roland kept his arm around the boy and beamed at the others. "I am proud of all of you."

"Well, *I'm* not proud of you, Gareth," Nikki said. "Not

until you make her hair come back."

Gareth looked back toward the bed. "I don't think I can."

"It will come while she sleeps, by day," Eric said, running a hand over his bride's shiny scalp and gazing down at her, his eyes brimming with love. "Thank you, Gareth. I couldn't have borne losing her. You children…all of you, you're very special. I hope you know that."

"You're back!" Christian's voice boomed from somewhere down the hall, and the children turned and ran to greet him. Blue lagged behind, nervous, but Nikki tugged her along by the hand in spite of that, shouting, "And we found our sister, Christian!"

Roland took my hand, brought it to his lips, kissed it softly. "It's nearly dawn. We must rest."

I nodded, but sadly.

"Tonight, when we rise, let's put everything else aside, my love, and spend some time with them. Let's do nonsense things, like…like carving jack-o-lanterns as we promised we would."

"Roxanne has bought a half dozen more pumpkins since they've been here," I said, but my heart was heavy. I knew my Roland's mind. I knew his soul. My love was convinced that the coming night had to be his final one, and he wanted to spend it with the children. And with me. "Go on down, I'll join you in a moment," I said. I leaned up and kissed his soft lips. I knew them by heart, his lips.

Roland nodded and went after the children, his limp worse than I had ever seen it.

I moved to the bedside, bending over my friend Tamara. Her eyes were open.

She smiled at me. "It doesn't hurt anymore."

"I'm very glad. I'm so sorry about what happened to you."

"What did happen, Rhiannon?" Eric asked. "Sarah Bouchard, is she…?"

"She admitted there's another remote control that can be used to control Roland's mind. It's in the desk of her superior, one Colonel Patterson, back at The Sentinel. Not that it matters at this point. She's quite dead. And before she went, I drank from her, and read all she knows. The device inside Roland will explode if we try to remove it."

Eric looked stricken. "But there has to be a way to disarm it!"

"Not according to Bouchard, and I probed her quite thoroughly. Eric, Tamara, I am aware this is a terrible thing to ask of you, especially considering that Blue just nearly killed you, Tamara."

"Blue?"

I nodded. "Nikki's sister. Bouchard had her, and she has the power to incinerate at will. But she's only a child, and she was led to believe you had come there to kill her."

"Unbelievable," Tamara whispered.

"And amazing," I agreed. "My friends, I need to know the children will be cared for, in case Roland and I–"

"Rhiannon!" Eric strode right up to me and gripped my shoulders. "Do not even think that way. We will find a way out of this. We'll do it together."

"Yes, of course we will," I said. And even to my own ears, my voice sounded lifeless. Hopeless. "But all the same, I need to know—Tamara, you're a modern woman, you're half child yourself. They love you. I know they'll be all right with you. And I know you'll make them understand why we–"

"Yes, dammit, yes, we'd see to the children should something happen to the two of you," Tamara said. "But nothing is going to.

"Together," I said. "They need to be kept together. I promised them."

"Together. Of course, but Rhiannon, let's just talk about this." She sent a helpless look Eric's way. Eric only met my eyes and remained silent. I think he understood. "Bouchard is dead. Only one other person in DPI knows what she was doing, and I made her assure him she would return with the children tomorrow, to keep him at bay for the night. I suggest we kill him as soon as is feasible and destroy any records he kept about any of this."

"All right," Eric said. "All right."

But he looked at Tamara and as I left the room, I thought she whispered, "*Do* something."

CHAPTER SIXTEEN

The next night, we spent hours making a complete mess of Maxine and Lou's kitchen as we gutted pumpkins and carved faces into them. Nikki, Ramses, and Gareth actually giggled during the festivities. Roland and I locked eyes, smiling at the sound. It was their first laughter. Their very first. They were going to be all right.

Blue would learn to laugh, too. She would. But as it was, she took the creation of the Jack-o-lanterns very seriously. I understood that. The concept of fun, of doing something for the sheer pleasure of it, was alien to her. But she would learn. She would learn.

The children would be happy. They would be loved, and they would be protected. Tamara would be the best mother imaginable for these special children.

Tamara. She had awakened from the day sleep as good as new, and then she and Eric had taken off somewhere, I thought to give us time alone with the children.

Our six goblin-pumpkins finally finished, we carried them

outside and placed them on either side of the three steps leading to the front door. Maxine had found us some candles to use, and I showed the children how I could blow them alight, except for Blue's candle. She lit her own, using intense concentration and scrunching up her face quite comically, while the rest of us ducked around a corner, just in case. She seemed pleased when the candle lit without any major wildfires igniting. She would learn to control her power, to use it with care.

Then we walked down the driveway a bit to get the full effect, so to speak, by gazing at them from a distance.

Nikki yawned. "I'm tired." And no wonder. It was well past midnight.

This was it then. This was goodbye. How could I bear it?

I took my little girls by their hands, and led them back to the house. Roland did likewise with the boys. Upstairs, we supervised the changing and washing up, escorted them in to say goodnight to Roxanne, who was looking much improved. And then we tucked them into their beds and kissed them goodnight.

I lingered beside Nikki, stroking her silken hair. "I love you so very much, Nikki," I whispered. "If ever I should not be with you, you must remember that. I love you."

She smiled at me. "I like this life. You were right about that. If only we could stop having to run away from DPI all the time."

"That's the very next thing on our to-do list. To fix things for you. No more running. No more connection between you and DPI. You're going to have a wonderful life, darling. A wonderful, long life."

"How do you know?"

"I just do." I hugged her gently, then let her go and she lay down and snuggled into her covers. "I'm very glad to have my sister back," she said.

"I'm glad too. Good night, precious Nikki. Never forget who you are."

"Who am I?" she asked, crinkling her nose at me, then settling down into her pillow and closing her eyes.

"Don't you know?" I asked. "You are the daughter of Rhiannon, born Rhianikki, daughter of pharaoh, princess of Egypt. You will grow to be a goddess among women, adored by men, and feared by all. You are special, Nikki. And you must never ever forget it."

She didn't respond. She had fallen asleep. I looked at her lashes resting upon her cheeks. "Good night my precious child," I whispered, running my hand over her silken hair one last time.

Then I got up and left her, and it felt as though the shattered bits of my heart left a glittering trail across the floor behind me.

* * *

Roland and I slipped out of Maxine and Lou's beautiful home in the depths of the night. We walked for a time, relishing the moonlight that spilled down as if to bathe us. The moon was the closest thing to sunlight we had, as vampires. And yet its reflected light was not strong enough to do us harm.

I wondered if there would be sunshine on the other side for us. When vampires died, did we go to a dark heaven reserved for us alone? Or was it the same bright and beautiful place to which all souls returned?

We'd been human once. Though, it was so long ago now that I barely remembered. I'd been so young when I was turned.

It had been a good life. A long one. I had not one single regret.

Roland slipped his arm around my shoulders, pulling me closer. "I know what you're thinking," he said.

"Of course you do. How could you not, after the centuries we've been together?" I shook my head. "How did you keep me from sensing your presence when you came into the woods to lure the children away?"

"I don't know. Maybe that device in my head emits a thought

barricade as well as toxins and poisons and explosives."

I lowered my head. "I believe we know everything about the device. Bouchard created it, after all. She designed it. I explored every bit of knowledge she possessed about it, my love."

"I know you did, Rhiannon. I know. If there was a solution, you would've found it there." He turned to look down into my eyes, gently moving my hair back off my face, and bending to kiss my forehead. "I want you to stay, Rhiannon. I want you to stay, to live. For the children."

"I want you to make love to me," I said. "For hours and hours until the dawn comes. I want to fall asleep in your arms, one last time, my love." My lips trembled, my heart squeezing tight in my chest. "And I want you to stop asking the impossible of me. For I can no more exist in this life without you, than you could without me. And I think you know it."

He scooped me right up into his arms then, and he ran as only a vampire can run, taking long, graceful leaps rather than short and choppy steps. And while his gait was uneven and his prosthetic, quite painful, he poured on the speed until we were bounding along the beautiful driveway of the home that I'd hoped would be our haven. Our Serenity. The place where we'd intended to raise our children. He kicked the door open, and carried me up the stairs to our bedroom, dropping me onto the bed, coming down onto it with me.

Our mouths locked together and we kissed as passionately as we had ever done. More passionately, perhaps, as my love stripped my clothes away, and threw them aside. And as he undressed me, he trailed his mouth down over my chin, and along my jaw. He kissed a trail over my neck, nipping me there, and then lower, to my breast, which he lavished with affection. To my other breast. To my belly. And lower, loving me so thoroughly and with such intimate knowledge of my body that I was shuddering within seconds. I grabbed his head, and unable to get a good enough grip to suit me, I tugged loose the band that held his queue, so I could run my fingers through his long, dark hair. And all the while he pleasured me with his mouth, with his tongue and teeth until I screamed his name and pulled that gorgeous hair of his harder than was kind.

He climbed up my body again, nude now, though I'd been unaware of him removing his clothes. When he slid inside me, it was like coming home. It had always been this way, making love with him. It was as if one of us was never quite complete until we interlocked in this way. Connected physically to match how very connected we were spiritually, emotionally and in every other way.

When my Roland made love to me, I was whole. Complete. At peace, and in absolute bliss. And there was nothing, not even the children, that could convince me to let him cross that dark void without me right by his side. It was where I belonged.

"Stop thinking, my love," he whispered, his lips moving against my ear, cool breath tickling deliciously. "Just feel."

I fought to close my mind down and shifted my attention to the sensations instead. The length of him, moving deeper inside me, sliding back again, a gentle rocking rhythm that took me higher with each repetition. The strength of his palm, sliding beneath me to cup my buttock, tilting me upward to the exact angle that gave me the most pleasure, while his other hand tangled in my hair, holding my head back to give him better access to my neck and breasts. He took turns delighting and tormenting those sensitive places, nipping me now and then, tasting my blood. He made it very easy for me to keep from thinking.

I returned every bit he was giving to me, arching my hips to meet his thrusts, running my fingertips up and down his spine, nipping his shoulder.

We knew each other's bodies. We knew every trick, every secret, every stroke and touch and kiss that would inflame each other beyond reason. The pace of our movements increased as if we were of one mind. And I often thought we were. And soon the orgasm tore through me like a rip current, and

I felt the answering tides of his own release. We clung to each other. He held me to him from my hips to my shoulders, those strong arms wrapped around me, making me feel small and delicate within their embrace,

Love was not a strong enough word to describe what I felt for my Roland.

There was no word. No description. Nothing could express the feelings rushing through me just then. And I said to my beloved, "I will not let you go without me. Do not ask it of me. And if you try, I'll follow you anyway, my love. You cannot leave me behind. This is my choice, my life, and I choose to go with you."

"But the children…you love them too."

"I do. And so does Tamara. They'll recover. They've only been with us for a few weeks. Tamara and Eric will raise them for years to come. Their hearts will heal. Mine will not, Roland. We've been together for centuries, my love. I cannot let you leave me behind. I will not."

I could not see his face, as we were so tightly entwined, but I felt him move his head, a slight nod, as he whispered, "I know."

* * *

They'd made love the night through, and it was still not enough. Roland almost hoped there was oblivion ahead of him, rather than some afterlife. For any life without Rhiannon in it would be unbearable. Being without Rhiannon would transform heaven into hell for him, and yet, he would not allow her to cross the void by his side. She had to remain, or it had all been for nothing.

They'd taken the time to shower—together, always together—and then he'd donned one of his finest suits of clothes, along with his favorite cloak. Rhiannon put on a skintight red dress, with a plunging neckline to reveal the swell of her breasts for him, and a slit that went almost to her hip on one side. Hand in hand, they walked outside, beyond the backyard where the children would play, away from the pool area, and they found a green, grassy spot without too many shade trees above it.

There, Roland spread his cloak on the ground and sat down. He'd carried a bottle of liquid life with him, and two elegant champagne flutes. Rhiannon had borrowed a couple of the tranquilizer darts from Lou Malone's arsenal. At least it would be painless. She sat on the cloak and laid the darts upon it in front of her.

Roland poured. Then he took one of the darts, broke it open, and emptied its contents into Rhiannon's glass. He broke the other one, and pretended to empty its contents into his own.

Rhiannon lifted her glass and looked down into the ruby red liquid. "We will fall asleep, all entwined around each other. The last thing I'll feel is your arms around me, and your chest beneath my head. We shall be deeply asleep before the sun rises, and then when it does, our bodies will burn, leaving nothing but ash that will scatter in the breeze. Nothing for the children to find. No trauma for them. And the letters we've left behind will explain as well as anything can."

"Yes," he said, waiting, eager for her to drink.

"Our spirits will fly free. Together, my love. Always together."

"Always together," he said, and he clinked the rim of his glass against hers, drew it to him, and drank. He drank deeply.

Nodding, her decision made, his beautiful Rhiannon did the same. And then she lay the glass aside and snuggled against him. They were still sitting upright, just wrapped in each other.

"I love you, Rhiannon. You must always remember how very, very much I love you."

She frowned a little, started to lift her head, but only a little. Then it dropped to his shoulder again. "I love you...." she whispered, the words slurred and soft.

He got to his feet, scooped her up into his arms, and carried her quickly back to the house. When she saw the children's devastation at losing him, she would understand why she had to stay behind. They needed her. And she needed them.

He carried her into the house and up the stairs to their bedroom, laid her gently upon the bed where they had made love for the past several hours. And then he bent to kiss her mouth. "Goodbye, my love. Goodbye. Thank you for loving me. You have made my life so precious. You are...everything, Rhiannon. You are everything."

It was all he could do to rise from the bed, to leave her, knowing he would never see his beloved again. The pain of that was brutal, and it was the need to escape that pain that gave him the strength to walk away as fast as he possibly could, and make his way back to the spot where his cloak and their empty glasses still lay.

He refilled his glass. Picked up the dart, and emptied its contents into the red liquid, swirling it with his hand. As he stared at the contents, he knew he had no choice but to follow through. Somewhere a man possessed a remote control that could take command of his brain and cause him to hurt the people he most loved. There was no way to remove the devices implanted inside him. Anyone who tried would die in the effort. And there was no way he could go on living, being a risk to Rhiannon and the children. Nor could he leave them. He would never be able to stay away if he were alive. This was the only way. They both knew it, but Rhiannon was not coming with him into death as she had hoped. He could not allow it.

He lifted his glass to the sky, and said, "What I do, I do for love. There can be no motivation more pure, and no cause more worthy. If the gods are kind, then one day, I will see my Rhiannon again."

Then he drained the glass and flung it against a nearby tree where it shattered. He lowered himself down upon the cloak. Daylight was ten minutes away. He wondered how long it would take the drug to steal away his consciousness, and he put Rhiannon's face in front of his mind's eye so it would be the last thing he saw in this life.

* * *

I did not understand what was happening when small hands clasped my shoulders, pulling me upright and shaking me.

I was supposed to be on the other side with my Roland by now. But this did not feel like the afterlife.

"Rhiannon, wake up!" Nikki cried. She was shaking me, shouting at me. "Where is he? Where is Roland?"

I pried my eyes open. Her little face swum before me, and my head fell sideways, as if my neck were too weak to hold it. And then I saw Gareth, beside her, and Ramses and Blue at the foot of the bed.

I was aware of being in our bedroom, and that the sky beyond the window was a deep shade of gray. "Is it night again?"

"It's not morning yet. Where is he?"

I frowned, then, trying to make sense of it all. "Why am I here? I'm supposed to be outside...in the grove with my love."

"The grove," Eric's voice shouted. "Hurry!"

I didn't know who he was talking to, but when the children released me, my body fell back onto my bed, and my eyes fell closed again. Nikki crawled up into the bed beside me. I felt her curl into my arms, her head on my chest, and she whispered, "You can't go and leave us, Rhiannon. You are our mother, and we won't let you go."

* * *

When my senses returned to me once again with the setting of the sun, I knew it was night. I felt the arrival of night as I had always done, and I felt my beloved lying close beside me. I sat up suddenly, waking all at once, and I looked down at him. His beautiful face, his chiseled jawline and noble nose, and those eyes of his, which blinked open while I gazed at him in love.

"Heaven is apparently much like home," I told him.

Frowning, he sat up quickly, looking around. "What happened?"

I shrugged. "I have a vague recollection of...." I blinked. "Of the children. And Eric."

Roland looked shocked. He flung off his covers, surged out of the bed, and went running out of the bedroom, his limp more pronounced than ever. He even sucked air through his teeth at the first steps. "Eric, where the hell are you? I know you're here, I feel you!"

"Easy, man, you'll wake the household." Eric's voice was casual, and came from further down the hall.

I quickly got up to go and see what had happened, although I was already piecing it together. Eric had figured out our plan and had thwarted it. That much made sense. What did not was that he had involved the children. We'd wanted to spare them. What if they'd arrived too late only to see us die?

"How dare you?" Roland asked.

In the hallway, I saw him advancing on his best friend. His tone was furious. "You have no idea how difficult it was to take this step. It was my decision to make, my life to end. You had no right."

"I might say the same to you, Roland," I said softly. "Tell me, my love, how did I get back into the house? Back into our bed"

He ignored me. Eric said, "It was a bone-headed decision, and you were in no condition to make it. You've got enough hardware in your head to screw up anyone's thinking. You," he added, looking at me, "have no such excuse. Thank goodness the children knew what you were up to and came after you here."

"The...the children?" Roland asked, turning to meet my stunned eyes.

"Yes, the children. I didn't even know what they were up to, but I had to come after them. By the time I arrived, Roland, they were already dragging you up the stairs, feet first." He smiled a little. "It was quite the sight, actually."

"It won't matter," Roland said. "There's no other option for me."

"And I will not live without you. Leave me and I will follow the very next sunrise, I promise you that, Roland. You cannot–"

"Oh for crying out loud, will you tell them already?" Tamara shouted while racing up the stairs to join us in the hall outside our bedroom. "The melodrama in here is going to reach toxic levels soon."

I moved up beside my Roland, unwilling to be furious with him for trying to prevent my death. I was furious with myself for not anticipating he would do something like this.

"Tell us what?" Roland asked softly, sliding his arm around me and holding me close.

"Roxanne flew Max and Lou and Christian back there last night," Tamara said. "To DPI's Sentinel. They got that stupid remote from Colonel Patterson's desk, wiped all the computers including the backup servers, and got a little something else, too."

Eric pulled a tiny black notebook from his breast pocket, flipped its pages, and then, holding it open, handed it to Roland. It was filled with schematics, drawings, and they were very familiar to me. "I saw all of this when I drank from Bouchard," I said. "This is everything she knew about the device. How did you get it?"

"Christian drew it for us. Right after he drank Colonel Patterson dry."

"Christian?" My eyes felt wide enough to pop.

"He was determined that man would never come after the children again," Tamara said. "He really loves those kids."

Roland took the book and we both gazed down at the pages.

Eric said, "The explosive liquid will not go off at extremely low temperatures, and according to Ramses, he can bring about extremely low temperatures."

"I can't believe–" Roland began.

"Believe this, my friend," Eric went on. This is our answer. I'm going to operate on your brain. Gareth is going to keep you from bleeding out while I do and Ramses is going to keep the explosive so chilled that it can't go off."

Roland looked at me, and I stared back at him, hope sparking to life in my chest. He gave his head a subtle shake, not yet ready to believe. "If the children are close to me, and it goes off–"

"Roland, it's not going to go off. I wouldn't risk the children any more than you would. Ramses can chill the explosive down to absolute zero if need be, and we only need it to hit minus twelve."

Tamara slipped a hand over Eric's shoulder. "Don't you two get it? Thanks to those amazing kids of yours, you're still alive, and we can take the stupid machinery out of your head and keep you that way. You guys need to work on cultivating a more positive attitude, for crying out loud."

There came then, the unmistakable sound of children, banging into the house below and racing through it.

"Come on, Blue, you have to see the pool!" Nikki shouted.

My heart, it seemed, was healed by the stampeding of small feet through the house. I felt Roxanne come in behind them, walking slowly with help from Christian, and then I heard Christian's huge feet pound over the floor after the children, shouting, "Wait for me!"

I stared into Roland's eyes. He held my gaze, solemn, and then, slowly, his lips pulled into a smile. I smiled back and then I laughed. "It's going to be all right," I said. "It's truly going to be all right."

He laughed too, sweeping me into his arms and picking me up off my feet to twirl me in a circle, but he stumbled a bit, and we both wound up on the floor, laughing all the way down.

I sat up, running my hands over his hair and feeling weightless and light in a way I don't think I ever had before. "Thank you, all of you. Thank you for stopping us." But I couldn't look away from my beloved husband's eyes. I loved him so much I ached with it.

"Yes, my friends. Thank you," Roland said, his eyes devouring mine.

I sniffed, brushed away a tear, and got to my feet, reaching down a hand for my love. But he didn't take it. Instead, still smiling he began unlatching the buckles of his ingenious prosthetic. Taking it off, he held it up. "Perhaps, Eric, you can apply your genius to this device of mine. Something is making it chafe me terribly."

Eric took the device as Roland peeled off the sock he wore beneath it, and rubbed the sore spot gently.

The house had gone quiet as the children raced out the back, but they soon came crashing back inside. "Now you should pick your own room," Nikki was saying loudly. "You can take the one right next to mine. Or we can share!"

They came bounding up the stairs as Roland got to his feet, taking my hand and letting me help him.

The children ran through the hall, spotted us and waved hello, then kept right on going into Nikki's bedroom, all four of them talking at once about bedrooms, and Halloween, and how they were going to put on disguises and go 'round saying 'trick-or-treat' to get candy from the people in the nearby town.

The children vanished into Nikki's room, but then Ramses stepped back out into the hallway again, and he met my eyes.

Never try to leave us again, those eyes told mine. And then the words that nearly did me in. *We need you. And...we love you.*

My heart seemed to swell to bursting. *I love you, too, Ramses. We both do. We love you all. And yes, I promise never to try to leave you again.*

Ramses nodded once, then vanished into the bedroom to join his boisterous siblings.

Eric was examining Roland's prosthetic and saying, "I don't see anything wrong with it, Roland," and then he dropped down into a crouch and looked at the stump that remained of Roland's long-lost leg. "Oh, now I see the um...problem."

He rose again, clapped Roland on the shoulder, and said,

"The prosthetic no longer fits, my friend."

"You're mistaken. It fits fine."

"It did," Eric said. "And now, it doesn't. Roland, your leg is re-growing."

Roland was silent. He opened his mouth, closed it, looked down, looked up again. "It's...growing?"

Eric nodded and his grin was so wide I thought it could have lit a small city.

Roland hopped upright on one leg, and hugged me in celebration, and I bounced up and down in his arms and said, "It's growing! Oh, Roland, you'll have your leg back!"

He stepped back from me just enough to stare into my eyes.

"Everything is going to be all right," he said softly. "It truly is."

"It truly is," I replied.

And then he kissed me, and I clung to him as if I would never let him go. Because the truth is, I never will.

EPILOGUE

I stood on the edge of a suburban street in the outskirts of the village of Cornucopia while the children raced to the very first door, rang the bell and shouted "Trick-or-Treat" in unison when it opened.

A smiling woman, an ordinary mortal, praised their costumes, and dropped candy into their hollow plastic pumpkins.

Don't forget to say thank you, I thought at them. And they all obeyed and raced away from the door, heading immediately to the next one.

Roland and I, dressed as Gomez and Morticia Addams, which really hadn't involved much creativity aside from drawing a thin mustache on Roland's upper lip, walked to the next house at a slightly slower pace, never letting the children out of our sight.

"It's a relief to have that hardware out of me," Roland said. "The headaches are gone, and I'm almost feeling like my old self again."

"You almost *are* your old self again," I told him. He had six inches of new growth on his leg, including a newly formed knee that seemed perfect in every way. "At this rate, you'll be as good as new by Thanksgiving."

I watched the children. They remembered to say thank you on their own this time, and raced to the next house. It was fully dark, of course, and most of the other trick-or-treaters had completed their rounds and returned home by now, but there were a few stragglers. I noticed how our children avoided interacting with the others, but also how they watched them, curious and wary.

"Eric has completed his hack into the DPI computers," Roland said. "He's convinced Bouchard never recorded anything about where we lived, nor Max and Lou either. She made me track you, but by then you were on that back road in the woods.

"Which works out very well for us," I said.

Ramses and Gareth took a break after five houses to sit on a stump and sample some of their treats. We joined them there. Watching them devour chocolate made me almost envious that I couldn't imbibe.

But what I had was ever so much better than chocolate. More precious than diamonds. More rare than snow in the desert. And more vital to me than my own heart.

What I had was a love that was deep and strong and very old, a love that continued growing bigger and broader with every day of my existence.

And now it had expanded to include four special children, with powers we still didn't fully understand and hearts that were like fallow fields. They needed love to fill them. And Roland and I had enough to spare. Enough to fill their little hearts until those vessels were overflowing with it.

If they could love the way we did, then they would need nothing else in life. If they could love the way we did, then they too, would be the most blessed beings in existence. Just like my Roland and me.

THE END

For now....

Wings in the Night: Reborn

ABOUT THE AUTHOR

New York Times bestselling author Maggie Shayne has published more than 60 novels and 23 novellas. She has written for 7 publishers and 2 soap operas, has racked up 15 Rita Award nominations and actually, finally, won the damn thing in 2005.

Maggie lives in a beautiful, century old, happily haunted farmhouse named "Serenity" in the wildest wilds of Cortland County, NY, with her husband and soulmate, Lance. They share a pair of English Mastiffs, Dozer & Daisy, and a little English Bulldog, Niblet, and the wise guardian and guru of them all, the feline Glory, who keeps the dogs firmly in their places. Maggie's a Wiccan high priestess (legal clergy even) and an avid follower of the Law of Attraction

Connect with Maggie

Maggie's Website www.MaggieShayne.com
Maggie's Bliss Blog www.MaggiesBlissBlog.com
Twitter @MaggieShayne
Facebook www.Facebook.com/MaggieShayneAuthor

Made in the USA
San Bernardino, CA
10 September 2016